SILENT KNIGHT

A FOG CITY NOVEL

LAYLA REYNE

LAYLA REYNE
ADRENALINE-FUELED ROMANCE

Silent Knight

Cover Design: Cate Ashwood Designs

Cover Photography: Wander Aguiar Photography

Professional Beta Reading: Leslie Copeland

Developmental Editing: Edits by Kristi

Line & Copy Editing: Susie Selva

Proofreading: Lori Parks

First Edition

May, 2021

E-Book ISBN: 978-1-7341753-7-0

Paperback ISBN: 978-1-7341753-9-4

ABOUT THIS BOOK

I won't let anything happen to you.

Fourteen years ago, Braxton Kane's feelings were forbidden.
As an officer, he couldn't fall for an enlisted... no matter how much he longed for Holt Madigan.
Now—as a police chief in love with a digital assassin—his promise to always protect Holt is becoming harder to keep.

I'll protect you.

Holt doesn't understand why his best friend has been pushing him away for months.
But when Brax's life and career are threatened, Holt refuses to allow the distance any longer.
The Madigans protect their own, and Brax is family, whether he believes it or not.

I won't let anything happen to you either.

Forced together, Holt realizes his feelings for his best friend have changed.

His desire to explore the promise their single night together held is undeniable.

His resolve to protect the man who has always protected him is unshakable.

But if Holt wants a future with Brax, he'll have to search and destroy the person who attacked him—before Brax activates the kill switch and sacrifices himself.

Love and devotion. Friendship and trust. Family. It all comes down to this. Holt and Kane, together at last, in the final book of the Fog City romantic suspense series.

For Rachel,
who has been Holt's biggest fan from day one.

I

BRAX

CHAPTER ONE

Fourteen Years Ago

Captain Braxton Kane stood at attention next to his commanding officer, waiting as a C-130 lumbered down the runway. Sweat dripped down his spine, and he squinted behind his shades, rays of blinding sun glimmering off the tarmac. The bird reached the end of the runway, engines revving a final time and kicking up a blast of heat hot enough to wilt the wild poppies that grew alongside the airstrip.

The pilot cut the engines, and the ten or so seconds that followed were Brax's favorite of the day. Before his ears readjusted and the sounds of the base returned. Before his brain realized it had been fooled into thinking he was cooling off as the plane's heated gust dissipated. Before a new unit of soldiers disembarked and his chest ached at the truth that not all of them would board a plane home.

Reprieve over too fast, Brax followed Colonel Ayers to the rear of the transport. As the handling door lowered, shadows were visible moving around inside the belly of the plane. Orders were barked, and the dark shapes formed two lines. Soldiers descended the ramp, side-by-side, packs on their backs, helmets in hand. When the last pair stepped into the light, Brax's breath caught. Lodged itself in his throat with his heart. For the first time in years, he was glad for the searing sun overhead, glad it forced him to wear shades, and glad it left his skin a permanent shade of pink.

The enlisted soldier at the end of the line was a giant of a man. Built like a linebacker, he was a couple inches taller than Brax, more than a few inches broader, and his skin was several shades more red. Sunburn more intense than Brax's. Fresher too, bits of dry skin flaking off the soldier's freckled nose. The lobster-red skin was an unfortunate, adorable clash with the bristles of reddish-blond hair atop his head. A contradiction, like the strong jaw belied by the dimpled chin. He was fucking beautiful—the most beautiful man Brax had seen in his thirty-six years on earth—and he was so fucking off-limits. Too young, an enlisted, straight for all Brax knew, and judging by the fear and pain that swirled in big brown eyes Brax could spend a lifetime getting lost in, too easy a target out here in the desert.

On multiple fronts.

The desire that churned in Brax's gut morphed, the ache in his chest intensified, and a new objective settled on his shoulders. Took root in his mind and spiraled through his veins. He'd do whatever it took to make sure *this* soldier walked back up that ramp and made it home when his tour was over. Of course that's what Brax wanted for every soldier in every unit that rotated through under his command, but it was more than want where this soldier was concerned. It was a need. He couldn't explain it, but after more than a decade of service, he trusted his instincts.

"Welcome to Afghanistan," the colonel greeted, and Brax tore his hidden gaze from the enlisted stranger.

Just in time to accept the clipboard full of paperwork the transport officer shoved into his hands. As Ayers briefed the new soldiers, Brax flipped through the papers. He checked the cargo manifest—all looked in order—and signed to acknowledge receipt. He removed the roster file from the clipboard, then handed the clipboard back to the officer who would work with his base counterpart to offload the cargo. Brax flipped open the roster file, checked the number at the top of the page, then counted the soldiers in front of him.

Match.

His gaze drifted again to the enlisted soldier at the back and to the insignia on his uniform. Chevron with a rocker, private first class. But which one was he? Brax squinted against the sun to read his name patch.

MADIGAN.

Irish descent. Made sense with the ginger hair, freckles, and lobstered skin. He'd known a few Madigans back home, but this kid didn't look familiar. He scanned the roster again. Private First Class Holt Madigan, San Francisco, California. Not one of the New York Madigans he knew. Twenty-years-old. Fuck, too young was right. Sixteen years between them. Brax had almost double the life on him, double the experience, including in the army, as evidenced by the apprehension lingering in Madigan's eyes and the tremors rippling through his at-attention frame. Fighting every instinct to shift on his feet and hitch his shoulders, channeling all his nervous energy into the balled fist at his side. He reminded Brax of the giant chestnut racing ponies his grandfather used to bet on at the track, always jittery in their stalls right before a race. Brax wondered if a gentle hand—

"Captain Kane will take it from here," Ayers said.

Brax snapped shut the folder and snapped shut his mind to reckless impossibilities.

Ayers departed and Brax stepped forward, lifting his shades. "Welcome, soldiers. I'm Captain Braxton Kane, your unit leader for the next six months here at Camp Casey." He took a moment to meet each soldier's gaze, his eyes clashing—and holding—with the big brown ones at the end of the line. "I'll be taking care of you."

He told himself he wasn't talking to only PFC Madigan. It was a lie. One he'd tell every day for the rest of his life to see Holt Madigan's broad shoulders relax, his puffed-out chest collapse from a held breath expelled, and the fear in his eyes chased away by a too tempting warmth Brax had put there.

"Where's Madigan?"

Before anyone in the gathered unit could speak, the raid sirens blared again. Brax didn't flinch, the sound familiar to him, but only a few months off the plane, several troops covered their ears while others instinctively crouched, taking cover from the incoming danger the sirens warned of. With half the soldiers hunched over, the absence of the unit's physically largest member was even more noticeable.

Not that Brax hadn't already noticed. The quiet, giant of a man was the first soldier he always looked for any time the unit gathered for instruction, meetings, or maneuvers, any time Brax entered their bunk for announcements or inspections, any time he watched them dine from across the DFAC where the officers ate separately. Ninety days had done nothing to dampen his unwise interest and over-protective feelings for PFC Madigan. Neither had the scant words they'd exchanged. A dozen at most, outside of call and answer, but as far as Brax could discern, Madigan barely spoke to anyone. Only the minimum words necessary.

Which was not how the private approached the rest of his duties. Madigan was always exactly where he was supposed to be, perfectly at attention, executing his tasks and maneuvers with eerie efficiency. Almost like he needed to be there, like he derived some peace from the routine. Definitely like he had premilitary training. His file backed up Brax's speculation. Top of basic training in weapons handling, marksmanship, and close-quarters combat. The snipers were eyeing him for their unit once he advanced in rank. Brax didn't think it would be a good fit. Not with the pain and sadness that still swirled in Madigan's eyes, casting a lure of vulnerability that Brax was helpless to resist. Had that vulnerability gotten Madigan into trouble tonight? Brax wasn't a fool. He knew hazing went on among the enlisted soldiers. Granted, Madigan was huge and had the skill set to take care of himself, but would he fight back if one of the jackasses on base—and there were plenty—harassed him? Attacked him? Was that why, for the first time in three months, PFC Madigan was not where he was supposed to be?

Brax ordered the troops into formation. They'd gathered at their designated location, awaiting orders as to where they were needed on base in case the first line of defense failed to divert the threat. More often than not, the camp's front line held or the threat was just that, a threat, but if the threat became a reality tonight, and if the front line didn't hold, and if Madigan was alone somewhere, injured... Or he could just be in the head. Or getting laid. In either of those situations, though, Brax would have expected Madigan to yank up his pants and assemble with the rest of his unit. Instead, Brax was missing a soldier.

"Has anyone seen PFC Madigan?" he asked again.

A chorus of "No, sirs" echoed in reply.

"Nothing, Bailey?" he said to Madigan's bunkmate.

"It's dark, sir."

"Not that dark." He gestured at the full moon overhead. "I think you'd notice if he were in his bed when you jumped down from yours."

"He wasn't, sir."

Worry spiked.

"I thought he was ahead of us," Bailey added.

Spiked higher. At most, Madigan would have been out

the door a half minute sooner than the rest of his unit, and if that were the case, Brax would have seen him as he'd approached. Brax's reaction to the sirens was immediate, whereas new soldiers typically experienced a brief disorientation before their training kicked in.

"You missin' one, Captain?" a major asked as he circulated through the gathered groups of soldiers.

"Clearing the bunk," Brax covered. He'd spent much of his career as military police before deciding he wanted to focus on better integrating new soldiers, not disciplining those who stepped out of line. That's what would happen to Madigan if Brax had given the major any other answer, and Brax was fairly certain that further isolation, an interruption of the routine the private thrived on, was the last thing Madigan needed.

The major nodded, seemingly satisfied with the explanation. "Take your unit to the armory. Resupply detail until the threat has passed."

"Yes, sir."

Brax's thoughts didn't stray far from the missing member of his unit even as he marched the rest of them to their station. Brax waited long enough to make sure his soldiers were well handled and well behaving, then slipped out. Using the shadows and increased base activity as cover, he hustled back to the unit's bunk, checking the bathrooms, showers, and DFAC on the way. No sign of PFC Madigan.

Toward the outer edge of Camp Casey, the unit's bunkhouse was dark inside, only a faint glow from the moonlight making the outline of furniture visible. Maybe he'd been too harsh on Bailey. He kept the lights off, per protocol and per his covert intentions.

"Madigan, you in here?"

No response. He waited another moment for his eyes to adjust, then carefully moved around in the dark, walking the center aisle between the bunks and checking top and bottom beds. Nothing. He checked the storage room at the end of the bunkhouse. No missing private there either. He crossed back to Madigan's bunk and laid a hand on his rumpled sheets. A trace of warmth lingered. He palmed Bailey's bed above. Roughly the same temp. If Madigan had been out of bed before the rest of his unit, it hadn't been for long.

"Private, if you're in here, come out."

Silence.

"You're not in trouble."

More silence.

Fuck, if Madigan wasn't here, where the fuck was he?

Brax headed for the door. His hand was on the knob when the raid sirens blared again. And something shifted behind him.

Inside the bunkhouse.

He whipped around. "Madigan, you in here?"

Another shift, and if Brax wasn't mistaken, the scraping sound had come from under Madigan's bunk. He hadn't bothered to look there; no way the hulking private would fit.

He crossed the room again and sat on the bottom bed of the bunk next to Madigan's. "You under there, PFC Madigan?"

A beat of silence, another, then a quiet, gruff, "Yes, sir."

"Don't expect it's too comfortable for a guy your size."

"No, sir."

"You want to come out?"

"No, sir."

While this hadn't happened with one of Brax's soldiers before, he'd heard tell of others. Some COs got angry, flipped beds, and shouted the soldier down for insubordination. Brax didn't see how scaring a poor kid who was obviously already terrified was gonna help anyone. Yes, the military required discipline, but leading people also required understanding and compassion. Not every situation was black and white; there was a fuckton of gray out there.

Brax slid off the bunk onto his knees, then, mimicking a push up, lowered himself onto his stomach on the floor between the bunks. One look under Madigan's bed and warring urges ripped Brax in two. Part of him wanted to laugh. Madigan was definitely too big to be hiding under the bed, his nose practically stuffed into the underside of the mattress. The other part of Brax, the stronger of the two urges, wanted to reach out and comfort the young man. Wanted to cover his balled-tight fist and wipe the tortured expression from his tear-stained face.

The sirens sounded again, and Madigan's entire body clenched, shaking the frame of the bed. His knuckles blanched, and another tear leaked from the corner of his tightly shut eye.

Amusement vanished. Brax wanted nothing more than

to comfort, and to do that, he needed to understand. "You don't like the sirens?"

Madigan shook his head, a single, sharp movement.

"Not used to them?" Brax asked.

The sirens quieted, and Madigan exhaled. "That's not it. It's fucking ridiculous given my family..." His words drifted off, swallowed by a choked sound, half laugh and half sob.

Brax changed tactics. "You make it a habit to hide under beds?"

The half laugh won, a watery chuckle escaping Madigan's lips before he sobered. "Only the second time."

"The first?"

Madigan rotated his face toward Brax. He opened his eyes, and even in the low light, the pain in their dark depths was fathomless.

Fuck holding back. Brax reached out and grasped Madigan's shoulder. "You don't—"

"The day my parents died."

Brax tightened his grip. "Fuck, Private, I'm sorry."

"It was a Tuesday. The outdoor warning sirens in San Francisco go off every Tuesday at noon."

"How long ago—"

"Four years." His dimpled chin wobbled. "I had to fight not to crawl under the bed every week until I enlisted. Until I left."

"And the sirens stopped."

"More like changed, but these, they sound..."

Just like the ones from the day his parents had died.

Brax knew something about that sort of pain, about

harmless associations that suddenly felt like crushing boulders. He drew his hand back and braced his weight on his elbows. Eyes closed, he recalled the sense memory he'd banished years ago. "You know those peppermint pinwheel candies you sometimes get with the bill at restaurants?"

"Yeah, you get them everywhere. They're fucking disgusting."

Brax smiled, impossibly, in the face of the memory of the worst moment of his life. "I used to eat them compulsively. Had one in my mouth the day I got the call. Lost my mom on 9/11. She worked in the Towers."

A gust of air blasted the side of his face. "Fuck, Captain, I'm sorry."

"Me too, Private." On active duty status, Brax had had less than twenty-four hours to grieve his mother, his last remaining relative, before he'd been on a transport to what would quickly become a warzone without one of his most basic comforts. At the time, even the sight of the red and white candies brought him to the verge of tears. The taste, he didn't doubt, would have triggered a full-blown meltdown. He'd had to find comfort somewhere else. His replacement addiction. He reached into his pocket and pulled out a gold-wrapped hard candy. "Switched to caramel."

Madigan chuckled, and sensing the break in tension, Brax pushed into the opening. They needed to get to the armory before their absence was further noted. And investigated. "How did you get out from under the bed?" he asked. "How did you keep from crawling back under it?"

"My brother lured me out with a jacked-up laptop. Always kept it with me. Kept me busy."

"Gamer?"

A sly smile turned up one corner of Madigan's mouth. "Not exactly."

"I saw your aptitude test scores. You've got some talent with computers." Not as much talent as he had with weapons, but tech was a close second. And a skill set that was a whole lot safer than joining the snipers. "I've got a buddy in signal support. I can put you on his radar."

Brax imagined the light that flared in Madigan's eyes was similar to what his brother had glimpsed that day four years ago. Hopeful, Brax shifted onto his knees and held out his hand.

Madigan's bear-sized paw enveloped his, then nearly crushed it when the sirens sounded again. The sheer strength of his grip set off a flood of inappropriate thoughts. Brax hastily shoved them into a tiny mental corner, slamming shut and locking the door on his id. Not the time. Never the time where an enlisted soldier was concerned. He gave a light tug, and Madigan scooted the rest of the way out from under the bed.

Brax helped him to standing. "I'll talk to my buddy later today."

The sirens stopped, and Madigan released his hand, eyes downcast as he wiped his face. "Why are you helping me? I wasn't where I was supposed to be."

"You were where you needed to be." Brax stepped into the aisle and gestured for Madigan to follow. "Finish getting dressed, Private, quickly, and if anyone asks, I was having you clear the bunkhouse."

The soldier snapped his heels together. "Yes, sir."

Brax turned for the door. "I'll be waiting outside."

The soft-spoken "thank you" behind him was way too gentle—way too tempting—for a man Madigan's size. Brax's id slammed itself against the locked door.

CHAPTER TWO

Thirteen Years Ago

Brax pushed open the DFAC doors and immediately regretted not taking a shower first. The blast of chilled air that hit his sweat-soaked skin sent a full-body shiver rippling through him. Thankfully, only a handful of people were in the chow hall, none of whom seemed to notice his Casper impression in their haste to rise and salute. A couple of late lunching privates in the far corner, several specialists playing cards around a center table, and two junior enlisted soldiers on KP duty with the cook, Luther.

Brax bade them "at ease" and hustled to the buffet, afraid the lunch leftovers would be cleared before he got any. "Hold up, Teague. Let me at least grab some cold cuts."

The private laughed. "Late transport again?"

"Third one this spring." Third time he'd stood outside on the tarmac for over an hour in triple-degree heat, watching the wild poppies sway while waiting for a C-130 that never showed. Weather still existed in other parts of the world, and storms managed to fuck up all manner of schedules, including Brax's.

"How late's this one?" Teague asked. "And why's it always on a Tuesday?"

"No idea. Fucking jinxed, I guess." Brax checked his watch. "Over ninety now. Revised ETA in forty." Which left him just enough time to scarf down the turkey and cheese sandwich he'd assembled. He snagged a bag of chips from the end of the line and a can of ginger ale out of the bucket filled with long-melted ice, the water lukewarm. When he went to set them back on his tray, two blondies drizzled with extra caramel were stacked on the corner.

Teague grinned. "Luther told us to save you a couple."

"Makes the wait worth it," Brax said with a grateful smile, and a "Thanks, Luther," for the cook prepping vegetables behind Teague.

Little things like that made the transfer out of MP to his current duty worth it too. He liked being the officer soldiers wanted to see versus feared seeing. Also worth it, the difference he'd made in the duty of the soldier sitting by himself in the other half of the chow hall.

Protocol dictated Brax sit separately—officers and enlisted soldiers rarely ate together—but fuck it, there were no other officers there and barely any enlisted personnel. He approached the table slowly, careful not to startle the big man wearing his over-ear headphones. Madigan was hyperfocused on a game of solitaire dealt out on the table. Brax set his tray opposite the line of cards, and brown eyes shot up to his. The man followed suit, standing so fast he yanked the iPod attached to his headphones off the table. He caught it with lightning-fast reflexes and tossed it, blind, to his left hand in a perfect pitch and catch. He yanked up his right hand in a salute. "Sir."

Brax didn't know whether to laugh or ask one of the many questions in his mental file labeled *Holt Madigan* that kept him awake at night. Since Madigan had moved on from Brax's command, Brax's daily internal battles had waned, but the curiosities lingered. How did a giant Madigan's size move so stealthily, so efficiently? And yet, also disregard—almost forget—his size half the time? Brax, however, didn't think that was a conversation for forty minutes. "Sit down, Private."

Madigan folded back into his chair and lowered his headphones to rest around his neck.

"You mind?" Brax gestured at the opposite chair. "I've got forty before the transport arrives."

"Not at all. You want me to deal you in?"

"Nah, you keep at it. I'll eat." He sat across from the private and dug into his lunch. "How's it going with the new gig?"

"Good. I like it a lot. Thank you again."

"Heard you put on quite a show." Word had gotten back to him that Madigan had cracked Camp Casey's firewall in record time. Faster than Emmitt Marshall, the camp's hot-shot cyber warfare CO. Brax wouldn't be surprised if Madigan was moved from signal support where he'd been the past six months to Marshall's team by the end of the year. The former was necessary to learn the systems and protocols, but Madigan's skills would serve the latter better. And cowboy that Marshall was, from his Texas drawl to the methods he sometimes used to get the job done—and he always did—he would want a weapon like Madigan in his arsenal. "Colonel Ayers owed the tech teams enough favors to swipe you from the snipers."

A shiver snaked through Madigan, not unlike Brax's when he'd first entered the DFAC, except there was no AC blasting in this part of the chow hall. "I'm much happier with my current assignment."

"Good." Brax took another bite of his sandwich. "You don't look nearly as sunburned either."

"Small mercies."

Brax chuckled, and Madigan relaxed further as he gathered up his cards.

Brax ripped into the bag of chips. "And the team there?"

"They're good too."

"But you didn't want to play with them?" Brax tilted his head to the other half of the DFAC where he'd recognized two other signal support specialists among the group around the center table.

Chin lowered, Madigan reddened as he riffled the cards. "Can I tell you a secret?"

Brax swallowed around the sudden lump in his throat. Was there a problem on the team? Or did he—No, he wasn't going to speculate. "Sure."

Madigan glanced at him through criminally long, red-gold lashes. "I'm really fucking terrible at cards."

A bark of laughter erupted out of Brax, the answer so

far from what he'd expected that the tension evaporated on a dime. "I never would've figured."

"No one does. Apparently my being a genius at ones and zeros does not translate to these." Madigan fanned the deck out on the table. "My brother gives me endless shit for it."

"Older?"

Madigan raised two fingers. "By two minutes, and he never lets me forget it."

"Twins?" Brax leaned back in his chair, one leg crossed over the other, bag of chips in hand. "There are two giant Madigans out there?"

Madigan rolled his eyes, but the gesture was belied by a fond smile. "Yes and no. Hawes isn't much shorter than me now, finally hit his growth spurt, but he's still leaner, all sharp angles. Our mom—" His voice cracked, and he closed his eyes a moment longer than a blink. For an interminable second, Brax fought the urge to reach out, crushing the bag of chips to stop himself, and then it passed, and Madigan opened his eyes and cleared his throat. "She used to joke I took up all the space in her womb, so Hawes came out first, screaming and squished."

Brax discarded the crumpled bag and snagged a blondie. "I don't think that's how it works."

"Of course it's not. But somehow I got stuck with 'Little H' as a nickname, and he's 'Big H.' Our younger sister, Helena's, doing." He riffled the cards again. "But Hawes is a giant in other ways. He's never been afraid to be himself, even when I had to help fight off the bullies."

"Because he was smaller?"

"And gay." The casual ease with which Madigan dropped that fact, the lack of any sort of judgment in his voice or interruption in the cards he was dealing, loosened a knot in Brax's chest. "For real, though, I think I played lookout for him more than protector. He was always getting into shit and fucking around with guys. And Helena's trouble with a capital *T*. Flirts with anyone and everyone and is smarter than me and Hawes combined."

The knot loosened more, almost loosened Brax's tongue enough to ask about Madigan's sexuality. Or more tempting, to confess his own. Both would be completely inappropriate and illegal under Don't Ask Don't Tell.

Madigan saved him the infraction. "That's another reason I tend to keep to myself." He lowered his chin again, and if not for the blush, Brax would have thought he was just focused on the game of solitaire he was butchering. "Not really here for the whose chick is hotter convo." He stopped midreach with his next card as if realizing his slip in candor. "Shit, sorry."

Too flustered for words, Brax waved him off and shoved the rest of the blondie into his mouth, preventing himself from committing infractions.

Welcome back, internal battles.

"Can't really have the whose guy is hotter conversation either." He cringed. "Shit, I'm sorry again. I'm from San Francisco. Not talking freely about this stuff is weird, especially given my siblings." He swept up his cards, the game lost. "It's frustrating."

Brax wiped off his hands and mentally guesstimated how many hours this new Madigan puzzle piece was going to keep him awake tonight. "I'm from New York, so I get it, and maybe you just haven't found the right person yet."

"Maybe." He shrugged one shoulder, chin still lowered. "In any event, I'd rather not get into the middle of"—he gestured toward the other table—"that, for multiple reasons."

"Fair enough." Wanting to see his eyes again, Brax offered a bit of his own truth in return, trusting he could give it to Madigan. And he wasn't *exactly* violating the law. "Not really one for the whose chick is hotter convo either, and not only because it's sexist as hell."

That did the trick. Madigan's gaze darted to his, brown eyes wide with surprise. Then with an acceptance Brax had forgotten how much he missed. The small smile and affirmative nod that followed confirmed he understood the implication. And it felt good—*so fucking good*—for someone there to know and accept that part of him.

Before Brax could say more, his radio crackled with word the delayed C-130 was inbound. Fifteen minutes early. He confirmed he was on his way, then stood. "Good to catch up," he said to Madigan. He put the leftover blondie on a napkin, slid it across the table, and lowered his voice. "You ever need to talk, or not, I will beat you at cards any time."

Madigan grinned. "Those soldiers arriving today are lucky to have you."

"Thank you." Brax let loose more of the warmth in his voice. "You know, I think this is the most we've ever talked, Private."

Madigan pointed at the patch on his shoulder. His

smile grew, the freckles colliding, much like Brax's insides. "Specialist now."

"You were a private under my watch."

Madigan snatched up the blondie and lifted it as if in a toast. "And you, Major, were a captain." He winked before shoving the treat into his mouth, and Brax didn't even want to think about how many hours that wink was going to add to his sleeplessness.

CHAPTER THREE

Twelve Years Ago

"Outta the way." Tray held aloft, Luther shoved aside Teague, who Brax had been congratulating on his promotion to culinary specialist. "Got a special order for this one."

Luther's Flatbush accent usually comforted Brax, but today it only worsened the homesickness that hung over him like a storm cloud. He wasn't often prone to the longing for home that plagued so many soldiers. He'd been in the military seventeen years, fifteen of them deployed, and had no family left back home. He didn't consider himself religious either. But always at this time of year, always at the start of Hanukkah, he missed the tiny apartment his mother and grandfather would trim in silver and blue, making sure he didn't feel left out in a building otherwise festooned in red and green. He missed the soft light of the glowing menorah and the rich aromas that would waft out of the kitchen. Hanukkah wasn't as big a holiday to

Jews as Christians made it out to be, but Hanukkah food was Brax's favorite. Beef brisket, pan-fried latkes, sufganiyot, and more. He missed his favorites so much he was hallucinating them, the familiar scents tickling his nose. Smells that intensified when Luther handed him the tray.

"What's this?" Brax asked.

"Like I said, special order." Smiling, the cook tilted his head toward the other half of the DFAC, toward the table Brax had shared almost every Tuesday the past year and a half with Holt Madigan.

The Monday after their first lunch together, Brax had received a message.

Oski15: Hey, it's Holt. Same bat time, same bat channel tomorrow?

Roger that, Brax had replied before he'd been able to talk himself out of it.

He had arrived that second Tuesday to find Holt eating a sandwich and cutting two decks of cards. They'd eaten and played double solitaire, Brax winning every hand, Holt explaining how his call sign was a nod to the mascot of the school where his twin was in college, plus the jersey number of his favorite Toronto Raptors player who had since left the team. It was still one of the funniest rants Brax had ever heard Holt go on during their lunches.

The same routine had repeated itself each week they were both on base and unoccupied. Occasionally, Luther, Teague, or the KP soldiers on duty would join them, and they'd change the game to hearts, which Holt loved the most despite being dreadful at it. Yes, Brax was well liked on base and appropriately social with his fellow officers, but there were few among them he considered real friends. None among them he trusted enough to be his real self around.

Not like he did Holt Madigan.

Lunch, though, wasn't typically waiting for Brax. Usually he threw together a sandwich or, if he was lucky, cobbled together a plate of lukewarm leftovers. Nothing about today's lunch looked thrown together or lukewarm. He set the tray on the metal rails of the buffet bar and peeked under the metal warmer covering the dinner plate. The sight confirmed the smells that had teased him. Beef brisket, latkes, and chopped liver. He lifted the napkin draped over the smaller plate. Sufganiyot.

Fucking hell.

He rested his weight against the rails, nostalgia and desire cutting him off at the knees. He needed a moment to battle back memories of a past he longed for and dreams of a future that multiplied each Tuesday. A future he could never have, even if his mind wandered there without permission. Frequently. It wasn't possible on base, him an officer and Holt an enlisted soldier, and he wasn't even sure Holt would want more than friendship. And while a part of Brax wanted more, another part of him was equally terrified to lose the man who had improbably become his best friend. *This* present was more than he'd ever had. Holt Madigan had done him a kindness no one else had thought to do in seventeen years.

Holt hadn't done it alone, though. Their other friends

had helped. Brax cleared his throat and shifted his weight, standing again on steadier legs. "Thank you for this," he said to Luther and Teague.

The cook patted his belly. "No complaints here, Major."

"And I got to make doughnuts for dessert." Teague grinned. "That's a good day!"

Smiling, Brax thanked them again, then carried his tray to the table where Holt, head bent, was dealing a line of cards. The green and red lights strung around the chow hall twinkled and danced in his ginger bristles, and Brax wondered if the short strands would burn like fire under his fingertips.

Movement snapped him out of his daydreams of an impossible future. Holt stood on the other side of the table, fighting a grin as he raised his hand in salute. "Captain."

Brax returned the gesture. "Private." Off the mark as their titles were, their original ranks were as much endearments as they were an inside joke between them. "At ease."

Holt loosed his grin as they sat. "I wanted to surprise you."

"You did. This is... unexpected."

"I got it right, yeah? Hawes is the chef in the family. He's been collecting cookbooks since we were eight. After you mentioned missing latkes last week, I asked him about those and other Jewish holiday dishes. He sent me some recipes, and I gave them to Luther."

Brax removed the warmer and stuck his nose directly in the path of the wafting steam, inhaling deep and savoring the smells of home. "Only thing missing from my mom's usual spread is the gefilte fish."

Holt cringed. "Hawes sent me a picture of that one too. Looked like fish SPAM. Pass."

Brax laughed out loud. "You made the right call. They'd probably kick me out of here for it." He wouldn't be surprised if he lost his friend over it, and he didn't want that. But the fact that Holt had considered it, had recruited his brother to the effort and Luther and Teague too... Brax blinked fast a few times and cleared his throat. "Seriously, though, thank you for this."

"They're all geared up for Christmas"—Holt gestured at the lights overhead and the tree in the far corner—"but it's not the only holiday this time of year."

Brax took a bite of brisket and couldn't contain his moan.

Holt smiled wider. "That's a good sign?"

"It's perfect." He wanted to devour it and the latkes and the chopped liver and especially the doughnuts, which meant he needed Holt to do the talking for a bit. "You celebrate Christmas?" he asked.

"Yeah, it's a big to-do at our house. My grandmother does a huge Christmas Eve spread. Wait, that's wrong. She *hires* someone to do it." He rolled his eyes, and Brax bit back a laugh. "Then we all go to midnight mass at St. Patrick's. That's where my grandparents go to church. The rest of us are twice-a-year Catholics, but they still go every Sunday. It's this big red brick cathedral in downtown San Francisco. Total throwback in the middle of a bunch of skyscrapers, but it's gorgeous. So, yeah, that was Christmas Eve, and then we'd do brunch and presents in the morning. It was special because it was the one holiday we could count on everyone being home."

Brisket and one latke down, Brax moved to the chopped liver. "Your family travels a lot?"

Holt suddenly shifted his attention to the cards he'd dealt. "Yeah, for work."

"What do they do?"

"Cold storage."

"There's travel in that?"

"Yeah."

The transition from verbal vomit to single syllable answers would have been hilarious if the overall shift in Holt's demeanor wasn't so concerning. A split second later, Brax made the connection and remembered how tough those first few holidays were without the call from his mom. When his grief was still too fresh to enjoy the nostalgia. "I'm sor—"

"What about your family's holiday traditions?" Holt asked as he continued to flip cards. "Besides the food."

Brax picked up the ramekin of chopped liver, mixed in the hard-boiled egg, and considered his words, aiming to tread more carefully. "My mom worked in HR. End of year was when she was busiest, so it was hard for her to get all of Hanukkah off, especially when it fell late in the calendar year. It was easier to get single days off for the High Holy Days, sometimes she could swing Passover too, but she always tried to get at least the first couple days of Hanukkah off and this"—he gestured at the tray—"was what she'd spend most of the time doing. Cooking. She knew these were the foods I liked best."

"And your dad? You never mention—"

Because he wasn't worth the breath. "Left when I was ten."

"I'm sorry."

"Don't be. Mom and I got by all right, and with my grandfather's help too, until he passed my senior year of high school."

Holt laid down his cards but didn't look up. "You miss them?"

"All the time, but especially at Hanukkah. I'm not practicing, and it's not a major Jewish holiday like Rosh Hashanah or Yom Kippur, but it was my favorite holiday, and they indulged me." He traded his empty bowl for the plate with the doughnuts, plucked off the top one, and set it beside Holt's stack of cards. "It gets easier. The nostalgia starts to outweigh the grief. I'm sorry about earlier. I forgot how fresh it can still feel."

"Thank you. Six years, I would have thought..."

"It takes time."

Holt nodded. "My grandfather was right. I needed this. I needed a chance to get away and do something on my own. But yeah, I miss home and my parents, especially this time of year." He scooped up his cards and the doughnut, the latter of which went a long way to cheering him up, judging by the light that crept back into his eyes and the upturned corners of his mouth.

"Fuck, these are good."

"Aren't they?" Brax bit into one and startled with

surprise. "Caramel?" he mumbled around a second mouthful of heavenly goodness. He'd only ever had jelly or lemon filled before.

"You're welcome." Holt's wink distracted Brax enough the big man was able to steal another off the plate. "Here's a question... What don't you miss about home?"

"Oh, that one's easy. The snow."

"Not a fan?"

"One good thing about the desert." Brax snagged the last remaining doughnut and moved his tray aside. "Deal me in."

Holt wiped his hands on his cargos and dealt the cards into two lines. "I understand the no snow thing. Was never a fan of Tahoe. But it's so fucking hot here all the time. I miss the fog."

"I've never been to San Francisco." Brax turned over his first three cards. "Hell, I've only been to a few states on the East Coast. I've been more places outside the US than inside."

"When we get out of here, you should come to SF. It's not hot, it's not cold, it's perfect. Maybe we could celebrate Chrismukkah together."

Brax was so stunned, so pleased, so irrationally hopeful, that an explosion of silver and blue streamers erupted in his belly. "I'd like—" His too eager acceptance was cut short by a commotion on the far side of the DFAC. Two soldiers had rushed in and were scanning the room, looking for someone.

They locked eyes on their table.

Fuck.

The soldiers made a beeline straight for them, and the happy streamers vanished. Brax's stomach sank. And sank further into total free fall as the color drained from Holt's face. Had someone reported them for this minor infraction of friendship? Impending loss settled on Brax's shoulders, but he couldn't let that show. Nor could he let his expression show the fear that was lifting the hairs on his arms. That wouldn't help either of them, especially Holt.

"Whatever it is, it'll be fine," Brax whispered low as he stood. Holt followed, and they exchanged salutes with the other officers.

"You're needed in command, sir."

"Let's go, then." Brax pushed in his chair. "Nice to catch up, Specialist Madigan," he said, summoning up the polite detachment that had flown out the window the night he'd found Holt Madigan hiding under a bed.

"Sir," one of the soldiers spoke. "It's Specialist Madigan that SpecOps requested."

Holt's gaze darted from the soldiers to Brax, his brown eyes wide and filled with fear.

Brax's chest ached, the sight reminding him too much of Holt's first day in the desert. He shifted slightly, his eyes shielded from the soldiers and softened for Holt's benefit, the best he could do when he couldn't inject his voice with the comfort he so desperately wanted to provide. "Report for duty, Pri—" He cleared his throat and corrected. "*Specialist*. You're ready."

If not for the fact he was a light sleeper, Brax might have missed the knock on his door. He wasn't sure that's what it was at first, the sound so soft, but when it came a second time, he rolled over in bed and glanced at his clock. He'd managed a meager ninety minutes of shut eye once he'd finally convinced his brain to stop worrying about Holt. He stood, raked a hand over his head, and searched in the dark for the nearest T-shirt and sweatpants, cursing as he stepped on fallen candies. No lights slashed through his windows, no sirens cut through the otherwise quiet night, and those knocks hadn't been loud or authoritative enough to be an impending summons. He suspected he knew who was outside his door, and his earlier worry returned.

Then ballooned as soon as he opened the door and confirmed his suspicion. A ghostly pale and terrified to the point of shaking Holt Madigan stood in the hallway. His cargo pants were wrinkled, his camo over-shirt unbuttoned, and his hands were fisted in the hem of the Raptors T-shirt he wore underneath. His voice cracked as he whispered, "I can't do this."

Brax stuck his head out the door and turned it either direction, checking the hallway. The common area lights were lowered, and all the other doors in the officers' quarters were closed. No one else in sight, he grabbed Holt by the biceps and dragged him inside his room, shutting the door behind him and flipping on the lights. "How did you get in here?"

"I waited for an opening in the guard rotations and hacked the cameras. No one saw me."

"Risky as hell, Private."

"I know, I'm sorry, but I... I... didn't know where else to go." Another crack in his voice belied the momentary burst of confidence and revealed the depth of fear that had driven Holt to take such a risk.

Brax gentled his grip and led Holt to the desk. He tossed aside the pile of clothes that were on the desk chair, more candies falling out of various pockets, then guided Holt to sit. "Can't do what?"

Brax's ass had barely hit the edge of the bed across from Holt, the only other place in the room to sit, when the other man shot back out of the chair. "I'm not even allowed to tell you."

"But I can guess." Brax rested his elbows on his knees. "The soldier that came for you said Special Operations requested you. This for one of their missions?"

Holt nodded as he paced the ten-foot length of the room, his arms dangling at his sides, fingers moving like they would across a keyboard.

Brax continued to draw conclusions. "They need someone from cyber." As he'd predicted, Holt had been moved from signal support to cyber warfare earlier in the year.

Another nod.

"You're the best hacker on base. Whatever it is, you can do it."

Holt halted and turned to face him. "But what they're asking me to do isn't on base." True to form, once on a roll, Holt didn't shut up. "Fuck it. They need me to go into some Taliban asshole's compound and hack his system."

A knot lodged itself in Brax's gut. Holt had been lucky

so far. No assignments or operations off base. And every day that passed that way—with relatively minimal danger —was another day closer to Brax fulfilling the promise he'd made to himself. A promise to put Holt Madigan, alive and well, back on that transport home at the end of his duty. Now, however, Brax's promise, which had grown even more important to him as his friendship with Holt had grown, was in danger, as was his friend.

"Why can't you hack it from here?" Brax said. "If the target is on the internet, can't you tap in or whatever? Or can't SpecOps conduct the raid and bring the computer to you?"

Holt shook his head and began pacing again, his fingers moving almost as rapidly as his lips, words tumbling out. "It's not him or what's on the computer they're after. They need me to hack in while it's still connected to the system and inject some spyware. *And* a kill switch that will erase the spyware if it's found."

"You can't put the spyware and kill switch on a flash drive and let one of the SpecOps guys load it?"

"I could, but whether someone else could hack in..."

"Marshall?"

"Maybe, but..."

"You're the best shot they've got."

"And it's a one-shot deal." The truth finally out, Holt collapsed into the chair, mirroring Brax's earlier posture, shaking hands running over his buzz cut. "Fuck, Cap, I don't know if I can do this."

Panic swirled in his dark eyes, mixed with a heavy dose of doubt. Brax needed to chase those storm clouds away.

Holt's life depended on it. He slipped off the side of the bed and knelt in front of Holt, forcing his gaze. "Listen to me, Private. This was always a possibility. You are trained for this. You are the best hacker here, you were the top marksman in your basic training class, and top three in knives and hand-to-hand combat. Those skills have only improved. You've run the urban combat sims. You can do this."

"But what if I get out there and freeze? Basic training and sims are one thing, and yeah, I can handle myself in one-on-one situations. My family made sure of that. But actual military combat and a whole army team on the line is another. I don't want anyone to get hurt because of me, because I couldn't do the job. I don't know anything about running point."

"Did they say you were running point?"

"No, Marsh is running point on cyber, and Turner and Kwan on the op. But—"

Brax laid a hand on each of Holt's bouncing knees. "You can do the job. *Your* job. That's what you worry about. The team will be there to back you up, and Marshall, Turner, and Kwan will make sure you and the teams get in and out. They're running point. That's not on you."

"I just—"

Brax squeezed his knees. "You can do this, Holt."

The following ten seconds felt like the longest of Brax's life, waiting for Holt to accept what he'd said and slump back in the chair, exhaling some of his fear and doubt on a long, slow breath.

Brax gave his knees a final pat then stood. "When's the op?" he asked on his way to the mini fridge in the corner.

"Christmas morning. Just before dawn. They're doing more surveillance and will continue to brief us on the specifics of the location."

"Okay." Brax grabbed two ginger ales and turned back around to find Holt out of his chair again, except this time he was picking up the pieces of candy on the floor. Brax bit back his smile, thankful he'd gotten through to Holt enough that the other man was momentarily distracted by Brax's mess and not his own.

And apparently distracted more as Brax crossed the room back to him. "Your tattoo." Holt eyed his right forearm, exposed by the T-shirt Brax had shucked on. "I mean, I've seen hints of it under your sleeve but..." Brax's skin tingled under the appraisal. "I like it."

"My mom used to knit. Blankets, afghans, her own clothes. This"—he held up his forearm—"was one of her favorite patterns, especially the fringe at the bottom. I got it after she passed." Brax handed him the drink. "You got any?"

"Not yet. Have an idea for a sleeve." He jiggled his right arm. "I just didn't have time before I left and wasn't old enough for the liquid courage."

Brax chuckled. "Alcohol does help dull the pain, though tattoos can be a sort of relief too. This one was. Helped me process her death and honor her."

"I'm glad."

"You'll have time to get yours, either while in the service or when you get home."

"*If* I get home." Holt sank back into the chair, doubt clouds returning.

"You will." Brax leaned a hip against the side of the desk and clasped Holt's shoulder. "I'm not gonna let anything happen to you. I'll protect you."

But the doubt in Holt's brown eyes lingered. Doubt Brax needed to chase away. Holt needed to feel comfortable and competent on the mission. He had those skills already; he just needed to be reminded of them. "We've got time."

"Time for what?"

"Time to go back over the basics of urban combat."

And time for Brax to finagle his way onto that SpecOps team. He had confidence in Holt; he'd do his job. But Brax wasn't trusting the other job—of protecting Holt, of making sure he got back on the plane home—to anybody else.

Brax waited as the colonel's assistant announced him. "Colonel Ayers, Major Kane to see you."

Through the partially ajar door, Brax saw Ayers and several other COs gathered around a table covered in satellite photos. Among the group were Major Turner and Captain Kwan from Special Ops and Major Marshall, Holt's CO from Cyber.

"Come in, Major," Ayers called.

The assistant held the door open wider, and Brax

entered, exchanging salutes with the other gathered officers.

"I only have a minute," Ayers said. "I need to meet with the chaplain before the Christmas Eve service."

Brax ignored the familiar twinge of being overlooked and nodded. "Of course, sir."

"What do you need, Major?"

"To be on the strike team going out tomorrow morning." No sense beating around the bush.

"How do you know—" Turner started.

"You all know as well as I do this place is a sieve."

"And for the past five years, you've been everyone's introduction to it," Kwan said.

Brax gave her a knowing smile. "Including yours." She'd been one of the first soldiers to come through under his command—a unit of junior officers—and she was still one of the best soldiers he'd worked with as proven by her rapid ascent through the ranks.

"They tell you everything?" Marshall asked.

Brax bit back a smile and shrugged as much as he was able with his hands clasped behind his back. "Or I'm just familiar enough none of you notice me in hearing distance."

"Why do you want on the op?" Turner asked. "You were MP, then orientation. When's the last time you were actually in combat?"

Fair question. He wasn't Turner or Kwan or any of their unit, who regularly saw action on the front lines. But he regularly sent other soldiers out there, including the one who mattered most to him.

"Enlisted soldiers and officers arrive here, and I spend six months with each unit, orienting them to camp and to the prospect they may see action on the front lines. I try to make them better prepared for you"—he nodded to Turner and Kwan, then to Marshall—"so they can be better prepared to do their jobs, which may include going into battle. I need to be out there with them, put my own skin in the game, so they believe the bullshit I'm shoveling them."

"Major," Ayers chided.

"Apologies, sir," he corrected out of deference, but by the twitch of Ayers's mouth, Brax knew his point had been made. "Lead by example. That's what you taught me." He cut a glance at the rest of them. "I'd like the chance to do that."

He'd rehearsed his argument a dozen times the past two days, during each spare second he wasn't occupied with his current unit or reviewing combat tactics with Holt. And Brax genuinely believed it. He needed the gathered officers to believe it too... and believe it was the primary reason he wanted on the team.

"What if we lose you?" Kwan said. "You don't think you're more valuable here?"

"I can be—"

"No, you can't be replaced," Ayers said. "Not easily. You're damn good at what you do, Major Kane. Since you've been in charge of orientation, morale here is noticeably improved among the enlisted personnel and the new junior officers. You make a difference in their lives."

"He's not blowing smoke up your ass." Marshall

crossed his arms and leaned a hip against the table. Brax could imagine him back home on a Texas farm, big body leaning against a post, cowboy hat lowered over his strong, handsome features. "I've seen it myself," he added, and Brax wondered if they were talking about the same particular enlisted.

"I'm glad," Brax said. "And this will further the effort, strengthen the message." He shifted his gaze back to Ayers, making the final pitch and needing it to succeed. "Give me a chance to show them that what I'm training them to do makes a difference in others' lives and in this war we're fighting."

Ayers glanced at Turner and Kwan, the latter of whom wore a small smile. "You willing to take orders from someone you introduced to base?" Turner asked.

Brax raised his hand in salute to Kwan. "At your command, ma'am."

She unleashed a smile, and that seemed to convince the others, including the final arbiter of the decision.

"All right," Ayers said. "Captain Kwan, get him up to speed. Major Kane, make sure you get yourself and all of them back home."

"Yes, sir." He'd do whatever it took to make sure his soldiers returned, especially Holt Madigan.

"I'm in." Marshall stood from where he'd been crouched in front of the door lock, picking it open. A skill Brax hadn't known his fellow officer possessed. And thank goodness for it. Surveillance had told them the compound's tech hub was on the third floor. It had not told them about the series of locks on the door they'd have to get through to access it.

Brax flicked off his flashlight and stepped back, and Kwan turned the doorknob, carefully pushing open the door. They'd picked up no heat signatures inside, but they entered cautiously, Brax on her six. Moonlight streamed in through the open window, enough to see without their flashlights or night vision goggles. Confirmed empty, except for the single neatly made bed in one corner, a small table next to it with a vase of poppies, two rolling chairs, and the desks pushed against the other walls, all laden with computers and wires.

"Clear," Kwan reported, and Holt entered next.

Brax almost laughed at the giddy delight that streaked across his friend's face. Marshall slipped in after him and made a similar assessment, whistling low. "Tempting."

"No time to play, nerds," Kwan chided, sounding all business despite her upturned lips.

She was right, though. They had a narrow access window before the occupants returned, and they'd already lost valuable time on the locks.

"Eagle," Turner radioed Kwan from his post downstairs with the rest of the team. "We've got bogeys a half mile out."

And their window just got shorter.

"Fuck," Kwan cursed.

"Go," Brax told her. "I'll cover them up here."

She took off for the stairs while Marshall claimed the

chair next to Holt. "Let's figure out which unit you need," he said. "Then I'll bag or rip the brains out of the rest."

The hackers sorted their tasks in less than a minute, and Holt went to work, typing furiously on one of the desktop units while Marshall attacked the laptops, disconnecting wires and shoving the computers into a pack. Brax kept watch, pacing from the door to the window.

His pulse ratcheted up another twenty levels when a flash of headlights appeared in the distance, cutting through the slowly lightening horizon. Brax had never been afraid in the field before, still wasn't where his own welfare was concerned, but for the man in the chair behind the computer... "How much longer?" he asked.

"Five minutes," Holt replied.

"You've got maybe three."

Holt's fingers flew faster as the chatter over their comms continued, Kwan and Turner moving their troops into position. Marshall sped up his efforts too, bagging the last of the laptops and dismantling the other desktops in the room. He'd just finished when AR fire erupted outside.

"Under fire!" Kwan radioed. "Under fire!"

"Fuck!" Brax cursed. He scrambled to the window, back against the wall, splitting his attention between the outside and the door. He did not like what he saw through the window. Two trucks were converging, men standing in the beds, AKs braced on the roll cages and firing at the ground floor of the building. Brax could provide cover, but doing so would give away their location.

Fuck, fuck, fuck.

They were sitting ducks if Kwan and Turner couldn't

hold back the enemy combatants. "How much longer?" he asked again.

Still typing, Holt hunched over more with each blast of rifle fire. "Almost there."

"Brooklyn, report," Kwan called, using Brax's call sign.

"Oski's almost got it," Brax returned. "Just needs a minute more. Hold them back."

"Roger that."

"Another truck spotted," Turner radioed. "Possible RPG on board."

Brax's thundering heart sank. "Fuck!"

Marshall hitched the loaded pack onto his back. "Anything I can help with?"

Holt shook his head. "Spyware is injected. Should be spreading. Just setting the redundancy on the kill switch."

Kwan appeared in the doorway. "We need to go!"

"I'll stay with Oski," Brax said. "Clear us a path out of here."

"Roger that."

Kwan and Marshall disappeared out the door and rifle fire erupted immediately. Much closer. Too close.

"Cap?" That awful tremble from two nights ago was back in Holt's voice.

"Keep going, Private." Brax started for the door. "I'll protect—"

There was a *pop* the opposite direction, then a second later, a bullet whizzed past Brax, so close he could feel the shift in the air next to his ear. He spun on his heel, fast enough to catch the moonlight's glimmer off a sniper's scope in the building across from them.

Another *pop*.

He threw himself at Holt, rounding over top of him, hunching him over farther as bullets screamed through the window. "Sniper fire!" Brax radioed. "From the structure to the west. Need cover!"

"Backup en route," Turner radioed. "ETA two minutes."

"Stay down," Brax said to Holt. "Birds are on their way."

Their location no longer a secret, Brax stretched an arm out over Holt and fired, aiming to keep the sniper back.

"RPG is gonna beat the birds," Kwan radioed. "Brooklyn, Oski, get out of there now!"

"Two more commands and I'll be done." Holt's declaration was greeted with another flurry of bullets through the window. Brax returned fire, holding Holt down. Until the other man pushed up violently against him.

"Stay do—"

With at least twenty pounds on him, Holt easily shrugged him off, and Brax saw the future he wanted but could never have flash before his eyes.

The two of them together in bed, naked and wrapped in each other's arms, Holt moving on him and in him.

Holt rolling his eyes as their kid, with Holt's same warm brown eyes, no trace of fear in them, hacked the DOD mainframe.

Two old men, one gone gray, the other starting to, sitting on a porch together someplace cool and green, sipping ginger ale and playing double solitaire.

Saw it all and with a single *pop* of a pistol saw it die.

Except the bloom of red he expected to see on Holt's chest didn't materialize. Nor did Brax jerk with the impact of a bullet. He spun half around, just in time to see an enemy soldier fall in the doorway as Holt lowered his weapon.

The big brown eyes from Brax's vision snapped to his in reality. "I saw his reflection in the computer screen. I had to protect you too."

Everything exploded inside Brax's chest.

"RPG incoming!" Kwan yelled.

And everything was about to explode around them. Confirmed by the terrifying high-pitched whistle that cut through the shouts and rifle fire.

Growing louder.

Closer.

"Take cover!" Marshall shouted over the comm.

The quietest voice was the loudest. "Cap?"

Brax threw his arms around Holt, hauled him to the ground, and rolled them under the bed, holding on to the other man with everything he had, holding on to his dreams of an impossible future, while the walls came tumbling down around them.

Falling, forever, and all the while the sounds...

Wood groaning, stone crumbling, all of it crashing to the ground below.

The shouts and AR fire that continued and the high-pitched whistle of another RPG headed straight for them.

A *BOOM* even louder than the one that had sent them tumbling.

The world around them shuddered, and they fell faster.

It was all so loud Brax would have covered his ears if he wasn't holding on to the man in his arms for dear life.

And then the descent ended, and blessed silence reigned, together with darkness. As if his eyes and ears and brain had given up. No more processing. He wanted to give up too.

But he had to be sure.

He started to move, and fire seared through his body, through his bones. He'd never felt pain like this before. Was this how his mother had felt the day the Towers had fallen? That thought, more than any other, cleared enough of the fog, made all the pain worth it, to tighten his arms around the body against his.

Around the most important person left in his life.

He hadn't been there to save his mother, but he was here now. He hoped like hell he'd managed to save Holt.

The arms around him clenched back, crushing and painful in their brute strength. The best fucking pain Brax had ever experienced.

Holt's body shook against his and his breaths grew ragged. For a terrifying moment, Brax thought he was losing him. Until wetness hit his skin.

Holt was crying.

Brax gritted through the pain and lifted a hand to cup the back of Holt's head. His knuckles scraped the splintered wood and rubble atop them, but the bristles beneath his fingertips were soft. So soft. Nothing like he imagined, and everything he ever wanted. He raised his other hand to the side of Holt's face, wiping away the wetness there. The warmth of Holt's skin was reassuring as was the absence of any sticky liquid. No blood.

Unlike the slow trickle oozing down Brax's temple.

"Breathe, Private." His voice was hoarse and rough, and forcing air through his lungs, words out of his mouth, sent another wave of fire crashing through him. But Holt needed the reassurance. Needed to keep breathing. Needed to not panic if he was going to get out of there alive. "You'll be okay."

"We're trapped."

Brax opened his eyes and ears to more than the crevice they were trapped in. Listened for other sounds. Looked for any break in the darkness. Muted shouts reached his ears and a streak of light filtered through the darkness, dust dancing in its beam. "They'll find you. Shh, listen."

Holt's lips trembled against Brax's neck. "What if they don't?"

"They will." Words were getting harder, more painful. An inferno burning through him. Maybe if he just shut his eyes again. Slowed his breathing.

"Captain!"

The body on top of his moved, began to lift and shift the rubble pinning them. Arms curled around either side of Brax's head, protecting him. Bringing more blissful darkness. The giant green scientist of Brax's favorite comic came to mind. "Hulk out." He chuckled, then winced.

"Captain!" Big warm hands framed either side of his face. "Stay with me. Please, Cap." Holt coughed, then raised his voice. "Help!"

"Did you hear something? Over there!" A woman's voice. Familiar. Kwan.

Good.

"You'll get home," Brax wheezed. "I'll protect..."

"Cap, no!"

"Here!" Texas. "I think I heard someone here!"

Lips against his forehead. "Come on, Brax, stay with me, please. I can't lose you too. I won't." Then a hand covered his eyes. "Keep these closed."

A mighty shout followed, a ragged howl, and more rubble and wood shifted around them.

So loud.

More shouts and scrapes.

Even louder.

Until light filtered through Brax's eyelids and the morning sun and desert heat hit his face.

They were out. Holt was safe. His job was done.

And the darkness called.

The beeping woke him up.

The hand around his, the man it belonged to, brought him back.

CHAPTER FOUR

Eleven Years Ago

Brax cheeked the caramel candy in his mouth and laid the two and three of hearts faceup on the chow hall table. "Two points for me."

Grinning, Bailey gathered them into the discard pile while Teague tapped the eraser end of his pencil on the table. "How many points, Madigan?"

Holt tossed his cards on the table, three heart-suited cards and the queen of spades. "Got stuck with the bitch again. Sixteen total."

"That's game," Teague declared, and everyone around the table rolled with laughter, including the several other soldiers from Holt's past and current units who'd joined them.

"Jesus, Madigan," Bailey said. "You really are bad at this."

"Leave him some dignity," came a Texas drawl from behind Brax.

The enlisted soldiers scrambled to stand and salute. Marsh must have come from duty, still uniformed.

Brax merely shoved the empty chair beside him back from the table with a grunted, "Marsh."

Holt had been Brax's most frequent visitor during the month he'd been laid up after the raid, recovering from a concussion, two broken ribs, and a fractured ankle. Emmitt Marshall and his portable chess board had been Brax's second. In the four months since, the other major had become a close friend. Someone Brax could share a beer with as they watched shitty replays of NFC East games, played chess, or talked base politics. Talk other politics, the UT-Austin grad was delightfully liberal.

Someone who'd been there that day, who'd argued with the infirmary staff to allow Holt access, who could talk computers with Holt when Brax didn't have the energy to pretend he understood, and who didn't blink twice at the close friendship between an officer and an enlisted soldier.

Someone who'd shown up at Brax's room one night, drunk off his ass, because his boyfriend back home had dumped him. Brax had handed Marsh a bottle of water and a shoulder to commiserate on. Had told him how he'd been deployed less than a year when his college boyfriend had done the same. It felt good to have someone else on base he could trust, could be himself with, and who was also in Holt's corner, even if he did rag on his specialist mercilessly.

"At ease, soldiers." Marsh caught the chair with his toe, turned it around, and straddled it backward. Total fucking cowboy. "Except you." He pointed at Holt. "I'm here to take the rest of your dignity."

More hoots of laughter, and the hilarity continued as Holt quickly ran up the count and lost another game. He groaned and face-planted onto the table. "I can't even go out with dignity."

"That's okay," Luther said, emerging from the kitchen. Holding a large rectangular sheet pan aloft, he rounded the table to stand beside Holt. "You can go out with cake." He slid the pan onto the table, the three-layer cake on it looking decadent with its cream cheese frosting, dusting of walnuts, and "Good Luck, Madigan" in orange-piped frosting, set off by two green-frosting clovers. Luther grabbed Holt in a playful headlock and knuckled his head. "Happy last night in the desert, kid."

Brax clapped and cheered with the others and pretended not to feel the cavernous hole opening up in his chest. Failed. Pretended not to notice Marsh's hand on his knee beneath the table, offering silent comfort. Failed again. He lowered a hand and tangled their fingers, clutching tightly. Marsh was losing his best soldier and protégé. Brax was losing his best friend. But he had another now and had Holt to thank for that too. It was hard to see any of that right now, though. All he saw was the dark abyss that lay ahead.

Fuck, he'd been in the army fifteen years before he'd met Holt Madigan. He'd had his share of tough moments while deployed—losing his first love, losing his mom, losing soldiers—and he'd carried on, never questioning his purpose and commitment. But *this* loss, this feeling like his heart was being cut from his chest, was like nothing he'd ever felt before. It made him seriously consider requesting his own discharge papers, except he was two years from his twenty... and sixteen years older than Holt.

Impossibilities...

"Carrot?" Holt's voice, laced with wonder, drew Brax back from the edge of misery. "We never have carrot cake."

"Special occasion," Luther said.

Holt's gaze, however, remained locked on Brax. "How did you know?"

"Might've asked Hawes."

Holt's smile widened, his chin dimple deepening. "Thank you," he said, but there was a gleam in his eyes that hadn't been there a second ago. It nicked another of Brax's arteries, threatening to bleed him dry.

Why had he thought this going away party was a good idea?

Because Holt deserved it. Because he'd come so far from the soldier hiding under the bed. Because Holt had saved him. Because there was another conversation they still needed to have.

He cleared his throat and forced words out. "Cut your cake, Private."

The party swung back into high gear. Holt and Luther handed out plates of cake while Teague dealt another game of hearts. Once Holt had lost three more hands and the cake had been demolished, the party began to wind down. Luther and Teague were the first to depart, owing to the need to be up early for breakfast. They gave Holt big backslapping hugs and wished him well. As the soldiers from Holt's units were lining up for hugs, Marsh pulled Brax aside.

"You gonna be okay?" he asked.

Brax unwrapped another candy and popped it into his mouth. "I'm fine."

Dark eyes rolled. "That's an even bigger lie than the one you fed Ayers last year to get on that op."

There was a downside, of course, to having close friends. They got to know you too well. Brax ran a hand over his head and clicked the candy against his teeth. "Okay, I'm not fine, but I knew this day would come. This was the reason I wanted on that op. To make sure he got home."

If the tears in Holt's eyes hadn't killed him earlier, the sympathy in Marsh's would. Marsh clasped the side of his neck with a strong, calloused hand, the hold sure and comforting. "You need me, you know where to find me."

"Thank you."

Brax looked on as Marsh joined the goodbye line, and when it was his turn, Marsh spoke quietly to Holt, then hugged him hard. That hug only bested by the one Bailey gave Holt. Those two had stepped off the plane together, but where Holt had decided to return home and serve out his time in IRR while getting a degree, Bailey had re-upped for at least another couple of years. Holt walked Bailey to the door, and Bailey handed him a sheet of paper that brought a huge smile to Holt's face. Holt tucked it in his jacket pocket, then hugged Bailey one last, long time.

"Good time tonight?" Brax asked, once it was just the two of them back at the table.

"Yeah." Holt dealt out two rows for double solitaire. "Unexpected. You have something to do with that?"

Brax shrugged. "What'd Bailey give you?"

Holt let his dodge go and pulled the sheet of paper out of his pocket. "I told him sort of what I was thinking for a tattoo sleeve, and he came up with this." He handed the paper to Brax. "It's amazing."

Brax gasped. The design was unique, beautiful, and scary all at the same time. It would look incredible as a sleeve on Holt's arm. "I had no idea he was this talented."

"I want to get it done before I go home," Holt said, with all the naïveté of someone who'd never gotten a tattoo before. Especially not one this intricate. "I heard there's an amazing artist stateside, near the base."

Brax knew the artist in question, and he was exactly the right choice for this work. "Wynn Keller. He did mine. He was in the service then. But this"—he slid the paper back across the table to Holt—"is more work than you have time for at base. Get him to do the line work, then finish the rest at home. It may help, actually, to have it started while you're a soldier and finished as a civilian."

Holt smiled softly. "I like that."

"Are you excited about going home and being a civilian again soon?"

Holt returned Brax's earlier shrug. "Yes and no."

"Tell me about the no part."

"I don't know what it's going to be like back there. Without them." He fumbled a card, and Brax knew without asking that Holt was talking about his parents. "I don't want to fall back into the place I was in when I left."

Brax continued to play, hoping the normalcy of the activity would give them both some comfort, especially for the frank advice he needed to give. He'd avoided the topic so far, too caught up in his own grief and wanting Holt to enjoy his last night with friends, but time had run out. He needed to make sure Holt was ready and that Holt knew his promise held, no matter the distance.

"I'm not gonna lie and say it's going to be easy. Reintegration is hard. That's why you've got a few months on base, stateside, before you head home."

"You mean they're not just trying to get some extra hacking out of me?"

Brax chuckled. "That too, but it's also to teach you coping mechanisms and set you up with a peer support contact. Too many soldiers ignore the offer of help." He reached out and covered Holt's hands. "Please don't, Holt. I can't be here and know you're suffering an ocean away."

"You're talking about PTSD?"

Brax nodded and withdrew his hand. "The nightmares don't stop when you leave the desert." Too often Brax woke up from them, more often the past five months. In his recent dreams, he was always falling, and his arms were empty when he hit bottom.

Holt clasped his cards, failing to hide his shaking hands. "But the peer support contact they give me won't be my best friend. They're not going to be the person who saved my life."

Brax laid down his own cards and stood. Rounding the table, he knelt in front of Holt like he had that night five months ago. "You saved mine too. And the best friend part, that's not gonna change, no matter where we are." He laid his hands on Holt's knees. "I will always protect you, even if I can't be there for you in person. Though, honestly, I'm not sure how much help I'd be this many years in."

Holt picked up Brax's hands and held them in his. "So I'll go first, then, and I'll be there for you when you get out. I won't let anything happen to you either." He tugged and Brax went into his arms, the hug as tight and as fierce as the one Brax had held him in the night they'd saved each other. "Deal?"

A light sparked on the other side of the abyss. "Deal."

CHAPTER FIVE

Six Months Later

Brax kept his promises. He'd promised himself he always would the day his dad had left. He and his mom had gotten by all right, but ten-year-old Brax swore he wouldn't be the kind of man who went back on his word.

I won't let anything happen to you.

A promise he'd made to a terrified giant of a man almost a year ago. A kind-hearted, quiet soldier—a hacker—who had no business being on the front line. No business being trapped in a crumbling building as RPGs and AR fire exploded around them.

They'd survived that night together. Become closer friends for it. A friendship that had continued over emails and messages the past six months, Brax still in the desert, Holt on base stateside, finishing his active duty service before entering the IRR and heading home to San Francisco.

Except Holt wasn't in San Francisco.

He was in DC, in one of the town's most popular gay nightclubs, his face bright red and his brown eyes as wide and as terrified as they'd been the day he'd stepped off that plane in Afghanistan.

I'll protect you.

A man of his word, Brax slid off his stool and wove through the crowd to where his soldier stood frozen, partially blocking the entrance. Club-goers skirted around him like cars around a construction barrel in the middle of the road. The orange plaid flannel, unbuttoned over a ribbed white tank, only cemented the image.

Brax raised his voice to be heard over the thumping music. "Private!"

Holt spun. "Cap?" His smile grew big, and he launched himself at Brax. "Oh, thank God." He wrapped Brax in a fierce hug so tight it might have startled someone who wasn't used to them. Make them fear they were about to be crushed. That was not what Brax feared as he reveled in the much-missed embrace.

Six months was too fucking long. And to think, he'd tried to avoid this. He hadn't wanted the reminder, would probably wish it away again in an hour, but right now, he was content. He was whole again. But while the stream of people entering the club could careen around one barrel, the two of them together were blocking too much of the road, and they were taking a jostling for it. Stepping out of Holt's embrace, Brax tugged him toward the bar, away from the door and away from the DJ and her wall of sound at the opposite end of the space.

"What are you doing here?" he asked once he could do

so without shouting. "You're supposed to be in San Francisco."

"Got held up a couple days on base, then my flights got all screwed up because of the weather. I'm stuck here overnight. Why are you here?"

"Brass called me in for a meeting. Tweaking the orientation program."

"They're not pulling you off, are they?"

Brax dipped his chin and ran a hand over his head. "No, they want me to update the SOPs for all the bases and run a training course for the other orientation officers."

Holt shoved his shoulder. "That's amazing, Cap. Congrats! Why didn't you tell me you were going to be here when we talked on Tuesday?"

An email had arrived for Brax that first Monday after Holt had left Camp Casey. **Same bat time, same bat channel?** It was the ass-crack of dawn for Holt in the States on the East Coast, but he'd been there every Tuesday the past six months, on email or online chat, whichever program was fastest that day. Including the Tuesday earlier that week.

"Plans weren't final yet," Brax told him. "And you were supposed to be home. I didn't want to interrupt or delay you."

Because Brax was afraid if he did, if he ran into Holt here, he would never be able to get back on the plane. That his feet would stay planted, his heart an anchor he couldn't budge.

Holt drew him into another fierce hug. "Fuck, I missed you."

The anchor dropped. "I missed you too."

"Hey, Daddy, can I get in on this action?"

Holt froze, and his gulp was so loud next to Brax's ear that Brax almost laughed out loud. "Follow my lead," Brax whispered, then shifted to Holt's side, leaving an arm slung over his massive shoulders. The guy who'd approached them was cute, like a petite version of Ricky Martin, and had Holt not shown up tonight, Brax might have taken him up on the offer. He'd gone to the club to cut loose a little, to be himself for a night in a space that was safe, before he had to put the uniform back on tomorrow and tuck this part of himself away. Except Mini-Ricky's eyes weren't on him. They were roaming over Holt in a way that made Brax's hackles rise with unchecked possessiveness. "The boy and I will let you know if we're interested."

"Whatever, Daddy." The twink turned back toward the dance floor, shaking his high and tight ass and shooting an impish grin over his shoulder. "Come find me."

"The boy?" Holt squeaked.

"Don't ask." Brax slapped his back, then dropped his arm, missing the contact instantly but needing to get some distance before the anchor became completely immovable. "Come with me." He led them to the bar, and as they waited for the bartender to return with two beers, Holt rolled up his sleeves, revealing unmistakable ink.

"You got the tattoo done?" Brax said. "Wynn?"

"Oh yeah!" Holt abandoned his shirt sleeves and shrugged out of the flannel altogether, down to his tank. Every head at the bar turned their direction. Holt, however, was oblivious to the attention, too excited to show off the new ink. "Just the line work, like you suggested."

He offered his arm to Brax, who took it lightly by the wrist, enough to twist and examine the tattoo sleeve. Even without color, the design was exceptional. The outline of teeth and jaws curved around Holt's arm as if tearing the skin away to reveal the muscle underneath. Brax wanted to ask what was behind the design, but he was afraid of the answer. Afraid it would make it harder to leave. He added it to the list of *Holt Madigan*-labeled questions that still kept him awake at night.

"Awesome line work," the bartender said as he dropped off their beers. "You want me to take that shirt for you?"

Holt grinned and handed it over. "Thanks, man," he said, likewise oblivious to the bartender's naked interest.

"Wynn does good work," Brax said.

"He does." Holt picked up the bottle, then almost spat out his first sip, his gaze drawn to the number the bartender had scribbled on the napkin beneath it. He glanced up, eyes darting around. Face heated, he took a long pull from the bottle. Maybe not so oblivious anymore. "Wynn gave me the name of someone in San Francisco to do the fill."

"Good." Eager to rescue Holt from the attention—for both their sakes—and to ask a question he desperately wanted the answer to, Brax led Holt away from the bar to a quieter, dimmer spot against the wall. "So, I get why you're in DC, but what are you doing here?" He gestured around them at the club.

Holt's blush deepened, and he drained the rest of his beer.

"Come on, Private. Don't get bashful on me now."

"Remember our first lunch, our conversation about how the hot chick talk never did anything for me? And we couldn't really have the hot guy convo at camp either."

Neither topic had come up again, both of them steering clear. "I remember."

"Well, I thought..." Holt mimicked Brax's earlier gesture, waving a hand at their surroundings.

"You thought you'd come here and see about the latter?" Brax chuckled and took a sip of his beer, nursing it slowly. "What did you do? Look up DC gay bars on the internet?"

Holt shook his head. "Hawes gave me a list. This one's down the block from my hotel."

And of course it would be the one Brax frequented when he was in town.

"What did Hawes say about this plan of yours?"

"He started giving me pointers, in graphic detail, so I hung up." Holt braced an arm on the wall and turned into it, hiding his flaming face.

Brax drank his beer and ran a hand back and forth over his mortified friend's back.

"I just wanted to try." Holt angled his face enough for Brax to see and hear. "I don't want to go home a virgin."

Brax's hand froze between tense shoulder blades. "What?"

"You heard me. I'm a fucking twenty-three-year-old virgin. Well, not fucking, which is kind of the fucking problem." He buried his face in his arm again with a muttered, "Fuck."

Fuck was right. Brax needed to leave. Needed to take his hand off Holt's warm, solid back and run straight for the door before Holt noticed the erection straining his zipper. But he couldn't leave. He'd made a promise, and Holt needed his protection now more than ever—from everyone else in this club who had no doubt also popped a chub the moment Holt had walked in. And if they hadn't then, they certainly had when he'd stripped off his flannel.

Fuck.

Option one: Get Holt out of there. Brax stepped closer and leaned a shoulder against the wall near Holt's arm. "There's no ticking clock on your virginity," he whispered low. "You don't have to do this tonight."

"I know that." Holt straightened, then turned and slumped back against the wall, the movement bringing him close enough for Brax to smell sweat and fancy hotel soap. "I just... I just want to feel that spark with someone." He tilted his empty beer bottle toward the crowded club. "I thought this was worth a shot."

Translation: Holt hadn't felt that spark with him. Brax doubted the implication was intentional, but it cut like a knife all the same.

Brax drained the rest of his beer and debated his options again.

Stick with Option one: get Holt out of there, then go lick his self-inflicted wounds elsewhere. Option two: Do what he'd come to do tonight—cut loose a little—and have fun with his best friend doing it. An unexpected gift, an opportunity he couldn't be sure he'd ever get again, seeing as he was back on a plane to a war zone tomorrow. His and Holt's lives were headed in opposite directions, but tonight they were both in the same place, in a safe space where Brax could be himself and Holt could explore. Try to find himself too. Extra safe with Brax watching over him, a buffer from the Mini-Rickys of the world.

Maybe it was the stupidest idea he'd ever had, but fuck if Brax didn't want this too. A night out with Holt to dance and have fun without the threat of death or court martial hanging over their heads. And maybe tonight was exactly what Brax needed to slam the door on reckless impossibilities once and for all. Holt was going to move on, meet someone, have sex, and fall in love, and the odds of that person being Brax were slim to none. Better to rip the Band-Aid off now than spend a lifetime wondering. Better for Brax to be his friend and keep his promise. Protect him. Make sure Holt got the life and happiness he deserved.

Brax pushed off the wall. "Okay, then, let's see what we can do about finding you that spark with someone."

The bottle slipped from Holt's hand, but, as Brax had come to expect, Holt moved fast enough to catch it with his foot before it shattered on the floor. "What?"

"As your best friend, it's my duty to be your wingman." He bent over, picked up Holt's bottle, and held it in one hand with his own empty. He held out his other hand to Holt. "Do you trust me?"

"More than anyone." Holt's bear paw closed around his. "Just don't call me boy again."

Brax laughed his id back into its cell. "Roger that, Private."

The night's turn of events had played out in Brax's favor. Holt Madigan unwound was something else, and Brax was grateful beyond words that he'd gotten the chance to see it, gotten this night out with him in case they never got the opportunity again. That thought had continued to play in the back of Brax's mind as they'd danced and jumped to the music, had continued to drive his need to take a mental picture of every moment. Arms slung over each other's shoulders, bodies grinding, spinning from partner to partner, then back to each other again. Brax looked his fill at the beautiful man whose freckled skin was red with exertion and glistening with sweat, whose ginger temples dripped beads of moisture, whose eyes were wiped clean of fear and were feverish with life instead, more life and freedom than Brax had ever seen in their warm brown depths. He could be content with the fact he'd given Holt this night out. Had been there with him to experience it. That had to be enough.

Holt spun away from the bartender who'd taken a break to join them and crowded close behind Brax, hands on his hips, drawing him back from the bespectacled bear Brax had been dancing with. "Let's get out of here," Holt said, loud enough to be heard over the music, close enough that his lips brushed the curve of Brax's ear.

There was no way Holt didn't feel the shiver that

snaked through Brax. "You're supposed to say that to the bartender," Brax covered. "Or to Mini-Ricky."

Holt laughed. "Definitely not to him." The rumble from deep in his chest pressed against Brax's back and rolled through Brax like fine whisky, warming him from the inside out.

Brax shifted, aiming to get a little distance, to see Holt's face and understand what he was truly asking. "You sure?"

"I'm sure." There was no trace of sadness on his face. Only bright, beguiling eyes and a big goofy grin. "I just wanna spend the night with my best friend."

Brax's dick responded to his words, even as his brain said to take them at face value. And to appreciate that Holt had had a good time and was no longer hung up on turning in his V-card. Brax had kept his promise. And while he'd had a blast tonight, dancing and letting go, he would happily spend the rest of it with Holt in a less crowded, quieter space. Someplace they could talk, Brax could beat him at cards, and they could enjoy what little time they had left in each other's company. "Lead the way."

They retrieved Holt's flannel and their coats, and once bundled up against the brisk autumn night, jogged down the block to the hotel where Holt was staying. As they crossed the opulent lobby, then rode the marble and mirrored elevator up, up and up, Brax caught Holt up on Marsh, Bailey, and the others at camp, while Holt filled him in on his six months on base.

When they disembarked on the top floor, which only

had four rooms, Brax whistled low. "Fuck, Private, a penthouse suite?"

"Not my idea." He swiped his keycard in front of the electronic lock and pushed open the door.

Brax hesitated over the threshold, afraid to sully the suite, the spacious room lit in soft yellow light from two lamps. He'd never stayed somewhere so nice. Possibly never stepped foot in a place so grand. "What did you say your family does?"

Hand to his back, Holt shoved him forward with a laugh. "Cold storage." The door clicked shut behind them. "It's profitable in San Francisco. Lots of shipping, fisheries, and restaurants. Research labs too."

"This profitable?" Brax stumbled into the living area of the suite and spun in a circle, taking it all in. Vaulted ceilings, a crystal chandelier, elegant furnishings, and windows on three sides, providing grand views of the Potomac and multiple national monuments, glowing in their halos of light in the otherwise dark night. To the right, up a small set of stairs, there was an ornamental bookcase, tastefully decorated with leather-bound books, vases, and other expensive trinkets. Through the open cubbyholes, Brax glimpsed the king-sized bed in another room full of windows and a door off to the side, likely to an en-suite bathroom. "This is—"

"Wasted on me." Holt toed off his shoes and crossed the room to a beverage cart positioned between two windows. "All I need is a fucking cot or bunk. But Hawes and Helena wanted to do something nice since I got delayed and all." He lifted a tall bottle of amber liquid with a distinctive blue label. "Had this waiting for me too. Belated twenty-first birthday gift."

Speaking of fine whisky. "Two and a half years belated but trust me, JWB more than makes up for it." Brax had only had a glass once—in Ayers's office when Brax had been promoted to major—but he'd never forget that bottle or the smooth blended scotch inside.

Holt smiled. "Have a glass with me?"

"Not gonna say no to that." Brax ditched his shoes next to Holt's and settled on one of the two sofas in the middle of the room. They faced each other, a coffee table between them with a vase of fresh-cut flowers in the center. Fuck, what did a night in a place like this cost? Cold storage really paid this well?

Holt appeared at his side with two full-to-the-brim glasses of scotch. Brax bit back a laugh. Apparently, no one had ever taught Holt that two fingers' worth was a generous pour. Brax sure as fuck wasn't going to be the one to do so now, not when offered four Holt-sized fingers' worth of top-shelf scotch. He took the glass, and surprising him, Holt sank onto the sofa next to him.

"Cheers." Brax tapped the rim of his glass against Holt's, a slosh spilling over the lip of both their glasses. He took a sip before any more was wasted, enjoying the smooth, subtle flavors—oak and vanilla, caramel and spice, a touch of peat—as they burned across his tongue and down his throat. Not a scorcher like some bourbon and whisky, and not smoky and peaty like other scotch. Just a pleasant warmth. He licked his lips, making sure not to waste a drop, then looked up in time to see Holt quickly divert his gaze.

Warmth of a different sort prickled the base of Brax's spine, but he ignored it, keeping his desire locked away. It had been a good night, one they would both remember fondly. He wouldn't ruin it with impossibilities. "Sorry I was a shitty wingman tonight."

"Not your fault." Holt gulped half his scotch, then gasped, apparently not having had the sipping lesson either and not expecting the whisky's heat. Or maybe it had been intentional, his face falling. "I'm gonna go home a virgin still."

Brax had thought, had hoped, Holt was past that. He took another sip of his scotch and shifted on the couch to face Holt, folding a leg under him, then putting it back down after thinking better of it. Feet on the furniture was probably frowned upon in a hotel like this. "From what you've told me, it doesn't sound like your family would be the type to judge."

Holt grabbed Brax's leg by the knee and hauled it back up to where Brax had intended to put it. "Be comfortable, and you're right, they're not. At all." He took another healthy gulp of scotch. "But I thought maybe…"

"No spark with anyone at the club tonight?"

"There was one."

Brax drowned his aching heart in scotch before offering to go back there. "The club is open for another few hours." He didn't really want to go, but if this was important to Holt, if this was what he needed, Brax would make it happen.

"We don't need to do that." Holt threw back the rest of his drink, set his glass on the table, and when he returned his gaze to Brax's, his eyes were a storm of fire and fear. And his face had caught fire too, a bright scarlet red clashing with his hair and orange flannel shirt. "The person I felt a spark with is right here."

Whisky sloshed over the rim of Brax's glass again, coating his trembling fingers. Had he heard that right? Translated it right? Holt wasn't saying what Brax thought he was saying... was he? "Private..."

Holt pried the whisky from Brax's hand, gulped down the rest of that glass too, then set it on the table next to his. "Don't get me wrong, the bartender was hot, the maid of honor in that bachelorette group was gorgeous, the Georgetown grad in the bowtie was fly as hell, but I wasn't attracted to any of them. I didn't want any of them." He shifted closer to Brax. "But you... You were amazing tonight, sexy and uninhibited, and I trust you. I know you. I feel connected to you. Safe. And for some reason, that turns me the fuck on. Not anyone else tonight. No one in the past either. Just *you*. I want *you*."

Brax stared across the room, certain he was about to burst into flames. From the heat of Holt's leg next to his, from his too tempting breath on the side of his face, from the promise of his words. All of it more scorching than any whisky he'd ever tasted, top-shelf or not.

"But if you don't want to..."

Brax whipped his gaze back to the brown one beside him. "I didn't say that."

One corner of Holt's mouth twitched, fighting a smile

as if he could smell the victory. Or, more likely, see the bulge in Brax's jeans. "All my good memories the past three years involve you, Cap. This last one should too."

"Captain. That's why—"

Holt laid a hand on his thigh, and Brax's words died. "But you're not anymore, are you? You're a major." He slid his hand higher and spread his fingers, grasping the inside of Brax's thigh. "And I'm not a soldier anymore—"

"Technically—"

"Fuck technically."

If Brax hadn't been erect already, Holt's sharp, tortured growl together with the press of his fingers would have done the trick. As it were, a lightning bolt of desire ripped through Brax's veins, tripping circuits and standing all his hairs on end.

Making his dick ache with need.

"I'm sixteen years older than you." One last-ditch effort.

Which Holt easily batted down. "Good. You'll be better at this than me." He leaned closer, bringing them cheek to cheek, and slid his hand into the crease of Brax's groin. "I don't give a fuck about your rank or age. I want you. I want this. Please, Brax."

The last time Holt had used his name he had been desperate for Brax to live. Tonight's desperation was nothing like that. It sounded an awful lot like the desperate id Brax had kept locked away the past three years. Holt was prying open the lock—his knuckles brushing Brax's dick, his heavy breaths in his ear, the heat of his words and skin all around.

The desire that smacked against and recognized Brax's own.

"Please, Brax."

Desire Brax was powerless to resist now that the door had been flung wide open. "Fuck." He angled his face toward Holt's, and that was all the invitation Holt needed, chasing after Brax's lips and sealing their mouths in the kiss Brax had craved for years.

It wasn't smooth, or sweet, or seductive. It was sloppy, needy, all teeth and lips as Holt's inexperience collided with Brax's hunger.

It was perfect, and Brax was undone, groaning, opening his mouth under Holt's assault and sucking in his tongue when it pushed between his lips. Tasting beer, whisky, and the hint of something he couldn't define. He wanted more, more, more. Taking the cue, Holt kissed him deeper, pulled him under, drowning him in lust and his big body. He climbed onto Brax's lap, surrounding him, knees on either side of his hips, arms draped over his shoulders, torso blanketing his. Rocking an impressive erection against Brax's abs. It was long and thick, and Brax's ass clenched with eager anticipation. God, he wanted that inside him, wanted Holt inside him. He'd never let himself think that far before, never imagined—

Holt cupped Brax through his jeans.

Fuck.

Brax couldn't think anymore at all. He tore his mouth away and dropped his head back on top of the cushions, panting. Then groaned louder as Holt's lips and tongue burned a path down his throat. He nipped and sucked on a tendon, too hard, no doubt raising a bruise, and fuck if that didn't make Brax harder, make him want Holt to mark him all over. "More." He held Holt's head in place, fingertips crushing the soft bristles, as Holt's fingers around his cock tightened and slid down the growing length.

"Fuck yeah." Holt nipped the underside of his chin. "You're as hard as I am. You about to blow too?" As if to prove his point, Holt withdrew his hand and thrust his erection against Brax's abs again. "Fuck, it hurts, but it's good. So good."

Brax grabbed a handful of firm round ass cheek and held Holt tight against him. He rocked forward, making Holt feel even better, savoring his tortured gasp.

"Fuck," Holt keened. "I didn't know it could feel like this. I didn't know." Brax kneaded his ass cheek, rolled his own hips, rutting, and Holt's chants continued. "I didn't know."

So much he didn't know, and Brax only had one night to show him.

"Fuck, you keep doing that and I'm gonna come."

And with a twenty-three-year-old virgin's hair trigger climax too. Brax had to pull back if he was going to make this good for Holt. Good for both of them. He flattened his palm and rubbed it gently over Holt's ass. With his other hand, he grasped the back of Holt's head and guided his face out of the crook of his neck. "Ease up, baby. Breathe."

Holt panted against the side of Brax's face as he struggled not to thrust. He ran a hand up Brax's torso, over his T-shirt. Cotton was no match for the trail of heat in the wake of Holt's touch, for the explosion a pinch of his nipple set off. Brax gritted his teeth. "That's not easing up."

Holt circled his nipple with his thumb and licked at Brax's tense jaw. "I want to feel all of it. I didn't think I could... Wanna keep this feeling. Want to feel you."

Brax lightly slapped the redwood trunk of a thigh on his right side, intending to get Holt to move, intending to get them off the couch and to the bed where two six-foot-plus men could more fully enjoy each other, but Holt froze, a slab of granite braced above him. Brax panicked, afraid Holt had misread him, afraid he'd unintentionally gone too far. But then Holt moaned, low and needy, and Brax's toes curled.

Spanking turned Holt Madigan on. Not a fact he needed to know.

Before his imagination ran wild and he came in his jeans, Brax pushed off the back of the couch, scooting to the edge, his momentum forcing Holt to his feet. And putting his rigid cock right in front of Brax's face. Brax wanted to lean forward. Wanted to mouth it through the denim. Wanted to peel open the zipper and do the same through cotton until Holt was leaking and desperate, out of his mind with need like Brax.

A gentle, shaking hand skirted over his head. "I'm gonna come if you keep staring at it like that."

Brax wrapped his hands around the backs of Holt's thighs and looked up, not bothering to hide his need. "I want this too. As much as you do."

Maybe more.

Holt wanted an experience, one Brax was uniquely

able to give him. Brax wanted to make love to him. No denying that now. The heavy feeling in his heart and his dick wasn't only about lust. Wasn't only about getting off. Could they meet in the middle somewhere? Could he give Holt what he needed and not ruin himself forever? Probably not, but not knowing if he'd ever get this chance again, Brax couldn't pass it up. And he couldn't leave Holt like this, vulnerable and aching. He hadn't had this before, and just getting this far was obviously big for him. What would it do to Holt to deny him the rest? Brax was as terrified to stop as he was to keep going.

I'll protect you.

He couldn't be the one that hurt Holt. Wouldn't be. If Brax had to suffer from here to eternity to avoid that, then fine, so be it. And no matter what, he'd have this night. One impossible night to look back on and cherish. One night with the man he loved.

As if sensing the mental gymnastics tearing Brax apart, Holt lowered his hand to Brax's cheek, gently stroking it. "Tell me this won't fuck things up between us."

"It won't." Brax wouldn't let it. "But if you want to stop, we stop."

"That's the last thing I want." He smirked and thrust his hips forward, presenting evidence. Too close. Brax slid his hands up the backs of Holt's thighs, cupping his ass, and Holt pressed back into them, giving Brax an inch more space. And a whole other set of mental images. Images that vanished when the corner of Holt's mouth dipped. "Well, second to last."

"The last?"

"To lose my best friend."

Brax nudged him back enough to stand, skimming the front of Holt's hard body as he rose. Holt was no less aroused, just cautious. Mind set, Brax aimed to wipe his worry away. He lifted both hands and cupped Holt's face. "You won't lose me. I promise." He leaned in and kissed him softly to seal it. Then began trailing his lips over Holt's jaw, sucking and nipping at the tendon of his neck, leaving a bruise to match his, as he dragged the flannel down Holt's arms and shuffled them back toward the bedroom.

"I don't want to hurt you either," Holt mumbled, even as he pushed Brax's T-shirt up, big hands gliding over his torso, sending ripples of pleasure through Brax. Was this going to hurt tomorrow? Like hell. Was he going to stop it tonight? Hell no. Because Holt's hands on his skin, tweaking his nipples, his lips sliding over Brax's, his breath mingled with his own, the shivers racing down Brax's spine were the furthest thing from pain.

Brax ripped his shirt off over his head, then did the same with Holt's tank. There was so much skin, so much Holt, Brax didn't know where to start. "You are a gift, Holt Madigan." He nipped across his collarbone. "This night has been a gift." Licked into the hollow of his throat. "Gifts are a good thing." Kissed the divot between his pecs. "And I'd like to spend the rest of the night unwrapping you."

"But if this is awkward..."

"One advantage of you being on your way to San Francisco and me being on my way back to Afghanistan." He turned and walked backward up the steps, giving Holt an out, making sure he still wanted to follow.

Holt chased after him, lips colliding and hands roaming, never more than an inch, a breath, between them. "Sat phones are awkward anyway."

"Yeah, they are." He hooked his fingers in the waistband of Holt's jeans and steered him to the bed. "One night together. We enjoy each other before our lives take us opposite directions." He could die next week; so could Holt. If he had this one chance, he would go for it. He was only hurting himself. "I'm okay with that if you are?"

Holt laid a hand over one of his and dragged it along his waistband to his belt buckle. "Better than okay."

Brax leaned against Holt to catch his breath, his balance, his knees swept out from under him by this impossible reality. Holt held him up, a hand at the base of his skull, the other slinking down his spine and into the waistband of his jeans. The touch Brax really wanted just out of reach. He covered his swoon, his moan, by nuzzling Holt's chest and inhaling deep, more of that fancy hotel soap mixed with sweat and Holt. Brax wondered if the San Francisco fog had a smell. If that was the indefinable scent, the taste, that hung around Holt. He lapped it up with his tongue, then lapped at Holt's nipples while he worked open his buckle and fly. The jeans dropped with the heavy belt, and Holt kicked them away.

Brax stepped back to admire him. Cast in the moonlight and the ambient light of the living area, Holt looked like a ghost on fire—his pale skin dappled with freckles and red blotches of heat, a smattering of auburn hair, and his cock tenting his red plaid boxers.

Holt lifted a hand to Brax's fly, the line work on his

right arm coming to life, twisting and turning. "Where do we start?" he whispered.

"That's as good a place as any," Brax replied, then halted the movement of Holt's hand. "But first, you need to know I'm tested regularly, and I'm okay. You need to ask that of any partner if they don't tell you like I just did." He hated thinking of Holt with anyone else in the future, but he hated not giving him this lesson more. "And you need to tell them about you too."

Holt dipped his chin, the red creeping up his cheeks again. "I'm okay too. Tested, because regulations, but I haven't been with anyone else like this, so..."

"Okay, then." Brax leaned in and kissed his embarrassment away, breaking only when Holt tugged at his waistband again, impatience and need revved back up. "As you were, Private."

Holt unbuckled and unzipped Brax's pants, pushed them down, and Brax hissed as Holt skirted his knuckles down the length of his cock. Then hissed again as Holt dipped his fingers inside the slit of his boxers and teased the bare underside of his shaft. "I did this." He lifted his eyes to Brax, and they were full of awe, hunger, and pride.

"You did," Brax replied. "And I'll let you do something else about it soon. But first, I need you to sit on the end of the bed so I can suck your cock."

Holt wobbled, and all it took was a slight push to the center of his chest to topple him onto the bed. "Fuck, you keep talking like that and I'm gonna blow before you get the chance to."

Brax leaned over him, hands braced on the mattress,

stealing a kiss, then escaping Holt's incoming touch at the last possible second. Arms flailing, Holt laughed, the sound warm and lust drunk, as Brax kissed a path down his chest and abs. It was all Brax could do not to detour, to not set about tasting every inch of Holt's big, hard body, but if the other man's squirming, if his straining cock, if his muttered pleas and clenched fists were any indication, he wouldn't be able to hold off his orgasm for long.

And if there was anything Brax wanted tonight, it was to feel the hot hard length of Holt's cock, to taste his come on his tongue. Sensing Holt careening toward his climax, Brax dropped the rest of the way to his knees, taking Holt's boxers with him.

Some sense of modesty must have kicked in because Holt moved to bring a hand down to cover himself. Brax grabbed it, tangled their fingers, and pinned Holt's hand to the mattress. "No hiding. You're beautiful. I want to see all of you." Using his other hand, he spread Holt's legs farther apart, making room so he could suck a bruise on Holt's inner thigh before burying his face in the thatch of auburn hair at the base of his cock.

"Oh God. Brax, I can't—I'm gonna—"

Brax cupped Holt's balls and waited for his breaths to slow. "Not yet." He lowered his head and licked a stripe over Holt's taint, removed his hand and licked around each of his balls, then let his lower lip glide up the length of Holt's cock. Holt's hand in his clenched, all that strength that had tempted Brax was also tempting him right to the edge. "Fuck, Holt, what you do to me."

"Jesus fucking Christ, Brax, I'm gonna blow."

The precome leaking from his slit foretold as much. Brax lapped it up, then without preamble, the time too short, took Holt into his mouth, all the way to the back of his throat.

"Holy fuck, that's hot. Too hot." Holt thrust his hips off the mattress, and Brax rode the wave with him, pulling back enough not to gag, sucking on the way, then flicking his tongue against the underside of the head before sliding back down. "Oh fuck, Brax, please." The cock in Brax's mouth swelled and heat spread under Holt's skin, the blush and blood running ragged through his body. He arched his back and Brax sucked hard. "Yes, fuck, yes!" Holt shouted.

Hot, thick come hit the back of Brax's throat, and he swallowed it down. Greedy, feeding the hunger, sucking every last drop, and licking Holt clean until laughter above him broke through the lusty haze. Brax pulled off and glanced up.

Holt's arm was thrown over his face, but he lifted it enough to peek at Brax. "Jesus, that's what they call high-school-level embarrassing, wasn't it?"

Brax gave Holt's hand still in his a squeeze. "But was it good?"

"*Good* is an understatement." Holt used their hands to tug Brax up and onto the bed beside him. "I didn't think I could do that with anyone."

"You definitely can." Brax nuzzled his armpit, desperate for more of his scent. He inhaled deep, dizzy on it, stoking his own still raging need. He reached a hand down to stroke his cock.

Holt intercepted it. "Can I?"

"Please." Brax shoved his boxers down and off, and when Holt's hand closed around his shaft, he forgot what he was doing, forgot his own fucking name. "Yeah, just like that."

Holt's grip was a little dry at first, a little tighter than Brax usually liked, but precome made the glide smooth after only a few strokes, and the tightness revved him up faster. He rolled onto his back and spread his legs, opening himself for more.

Holt rolled with him, front pressed against his side. "Fuck, Brax, seeing you like this, knowing I did this..." He fondled Brax's balls with his other hand. "Fuck, it's making me hard again already."

Brax chuckled. "Stamina of a twenty-three-year-old."

He thrust his dick against Brax's hip. "You complaining?"

"Fuck no. Youth can win this one." He pushed up into Holt's grip and rolled his head to the side, opening his eyes. His heart clenched at the sight of Holt watching with rapt attention as he stroked Brax's cock. "Feels good." He slipped his arm under Holt's and held his pelvis against his hip, eager to feel him, letting his imagination wander to how Holt's dick would feel pounding inside him. Except as much as he wanted that, it really would ruin him forever, and possibly blow Holt's mind completely. But they were both building, and fuck if Brax didn't want to come together this time. Wanted to share that with Holt too.

"Come here." He rolled Holt more fully on top of him

and maneuvered him between his legs, their cocks lining up.

"Oh fuck," Holt cursed. But the "fuck" that followed did not sound like the good kind. Neither did the stillness that washed over his body. He lowered his weight onto his elbows and buried his face in Brax's neck. "I fucked up," he mumbled. "I don't have condoms and lube. I was in such a hurry to get to the club, afraid I'd talk myself out of it, and I figured if I went home with somebody, they'd have that stuff. Do you?"

Brax couldn't help but laugh, some of the tension easing with Holt's familiar verbal vomit and with at least one decision made easier. "One, don't ever count on that. Two, I do, but it's back at my hotel room." Holt's face fell until Brax hitched his legs higher, sliding them along Holt's flanks, grinding their cocks together. "More than one way to have sex, as we've already proven," he said. "And this is more than enough." More than he thought he'd ever get. Using both hands, he held Holt's face above his and kissed him long and deep, pouring every ounce of gratitude and desire he could muster into the kiss. When they came up for air, he grasped Holt's wrist, brought his hand to his face, and licked Holt's palm.

Holt shuddered. Shuddered again when Brax guided the slick hand around their cocks. "Oh shit, Brax."

Brax nipped his ear. "Make us come, Holt."

Holt's grip around them was just right, and Brax tried to memorize everything. More mental pictures. The feel of Holt's body blanketing his. Holt's thick, hard cock rutting against his. Holt's strong sure grip jacking them together.

Holt's smell amplified to the max. Holt's grunts and "fucks" in his ear. Holt's taste as he kept returning for more kisses.

When Holt's rhythm began to falter, Brax covered his hand, steadying, guiding. Two strokes later, Holt howled and came within their grip. The added slick and riotous heat were exactly what Brax needed to follow him over the edge.

"Holy shit, Brax, that was..." Holt collapsed on top of him, then shifted to the side, streaking come across Brax's hip. "That was fucking amazing."

Brax buried his nose against his temple. "You were amazing."

Holt yawned, his body growing heavier. A twentysomething's ability to pass out right after sex too. "I'm happy you were my first," he mumbled.

Brax knew he should get up, get a rag and clean them off, but everything felt so good—the soft mattress at his back and Holt right where he was supposed to be, in his arms and snoring lightly. His promise kept. "I'm happy it was me too."

Brax patted down his pockets, making sure he had everything. Keys, phone, wallet, candies. He popped one of the latter into his mouth, a deterrent. If he was sucking on it, he wouldn't be able to suck on something else he wanted more. If he gave in to that temptation, he might never leave this hotel room, might irrevocably wreck the most important relationship of his life. Would definitely miss his wheels-up time.

He eyed the lofted area, listening to the man snoring in the bed up there. He should just turn out the lights and go. But fuck, he did not want to leave that way. Not after the most incredible night of his life. Not when an ocean and a war were about to be laid between him and Holt with no guarantees when—*if*—they'd see each other again.

He clicked off the lamps, the room cast in the waning moonlight. Outside, the dark sky was beginning to lighten from black to blue, the sun working its way up to the horizon. Brax approached the stairs with the same slow speed, taking the time to gather and fold Holt's clothes, setting them at the foot of the steps with Holt's phone on top. Climbing the stairs, he paused at the top, snapping another mental picture and adding it to the album from the previous night.

Holt was on his back in the middle of the bed, a single sheet slung across his hips, his tattooed arm on the pillow above his head and his other arm stretched toward where Brax had slept too few hours beside him. The splotchy blush from last night was gone, leaving his skin pale, freckled, and lightly furred, but for the bruise on his neck that matched the one on Brax's. And the one on Holt's thigh Brax couldn't see for the sheet. All that strength, all that muscle, was gorgeous at rest, same as it was in uniform executing maneuvers, or in a tank dancing at the club, or writhing naked below Brax as he sucked his cock.

Brax's gaze drifted down, following the line of coarse hair to the not insignificant bump beneath the sheet.

Twenty-three, raring to go again, even in his sleep. Brax could just—He clicked the candy against his teeth, stopping the thought before it spiraled further.

He raised his eyes to Holt's face and kept careful watch as he crossed the room and lowered himself onto the side of the bed. Holt shifted toward him, blinking sleepily. "Cap?"

"Shh, Private, it's early. I'm wheels up at oh-six-hundred. I just wanted to say goodbye."

"I'll get up." He blinked more determinedly and planted an elbow on the mattress.

Brax cupped his bare shoulder and pushed him gently back down. His skin was so warm. Brax wanted to touch more of it, all of it, again. He withdrew his hand instead and folded it with the other in his lap. "Your flight home isn't until noon. You got an alarm set on your phone?"

Holt nodded.

"Good, go back to sleep. Phone is on your clothes at the foot of the stairs."

Holt relaxed back into the mattress, eyes fluttering closed, and Brax gave in to the urge to run a hand over his head, feeling the soft bristles one last time. Resisting the temptation to coast lower, Brax moved to stand, but Holt shot out a hand, grasping his wrist. Another question added to the list. Holt's reflexes were more honed than the military taught. What was it he'd said once? That his family had made sure he could handle himself in one-on-one situations? Brax quickly forgot the quandary, though, as he met Holt's gaze. Last night's fire was gone, just fear there now despite the power of the grip on Brax's wrist. "I don't know if I can do this without you. You're my best friend." His voice cracked. "Tell me I didn't fuck this up."

Brax settled back down and braced a hand on the mattress on the other side of Holt's head, forcing Holt onto his back. He leaned over and kissed his forehead, lingering there. "You didn't, and you can." He drew back, meeting Holt's eyes. "You've got your whole life ahead of you, Holt Madigan. Go live it."

Holt loosened his hold on his wrist and adjusted his grip, lacing their fingers together and resting their clasped hands on his chest. "What if I never find this spark again?"

"You will." It would hurt like hell for Brax, but the thing he wanted more than his own happiness was Holt's. Happiness for his best friend, for the man he loved. Even more after last night. But in the current space and time, there wasn't a damn thing he could do about it. They were headed in opposite directions for the foreseeable future, and Holt had years longer than him. He had to let Holt live his life, and he had to live his too. "Hopefully you'll find it with someone closer to your own age."

Holt blushed. "That didn't matter last night." He lowered his gaze and stared at their joined hands, his thumb caressing the side of Brax's. "What about you? Your life from here?"

"I'm gonna finish my twenty, then we'll see." Brax pushed off with his braced hand and sat up straight, leaving his other hand still in Holt's and giving it a squeeze. "But if you ever need me, I'm only a message away. I will always be there for you."

Brown eyes lifted to his. Some of the fear still swirled

there, together with an added touch of sadness, but also fondness and friendship that warmed Brax to his core. "I'm going to miss you. Not the desert, fuck the desert, but you…"

Brax chuckled. "Go home to your fog, Private." He started to stand, but Holt still wouldn't let go.

"Come visit me."

"I promise." He lifted Holt's hand to his lips and kissed his knuckles, sealing it.

And his fate.

CHAPTER SIX

The Next Day

There was a message waiting for Brax when he arrived back at camp.

Oski15: I'm home.

A picture was attached. Holt, in that hideous orange flannel, arms outstretched, standing on a pier with the Bay Bridge in the background. Only half the towers were visible, fog as thick as pea soup swirling around the bridge and around Holt, obscuring everything else in the picture.

Brooklyn11219: I thought you said the weather was perfect there.

Oski15: It is :)

Brax waited until later that night, when there was no one else in the office where the shared printer lived, to print the picture. He stared at it the length of one candy, then folded it and put it in his wallet. Back in his room, he tucked it in the frame behind the picture of his mom and grandfather.

He'd kept his promise. The private was home. And the desert had never felt lonelier.

The Next Monday

Oski15: Same bat time, same bat channel?

Their usual chat time had been the ass-crack of dawn with Holt on the East Coast. It would be the middle of the night in San Francisco. But maybe that's what Holt needed. To stick to his routine and to talk to a friend when the nightmares woke him.

Brooklyn11219: Roger that.

A Month Later

Oski15: I'm home but not.

Brax set aside his sandwich, his appetite waning on a tide of worry.

Brooklyn11219: Talk to me.

Oski15: I left at 18. Hawes and I used to share a room. Weird at 23. Third floor was our parents', but I couldn't yet.

There was a pause before the words continued, rapidly appearing onscreen, Holt's keystrokes no less maniacal now that he was home.

Oski15: I miss them, but it's not the same. Guess that part worked.

Another long pause during which Brax's worry ratcheted higher.

Oski15: I'm in the attic now, which used to be our bonus room. They offered to move my furniture up here, but all I need is a cot. It was simpler in the desert. Things are... not... here.

Holt adored his siblings, that much was clear whenever he spoke of them, but Brax had a hard time getting a read on Holt's relationship with the rest of his family. Holt missed his parents, though he never talked much about the time before their deaths, and he revered his grandparents, but there was a tension there too. Expectations, maybe? Would make sense in such a successful family. While the military was hard in its own way, in some ways, it had been easier for Holt. That's how it worked out for a lot of soldiers. Going back to civilian life was not easy from the stories Brax had heard. He hadn't been lying when he'd implied he was worried about his own reintegration one day. But that was for another time. Today, Holt needed his help.

Brooklyn11219: Reintegration is hard. It was hard integrating here too.

Oski15: But I had you.

Brax's chest ached and his hands shook, making it hard to type.

Brooklyn11219: You still do. But you also need to find people you can talk to there. Who

know what you're going through. Go to the VA.
Find a support group. Did they give you a list
before you left base?

**Oski15: I know, and yes, they did. Jeremy
reached out already. You have something to do
with that?**

**Brooklyn11219: Met Jeremy in OCS. He's a
good guy and there in SF. Thought he could
help.**

Brax had woken up from his own nightmare his first
night back at camp. Holt's brown eyes had stared at him
through a bank of fog, filled with the same despondent fear
and sadness Brax had seen in them the night he'd found
Holt hiding under his bed. The same night Brax had
learned something about the private that had set Holt on a
course to succeed, in the army and in dealing with his
fears. Holt needed to focus on something besides the fear
and the before and after differences he couldn't help but
notice. A touchstone that had always been there—before,
during, and after his service.

**Brooklyn11219: You also went home with
certain skills on hyperdrive.**

**Oski15: Are you encouraging illegal behav-
ior, Cap? Of the hacking sort?**

Brax chuckled.

Brooklyn11219: Me? Never.

Oski15: This room would make a good lair.

Brax imagined Holt in an office chair, spinning round
and round, devising a monstrous computer setup—

multiple screens, a line of keyboards, stacks of CPUs—like he'd had at his fingertips in Camp Casey's command center. Yes, that's what Holt needed, a project that put the skills that had rescued him, motivated him time and again, to good use.

Brooklyn11219: Find your focus, Holt, and you'll find yourself. Just like you did here.

After they finished chatting, Brax emailed Jeremy, thanked him for reaching out to Holt, and asked him to reach out again soon.

A Couple Weeks Later

Brooklyn11219: Do I have you to thank for tonight's Hanukkah meal?

Oski15: Least I could do. I have you to thank for this.

A picture downloaded. Holt stood in front of a wall of digital mayhem, exactly how Brax had pictured it. Sadness lingered in Holt's eyes, but not as bad as the night Brax had found him under the bed, and not as bad as Holt's words had led Brax to imagine a couple weeks ago. But the dark circles under his eyes worried Brax more than a little. Were they from long nights building computers, or were the nightmares getting worse?

A Few Months Later

Oski15: I've started going to the support group more regularly. It's good to know it's not just me with nightmares. But the nightmares…

Worry realized, Brax ignored his twisting insides and hurried to type back a message.

Brooklyn11219: You're not alone. You've got Jeremy, the group, and your family there. Me here.

Too fucking far away when Holt needed him most.

Holt's response surprised him.

Oski15: Are you alone? Do you have anyone there? Do you have nightmares?

Of Holt not opening his eyes that day in the rubble.

Of Holt on the dance floor with someone else.

Of a blinking cursor, no message incoming.

Of big brown eyes in the fog, full of sadness, too far away for Brax to fix.

Brooklyn11219: We all have nightmares. It's normal. And yes, I have friends here to talk to.

Thanks to Holt.

Brooklyn11219:   Marsh   keeps   talking computer at me like he thinks I'm you, and Luther and Teague feed me well. Helps me sleep better.

Worse, in fact, though Marsh's company on nights when the nightmares were too vivid, the worries too close to the surface—usually Mondays, the fear of the blinking cursor the next day riding Brax hard—was a comfort. But

Marsh wasn't his best friend; neither were Luther or Teague.

Brooklyn11219: You can message me anytime. It doesn't only have to be on Tuesdays.

Oski15: Okay, will do. Same to you.

He thought Holt was done but then another question came through.

Oski15: Have you thought any more about what you're going to do next year?

Brax coasted his fingers over the framed picture on his desk, thinking more about the photo behind the one displayed. Fuck, at this point, he was more afraid of leaving the desert than he was of dying there.

Brooklyn11219: I'm not sure yet. What do you think I should do?

Oski15: Counselor. You help people, Cap. All of us there, me now.

It was an idea. He had options. He was a twenty-year army vet with experience as military police and in orientation and training. Police department placements, feds, defense contractors, VA positions were all on the table. But that wasn't what the fear of leaving was really about for him.

Brooklyn11219: Maybe. Or cop or parole officer. I've got options. Not sure where though. Twenty years here, and no family left in New York.

There was a long pause, then an answer that twisted Brax's insides more.

Oski15: You have family. And you made me a promise.

Eight Months Later

They'd been chatting for almost an hour. It had been a four day stretch since they'd last caught up, long for them now. Brax had been off base in a nearby village for a training exercise with local law enforcement. Holt was filling him in on some of the IT improvements he'd made at Madigan Cold Storage, his family's business, while Brax updated him on Marsh's recent promotion, the marathon chess game they had going, and Luther and Teague's extravagant Thanksgiving dinner.

He was due in a meeting in thirty, but he wanted to tell Holt his news. Except he was nervous as hell. Nervous whether Holt would be happy about it or if he'd be disappointed or, worse yet, angry.

He was breaking a promise of sorts. Not that he hadn't tried to keep it. Holt deserved to hear that from him. There was also a part of Brax that was excited and wanted desperately to share the news.

Brooklyn11219: I made a decision. Put in my retirement papers.

Oski15: *clapping* So when are you coming to San Francisco?

Brooklyn11219: I applied for a job there.

Oski15: *no longer clapping* Why didn't you tell me?

Brooklyn11219: Didn't want to get your hopes up, which was the right call because I didn't get it.

Oski15: Fuck. Where you gonna be?

Brooklyn11219: Boston Police Department.

There was a long delay during which Brax feared he'd lost his best friend. His stomach sank, his chest ached, and sweat broke out across his brow. He nervously brushed his fingers over the keyboard, working up an apology.

But then a picture appeared. Holt in one of his ratty Raptors tees and a clashing flannel, holding a bottle of Dom Perignon in one hand and a champagne flute in the other. A toast, to him.

Relief washed over Brax, the wave so powerful he had to lay his head in his arms on his desk, catching his breath and waiting for his racing pulse to slow.

The computer dinged with another message. Brax peeked at the screen.

Oski15: Fancy for the fancy.

And laughed out loud. He straightened and put his fingers back on the keyboard.

Brooklyn11219: Ayers pulled some strings.

Oski15: Congrats, Brax. You deserve it.

The "Brax" drowned him in an even stronger wave. Of memories from their night together over a year ago. Holt laid out on the bed, legs spread, his back arched and his cock hard in Brax's mouth, chanting "Brax" among a string of lust-drenched curses.

Brax's dick ached worse than his chest.

Oski15: Keep me posted on the retirement ceremony. I want to be there.

Brooklyn11219: I'll send you the details as soon as I have them.

After they signed off, Brax took an unscheduled shower. Cock in hand, he brought himself off to the memories of Holt's smell, his taste, and his tight grip around Brax's cock. He muffled his groan in the crook of his arm and tried to wash away his love for a man who was still out of reach.

Two Months Later

Oski15: I learned something about myself today.

Brooklyn11219: What's that?

Oski15: I think I'm demisexual.

Brax had heard the term before but only recently. In preparing for his move to Boston, he'd been researching the local LGBTQ community. Where to live, where to hang out, where he might volunteer his time. Working in law enforcement wasn't the most queer-friendly career, but it would be more queer friendly than the military. Enough that he felt comfortable in planning not to hide, to enjoy himself, and to volunteer for causes that were personally meaningful to him.

He opened his internet browser and typed in *demisexual*, but before the results returned, another message from Holt popped up.

Oski15: Let me back up... Amelia, she works for the family, she's a nurse and a family friend. Actually, I think my grandfather likes her better than his own grandkids.

A nurse that worked for their family? In cold storage? But that wasn't the curiosity that most caught Brax's attention. There was a fondness in Holt's message, even in digital, that made Brax sit up straighter.

Oski15: She volunteers at a shelter for LGBTQ teens. She does checkups and stuff for them. Hawes and Helena volunteer there too. I went with them today. They needed some IT help. Amelia introduced me to one of the counselors who is demi. Mike only feels attraction to a person if there's trust and a deeper connection. The relationship comes first, not just any relationship either, and then the attraction.

Brax rewound to that night over a year ago, to him and Holt in a penthouse suite, to Holt scooting next to him on the couch. *"I trust you. I know you. I feel connected to you. Safe. And for some reason, that turns me the fuck on. Not anyone else tonight. No one in the past either. Just you. I want you."*

Holt's mind had apparently gone to the same place, judging by his next message.

Oski15: That's why I only felt a spark with you that night. We have a connection, a real one. A deep one. You're my best friend. I was attracted to you.

Was. If he dwelled on that word, Brax might never leave the service, might question every decision he'd made the past five years. He hedged instead.

Brooklyn11219: That makes sense. I'm sorry I didn't know.

Oski15: Don't be. The term is pretty new, and I didn't know either, but now I do. I don't feel so abnormal.

Brax leaped over the hedge, concern for Holt surging to the forefront again. Was that how he'd made Holt feel that night? *Abnormal.* He'd wanted to make him feel good, to do something wonderful for, and share something wonderful with, his friend.

Brooklyn11219: You were never abnormal, Holt. You were always you. I'm sorry if I ever made you feel that way.

Oski15: No, no, no. You didn't. Fucking chat. The tone is never right. I should have called.

Except that was never easy, and at the rate Holt was typing, he probably got the words out faster this way. Words that were flowing again.

Oski15: I wanted to thank you. For never

judging me and for being a safe space when I needed it.

Brax sighed with relief.

Brooklyn11219: You did the same for me, and I always will be, whenever you need me.

Oski15: Thank you for being my family, my friend.

Then.

Holt hadn't typed it, and Brax was certain he hadn't meant it. Brax was reading into meaning versus Holt leaving something unsaid, but once Brax had thought it, he couldn't unthink it. The dwelling, it seemed, was inevitable. He couldn't shake the knot that was forming in his stomach. Holt had all those things back now—family, friends, a safe space. How much longer would he still need him?

Later That Year

Brax had laid out everything he needed for the retirement ceremony. Uniform, medals, ribbons. There was just one thing missing.

The cell phone that had been waiting for him upon his return stateside—fancier than anything he'd ever used—rang. He snatched it off the desk, surprised to see an incoming call from Holt. Was he calling from the airplane?

"Hey, what're you—"

"Cap, I'm so sorry, but I'm not gonna make it. Family emergency."

Brax sank onto the edge of the bed, wrinkling his uniform, not giving a shit about it any longer. All his focus was on the phone in his hand and the man on the other end of the line. Hospital sounds were unmistakable in the background, and Holt's voice was rough and graveled with weariness.

"What's going on?" he said. "Talk to me."

"Something's up with my grandfather." A *snick* of a door, then the background noise quieted. "We're at the hospital. Been here since four this morning. Amelia—"

"The family nurse. You mentioned her before."

"Yeah, she's getting him seen. I know he's in good hands, but—"

There were no *buts*. Holt had flown a number of times over the past two years, and it seemed on every trip something went awry. "Do not fly across the country and get stuck here. Your luck with flights and weather is shit."

He chuckled, but it was more tired than amused. "I'm really sorry."

So was Brax, the disappointment *Titanic*-sized, but this wasn't Holt's fault. It couldn't be helped. And this wouldn't be the first time. More instances like this would occur, especially with Brax's new job. They had to get used to it. "Hey, it's okay. You need to be with your family."

"I know, but you're my family too."

A knock sounded in the background, followed by a woman's voice. "Babe, Papa Cal's awake."

Babe.

Iceberg ahead.

"I'll be right there," Holt said, then to Brax, "I'm sorry I can't be there, but you won't be alone. I promise."

Later that day at the ceremony, Marsh, Luther, Teague, and Max Bailey, who had just arrived back in the States, sat in the front row. The gathering was Holt Madigan's doing, making the impossible possible once again. As was the steak dinner afterward. Brax celebrated with their friends into the wee hours of the morning, playing more than a few rounds of cards in Holt's honor. The next morning, a package about the size of a shoebox and surprisingly heavy was delivered to his room. The return address was San Francisco. Inside was a note and two matching pieces of crystal.

The first, a nameplate etched with Captain Braxton Kane.

The second a candy dish with his retirement date and final rank—Lieutenant Colonel—etched along the rim and a poppy flower etched into the bottom.

He opened the note: *Cap, For your new desk. Love, H.*

Brax barely made it to the bed before his legs and heart gave out on him.

Several Months Later

Brax: You remember your bunkmate, Max Bailey?

Holt: Of course. Got his artwork on my arm.

Brax had still never seen the completed tattoo. Holt was always wearing a flannel in the pictures he sent.

Holt: He still on base there on the East Coast?

Brax: Yeah, but he's discharging later this month. His forwarding address is Daly City. I looked it up on a map. That's near San Francisco.

Holt: Yeah, a little south, but via BART, twenty minutes. What's up?

Brax: Help him with reentry? He was on an op before he left Casey that went south. Lost some of his unit. He wasn't in the best place when I saw him at the retirement ceremony.

Holt: I'm not sure I should be the person helping.

Brax smiled. He'd heard that line before, and he knew Holt had been getting better, work and friends and the shelter giving him new focus.

Brax: Jeremy said the same thing when I asked him to help you.

Holt: For real?

Brax: Yeah, for real. I think you and Max can help each other.

Holt: I'll be there for him.

The Next Year

Holt: You remember Amelia?

How could Brax forget? Holt had mentioned her with increasing frequency in their texts and conversations. He'd had a feeling this was coming. He'd prepared. Closing the police report he'd been reviewing, he stood from his dining table and made a beeline for the kitchen. He opened his baking cabinet and shifted the bags of flour and sugar around, retrieving the emergency bottle from the back corner. Johnnie Walker Blue. Same as he and Holt had shared that night four years ago. He poured two fingers' worth, tossed it back, refilled his glass, then returned to the table and his phone.

Brax: Yeah, your grandfather's favorite.

Jokes would ease the knot in his gut, right?

Holt: LOL, that's her. So, umm, we started dating a while back.

Wrong.

Brax: You've been holding out on me.

He was glad this conversation was over text. He could maintain the joking tone this way. Over the phone, it would be impossible to hide the dejection in his voice. Dejection he had no right to. He'd gone back to the desert, then to Boston. He'd told Holt to go home and live his life. Holt had done just that, and he'd found someone who made him happy. Someone closer to his own age. Someone else he had a spark with. He'd done exactly what Brax had told him to do. This was a good thing. Brax had to be happy for him.

Holt: Not intentionally. You know what this means to me. Kind of like you and the job thing, I needed to be sure.

Brax: I'm glad you found that spark with someone.

Else.

Holt: Spark isn't all there is to it. Amelia helped me understand that. She brought me to the shelter, didn't judge, and helped me put a word to it. I'm demi, and I've come to trust and care about her. We have a connection.

And she was there while Brax was a continent away. Brax took another swig of whisky.

Brax: I'm happy you found her.

Holt: I'm gonna marry her, Cap. I asked her, and she said yes.

Lowering the glass, Brax propped his elbows on the table, buried his face in his hands, and screamed.

The phone dinged.

Holt: Cap?

Cover. Divert.

Brax: I was just imagining how red your face is right now.

Holt: *flips you off*

Holt: Maybe a little. Nothing like those desert sunburns, though.

Brax: Congrats, Holt. I really am happy for you.

And he was, even if his own heart was breaking. Holt's happiness came first. Brax never wanted to see that look of sadness in his eyes again. He'd worried so much when Holt had first returned home, had seen it in his eyes again in that first picture, and Brax was terrified it would take hold when he was an ocean, then a continent away. But Amelia had entered Holt's life and given him answers and hope. She'd helped when Brax couldn't. She'd made Holt happy.

Brax would have to live with that. Somehow. He'd have to accept he was Holt's friend and nothing more.

Holt: Are we okay?

Brax didn't delay in answering, not wanting to dampen Holt's mood.

Brax: You're my best friend. Nothing is going to change that.

Holt: We're family, I know, I just—

Brax: I can't wait to meet her.

Once they finished their conversation, Brax stood, poured another glass of whisky, tossed it back in one shot, then hurled the bottle across the room.

The Next Year

Brax: A position opened up with SFPD. Do you still want me to come?

Holt: You made me a promise.

Brax: And I intend to keep it. But only if you want me there.

Brax had to ask. Had to make sure it wouldn't be awkward for Holt. They weren't exes, but they had slept together, and Holt was with someone else now.

For his part, Brax had gotten used to the mentions of Amelia, had wrapped his brain around Holt in love with someone else and accepted it. It had forced him to finally move on. Having Holt in his life was more important than losing him to an impossibility.

Holt was his family, and now he had the opportunity to be in the same town with him. But only if Holt wanted him there.

Holt: As long as you want to be here, my answer to that question will always be yes.

CHAPTER SEVEN

Six Years Ago

Brax peered out the airplane window. Normally, he wouldn't have the opportunity, always taking the aisle seat, his legs too long to be jammed into the window seat. Except he'd arrived at Logan this morning to find his seat in coach had been upgraded to first class, first row, window.

The gate agent had a note for him, along with the upgraded ticket: *Enjoy the view. Don't be freaked out by the tandem landing. —H*

If there was another plane out there on their wing, Brax couldn't see it. It was pea soup outside—like that first picture Holt had sent him—the fog so thick it left condensation on the window. Brax laid a hand on the plastic pane, fingers spread. Felt as cold as it looked. He'd left behind ninety-degree heat and ninety percent humidity in Boston... for fucking winter in July.

Confirmed when he stepped off the plane onto the

Jetway. Wind whipped off the Bay and whistled through the gaps in the mechanical walkway. Brax hitched the lapels of his blazer closer and cursed the lightweight material. Fuck. He'd need to go shopping. The moving truck with his box of wool suits wasn't scheduled to arrive until next week.

Holt thought this was perfect weather? For summer? Fuck, no wonder he'd been so out of sorts—and permanently sunburned—in the desert.

Brax followed the signs for baggage claim to the lower level of the terminal, but at the turnstile where his luggage was due, a suited man waited, Brax's suitcase and duffel already at his side. He held a paper placard that read *Braxton Kane*.

"You're here for me?" Brax said.

"Braxton Kane?"

Brax nodded.

"Then, yes, sir, and I already have your bags. A car is waiting outside."

"Did the department send you?"

"No, sir. Mr. Madigan."

Brax's insides were pulled in two different directions. Lightness from the laughter he had to bite back. *Mr. Madigan.* Heaviness from the disappointment that Mr. Madigan —who'd told him to come, who'd paid for his first-class ticket, who'd sent a car for him—wasn't there himself.

"Mr. Madigan had a work emergency," the driver said, answering Brax's unasked question. "He apologizes for not being here. If you'll follow me, sir."

They loaded into a town car and were out of the

airport faster than Brax thought possible. But there was no escaping the fog. It only grew thicker as they approached the city, like someone had laid a heavy wool blanket over San Francisco's skyscrapers.

"Is it always like this?" he asked.

"Summer in the city," the driver replied. "Though this week is a little drearier than usual."

They crested a large overpass, the ballpark on the right, and began to weave through the city's streets. San Francisco wasn't what Brax expected. A mishmash of old and new buildings, some short and others tall, but not like New York City, and even further from what he'd grown used to in Boston.

It felt different, wrong almost, like nothing he knew. He felt out of place, even more so than he had his first day in the desert. Brax wondered, not for the first time, if this whole thing was a colossal mistake. This was never supposed to be, never supposed to happen. Except for that one night in DC, he and Holt had never been in the same place outside of Camp Casey. Never had the chance to be friends in civilian life. What if this ruined everything?

Before he was able to tell the driver to turn around and take him back to the airport, the car pulled to the curb in front of a two-story building. One he didn't recognize. It was an older building, judging by the architecture, but newly renovated, judging by the black-framed gable windows and arched doorway. A rainbow was painted into the crenellations over the door. Not the police station, certainly not his rental, and not the Victorian mansion Holt had described to him as the Madigan family home.

"Are we in the right place?"

"Yes, sir. This is one of the LGBTQ shelters the Madigans sponsor."

"One of?"

"Yes, sir. There are several…"

The driver was still talking but Brax's attention was drawn elsewhere. To the big man pushing open the shelter's door and loping down the front steps. Bigger than Brax remembered, and the tattoo sleeve on Holt's right arm was on full display beneath short sleeves, an array of colors that contrasted with his pale freckled face and other bare arm. He'd let his hair grow out too, longer waves of reddish-dark blond on top, and a neatly trimmed auburn beard that covered his dimpled chin, making his jaw seem more square, more severe. Severity that was undercut by brown eyes wide with joy. Not a bit of fear or sadness in them. Holt looked good, happy, a long way from the man who five years ago questioned if he belonged back home.

Brax didn't question his decision to move to San Francisco any longer either. Especially not when Holt's lips curved into a huge smile, nearly splitting his face in two. Brax was meant to be where this man was. Period. He threw open the car door, and his feet hit the sidewalk at a brisk pace, embarrassingly almost running. But Holt was too, so fuck it. They collided midwalkway, throwing their arms around each other.

"Hey, Cap," Holt mumbled against his shoulder.

"Private."

"Fuck, I missed you."

Brax hugged him tighter. "Missed you too."

They stayed like that another minute or so before Brax drew back, needing to see Holt's face again. For real, in person. He was still smiling, and Brax felt his own lips curve to match.

"I'm sorry I wasn't at the airport," Holt said. "One of the kids here needed me."

Yes, Holt had finally settled into his life in San Francisco, where he was needed, and it pleased Brax to hear. "Thanks for the ride and the flight upgrade," he said. "Though I couldn't see anything outside the plane's window for this fog. I thought you said the weather was perfect here."

"It is perfect." Holt flicked his eyes up at the gray sky. "Nothing like summer in the city."

"Stop lying, babe," came a voice from behind them. "I can see the goosebumps from here. Your ass is freezing."

Holt stepped the rest of the way out of Brax's arms, shifting to his side and revealing a tall willowy woman coming down the shelter steps. She was beautiful with long dark hair, alabaster skin, and bright green eyes, and she moved toward them with a gracefulness Brax had to admit was a perfect counter to Holt's massive bulk.

"Someone I want to introduce you to," Holt said. The way his smile softened and love flooded his eyes, the way he slid an arm around her waist and held her tight, gave Brax that ripped-in-half feeling again. His heart sank for himself but flew high for Holt.

"This is Amelia," Holt said. "Amelia, this is Braxton Kane."

"I've heard a lot about you." She held out her hand. "It's a pleasure to meet you."

"Likewise." Brax returned the handshake, impressed by Amelia's strong, confident grip. Again, a perfect match for Holt.

"Thank you for making sure he got home," she said, drawing back her hand and patting Holt's chest. "The family will never be able to repay you."

"I didn't—"

"Yeah, you did," Holt declared. He stepped forward and yanked him into another crushing hug. "And now you're home too."

Brax couldn't argue the truth he felt in his bones. This hadn't been a mistake. This was, indeed, exactly where he was supposed to be.

The Next Day

"This will be your office." Chief Williams opened the door to the corner office at the opposite end of the hall from his own. Intentional, if Brax had to guess. Truth be told, he was surprised he'd gotten the job at all. His interview with Williams had been awkward, terse, and almost hostile, but he'd clicked well with the other officers with whom he'd interviewed. The others had assured him it was just the chief's way.

From the interview then, and the morning meetings and welcome lunch today, he had the distinct impression Chief Williams was not looking for an assistant chief to work with, but rather someone to work for him. Brax wasn't sure if that was in a do-my-bidding way or a do-the-shit-I don't-want-to way. Maybe both, more of the latter if Brax had to guess, especially given the afternoon tee time with several other law enforcement officials, including US Attorney Bowers, with whom Williams seemed particularly chummy. In any event, Brax could do the job. He was used to being the middleman, the one subordinates came to first. Brax would keep to his end of the hall, and Williams could keep to the other where Bowers was waiting for him now. He wasn't going to be a pleasant boss to work for, but it was worth it to be there with Holt.

"Kane." Williams's sharp bark jerked him back to the present where the chief had ventured ahead of him into the office. He was resting against the front of Brax's new desk. Mostly bare except for the computer and phone.

And three thick file folders stacked in the middle. Cases already?

Brax stepped into the office. "Yes, sir."

"Your captain in Boston said you had some experience with organized crime."

"Mostly cartels."

"We got those too, but let's start with this." Williams grabbed the folders off the desk and held them out to him. "Shake up happening with one of the city's crime families."

Brax glimpsed the name on the file tabs and almost dropped them.

MADIGAN.

Dread clawed up his spine. Surely not. San Francisco

had a sizable Irish American population. Maybe this was a different Madigan family. Some of the ones he knew back in New York. This would be like Holt's first day at Casey, when Brax had wondered if Holt was connected to any of those Madigans. He'd open the folders and just like last time—

Except it wasn't like last time. His blood ran cold, and his world came to a screeching fucking halt. He recognized these names.

Rose and Callum Madigan.

Noah and Charlotte Madigan.

Helena.

Hawes.

Holt.

There was no denying this. They were the same Madigans as *his* Madigan, further confirmed by Williams. "Patriarch just stepped down and the grandson, Hawes, is taking over. They run a successful cold storage business, but it's a front. Not all they do by a long shot. Only the big one is remotely clean, and that's because he's a good enough hacker to cover his tracks."

The big one. A good enough hacker.

The best hacker Brax knew.

Holt.

This was the answer. To all those questions that had kept Brax awake at night.

"This something you can handle?" Williams asked.

"Yes, sir. I'll get up to speed."

"Good." He pushed off the desk and headed for the door. "We'll discuss in a couple days after you get through the rest of department orientation." He left without another word, which was good since Brax didn't have any, his mind, heart, and guts a jumbled mess.

Hours later, Brax wasn't any less unsettled. He'd read through the three thick files, one for each generation. He struggled to fit his best friend, a person he thought he knew almost as well as himself, a man who still held a wide swath of his heart, into the bloody picture the files painted. There was no denying certain facts, certain statements that suddenly made sense.

Holt's parents' sudden death.

His brother's and sister's invincible attitudes.

The family fortune.

The skills Holt had come into the army with, the seemingly innate proficiency with weapons and hand-to-hand combat at odds with a man his size. They weren't innate, though. Holt had been trained. By his family.

Of assassins.

"I can handle myself in one-on-one situations. My family made sure of that."

The Madigans didn't just run a cold storage business. They were ghosts who haunted the city and killed and maimed in a cold, methodical fashion. Who had built an empire of fear and leverage. Who, over the past five years, had expanded their arsenal to include cybercrimes and digital assassination.

Only one explanation for that.

Brax flipped to the middle section of the last file. Thinner than the other two but the most dangerous to him. A picture of Holt stared back at him from the left flap.

Even if there wasn't an Amelia in the picture, even if Holt didn't look happier than Brax had ever seen him, this right here knocked the impossible future a tiny part of Brax's heart still clung to off the fucking cliff. A nosedive into the abyss. Why the fuck had he come to San Francisco? Why the fuck hadn't Holt said anything? He had to know this couldn't work. Brax, an assistant chief of police, and Holt, a digital assassin, among a family of assassins. Fuck, could they even still be friends?

The stab of loss cut deep, and Brax lashed out in pain, sending the files careening off his desk. The folders fluttered to the floor, the antithesis of violence, and not satisfying in the least. Just fucking silence. No pens clattering down, no stapler hitting with a *thunk*, no crystal candy dish shattering as it hit the floor.

Fuck.

Could he even put the name plate and candy dish on his desk without incriminating himself? Without looking at them every day and feeling like a traitor to one or the other of the two things he loved most in this world?

Anger and frustration escalated, searching for another target. He drew back an arm, preparing to swing at the computer.

"I wouldn't do that if I were you."

His arm halted midswing, and his gaze darted to the woman in the doorway. He'd been so lost in his head, in his pain, he hadn't heard her approach. Or maybe she was just that silent... and deadly. He recognized her from Holt's many descriptions—a petite powerhouse, long blond hair, dancing blue eyes, a teasing troublemaker's smile. A match to the photo in the last third of the last folder, the contents of which were strewn across the floor. For the subject of the SFPD's ongoing investigation to see.

Fuck.

"My brother would be upset if you did grievous harm to a computer."

She strode into the office and knelt to gather the scattered files. Brax remained frozen. From everything he'd read in those files, even though Hawes Madigan had been dubbed the "Prince of Killers," Helena Madigan was the deadliest of the current generation of assassins, but you wouldn't know it by her petite frame, designer suit, and flirtatious smile.

"What are you doing here?" he asked.

She rose, files in hand. "Meeting with a client."

A bark of laughter escaped. "That's right. Criminal law, specializing in the wrongfully accused. When Holt told me, I admired you. Now..."

"The irony, right?" She gave him a cheeky grin and tossed the files on his desk.

"Not what I expected."

"Expect not." She lowered herself into the guest chair, prim and proper, like a good little lawyer. Who could kill him with her dainty, bare hands. "Do you love him?"

The question knocked him for another loop. So hard he didn't hesitate to answer with the truth. "Yes."

"He loves you too."

Brax bit back his gasp.

"Talks about you all the time," she carried on, oblivious

to the earthquakes she'd triggered. "You're practically family, so I need to make sure this is going to work."

He let out a long slow breath and adjusted in his chair. "Why didn't he tell me?"

"Because he was afraid to lose you. After Mom and Dad died, Holt withdrew more and more each day. He was a shell of the big brother I loved when he left for the army." A flash of remembered pain streaked across her sharp features. She definitely favored Hawes more than Holt, but that lost look was the same one Brax had seen on Holt's face before. It was gone the next instant, her trial lawyer's mask back in place. She scooted forward in her chair. "You gave him back to us, to himself. It was touch and go there when he first got home, but you were his lifeline. Every Tuesday, then more frequently, a little more life was pumped back into him, enough to carry him through another week. He couldn't lose that—*lose you*—too."

"He could never lose me. I promised—"

"What did you promise, Assistant Chief Kane?"

He suddenly felt like he was being cross-examined and had been caught in a lie. He dodged. "I don't remember introducing myself."

She smirked. "I picked out the name plate, though the title's wrong.

"Inside joke."

"That's what Holt said. Now, answer the question."

Against his better judgment, Brax liked her. Liked her even more for being there on her brother's behalf, Holt's best interest at heart. This visit wasn't about the family business; it was about protecting Holt. *That* he understood. "I promised to always protect him."

"Good." She brushed her hands down her skirt and stood. "This will work then."

"How's that exactly?"

She paused with her hand on the doorknob and glanced over her shoulder. "There's a reason Holt's on digital."

The chief's words came back to him. "You're keeping him clean."

"As clean as we can."

"Why?"

Helena's features softened into a genuine smile, fondness melting the smirking mask. "Because he's the best of us."

CHAPTER EIGHT

Nine Months Ago

Holt had lied to him—again and again—with escalating and frightening frequency. Lies that had put lives and jobs, including his own, in jeopardy. Brax didn't know how to feel about that. Anger, betrayal, hurt, fear. Fucking hell, the fear. Not the same sort that had caused him to muscle his way onto a special ops team, that had left him no choice but to cover Holt from fire and yank him into his arms and under a bed as the world crashed down around them. In those instances, Brax had had a choice, a modicum of control, even if his heart had dictated his actions.

This fear was different. It had started five years ago when Helena Madigan had strolled into his office and planted the seed. Had hit its first major growth spurt the night Isabelle Costa—*no*, Special Agent Isabella Constantine—had been killed. Had bloomed beautiful, delicate flowers the day eight months ago when the little girl bundled in Brax's arms—his goddaughter, Lily—was born.

Had grown like a fucking fantasy beanstalk the past week and a half as everything in his life, everyone and everything he loved—Holt, Lily, the unlikely family he'd found, his job —were compromised.

He'd promised to always protect Holt, a promise that had extended to the Madigans and especially to Lily, Holt and Amelia's daughter, but how could Brax keep his promises when he didn't have all the facts? Granted if he had, he would have had no choice but to arrest his family. He understood, but he didn't like it. Didn't like having no fucking control over the situation, and the fear that lack of control brought was unlike anything he'd ever felt.

And when this latest chaos was over, what next? The present situation was untenable. He couldn't live like this, always half in the dark where his loved ones were concerned. But what was the alternative? How did this ever work? How did this fear, this life, not become a giant eucalyptus tree, layers peeling and ever changing on the outside, rotting from the inside, never knowing when it might fall and obliterate him? How did he keep his promise?

He was untethered, adrift, pushed around in dark waters by forces he couldn't see. Which Holt had kept from him. Same as he'd kept from him whatever they were up to this morning. Holt had shown up on his doorstep with Lily asleep in her carrier and her diaper bag stuffed full. He looked a wreck, still cut up over his own grand-mother's betrayal, a treason in which his wife had played a starring role. Brax had pulled him inside and into his arms and caught Holt's tears on his shoulder. But that was all the time he'd had with Holt before a text from Hawes called Holt into action. Before fear settled heavy on Brax's shoulders once more.

Did he still love Holt Madigan? Yes. Did he trust Holt Madigan? Not completely. Would he still do anything to protect him? Yes, and there was the fucking rub.

An hour passed, Brax circling his apartment, Lily in his arms, waiting for a call from the station to tell him about the latest tragedy involving his family. But it was a knock on the door—not the station ringtone—that interrupted him.

He was surprised when he opened the door to the woman dressed in boots, designer jeans, a knit top, and a blazer, her dark curls piled on top of her head. She was an unexpected visitor. But as Brax recalled his other interactions with Melissa Cruz over the past five years, her appearance now, in the middle of a shitstorm, made perfect sense. She was the eyes and ears of this town. Had been since she was the FBI Special Agent in Charge and was even more so now that she was a free agent.

But on whose behalf was she there? The Madigans had somehow stayed off the FBI's radar, which he suspected Cruz had something to do with. But she'd married into the Talley family a few years back, and they were tied to both law enforcement and shipping. And she was a bounty hunter. Fear settled even heavier. Down to his bones. Had an arrest warrant been issued? Or had someone taken an unofficial bounty out on his family? Only one way to find out.

"Cruz." He opened the door for her to enter. "What can I do for you?"

"I didn't come here for help. I came here to help *you*." She strolled past him and sauntered down the long narrow hallway to the living area at the back of his condo. She made herself at home at his dining table and pulled out the chair next to her. "Come have a seat, Chief."

Less is more. Let her lead.

He drew Lily's pop up crib closer to the table and settled her inside, making sure she was cozy and nestled in, still snoozing peacefully, before he took a seat.

Cruz leaned back, looking around him and into the crib. "You think she's going to be less trouble than this current generation of Madigans?"

A laugh escaped him, and with it, some of the tension he'd bottled up. "Oh, I'm pretty sure that's not gonna be the case. She's spoiled rotten."

"Danny and Aidan are the same way with their niblings, especially Katie. And that one has a US attorney wrapped around her finger too."

Tension rushed back in at the mention of the prosecutor. He was good. Fair, but good. And had a reputation in the military, as a SEAL and then JAG officer, that had crossed branch lines.

A hand landed on his back. "Breathe, Kane. Just breathe. I'm here to help. I won't let anything happen to them either."

And fuck did he need that—an outside ally and a break —and fuck if he didn't miss his other closest friend, Marsh, who'd gone off the grid after his retirement last year, their online chess game left open for months.

He propped his elbows on the wood table and buried his face in his hands. "I'm so tired, Cruz. So fucking tired of being afraid and so fucking tired of being kept in the dark."

"Not to mention just tired." She gave his back one last pat, then stood. She circled the table and crib, snagged the kettle off the stove, and filled it with water. "It's been a rough couple of weeks." Returning the kettle to the burner, she got that boiling, then dumped the old coffee grounds out of his French press and heaped in fresh ones. "It's about to get rougher."

"The showdown with Rose," he surmised.

"You're read in?"

"I know their grandmother was behind the coup to overthrow Hawes. I saw the video of Rose and Amelia plotting. But that's all I know."

"I'll tell you what else I know, and we'll sort it out." The kettle began to whistle, and she flipped it off before Lily roused. "I've got some experience with this whole straddling the line routine."

"No offense, Cruz, but you ended up out of the law as a result."

"None taken," she said with a smirk. She poured the piping hot water over the fresh coffee grounds. "My priorities shifted. I put my family and my heart ahead of the job. I don't regret it." She grabbed two mugs out of the drying rack and placed them on the table with the brewing press. "You've been juggling the same for a while now. Longer than I think most realize, and I suspect your priorities are shifting."

"Like fucking quicksand."

"The same decision freight train is headed your way, and I'll help you through that too when the time comes. But for now, let's make sure the right Madigans win." She reached a hand into the crib, lightly running her fingers over Lily's auburn fuzz. "For her sake and ours."

Lily's brown eyes blinked open, the same warm brown color as her father's, and Brax offered his pinky for her to curl her tiny fingers around. Yes, the danger and fear had grown, but so had the love, his heart more full—more at risk —than ever. One battle at a time. He'd sort out the rest if —*when*—they survived the current threat.

"Will you help me, Chief?" Cruz said. "Help them and her?"

He was scared to death, for Lily, for Holt, for his family and himself, but there was only one answer to the question. "Yes."

II

HOLT

CHAPTER NINE

Present

Three things happened at once.

The doorbell rang, Lily woke up, and Holt knocked his elbow against the leftover tub of concrete paint next to him. He tossed aside the grout gun and shot out a hand, catching the lip of the container with his index finger, only a drop escaping onto the freshly finished floor.

"One minute!" he shouted up the stairs. He grabbed a scraper and smoothed out the runaway paint, not wanting it to dry unevenly. He'd used a hard-to-find, hard-to-apply, nonslip finish. Safer for Lily. He didn't want an errant blip in the coating to trip his seventeen-month-old daughter as she toddled through the door.

Assuming they ever moved in. He tossed the scraper into the supply bucket. That was a decision for another day.

"Da-Da!" came another call from upstairs, right as the doorbell rang again.

"I'm coming!" he called to both.

He stood, flicked off the baby monitor, and grabbed a shop rag. He wiped his hands as he took the stairs two at a time to the entry foyer of the split-level house. Through the textured sidelight window, a seventies relic that still needed to be replaced, he glimpsed the shape of a petite woman with long blond hair, dressed in all black, a helmet in hand at her side.

He opened the door for his sister. "Thanks for waking Lily." Not waiting, he continued up the stairs to the main level, swinging open the baby gate at the top.

Helena trailed through the house behind him. "It's not her normal nap time."

In the middle of the remodeled living room, Lily stood in her portable crib, holding herself up by the siderail. "Da-Da!" She threw her arms into the air so excitedly she started toppling backward. "Yes!" she shouted her new favorite word.

"Whoa there, baby girl." Holt snatched her up and into his arms, giving her a toss for good laughing measure.

She giggled and squealed, a happy toddler. Even happier when her brown eyes landed on her aunt. She leaped from Holt's arms to Helena's. "Na-Na!"

"I'm not old enough to be your Na-Na... stinker!" Helena wrinkled her nose and pointed at Lily's diaper. "What time did your daddy have you up this morning anyway?"

"Couldn't sleep," Holt said as they worked in tandem to change Lily's diaper on the black leather sofa from Hawes's old condo. "Figured I'd come out and get some work done. We played a little when we first got here." He gestured at the scattered toys in the far corner of the room. "Then I fed her, and she napped. I was finishing up the floor downstairs."

"Where's your phone?" Helena asked.

He patted his pockets. Empty. "Shit. I must have left it in the car."

"That's why you need a coffee machine up in here." She finished buttoning Lily's onesie while Holt bagged the dirty diaper. "Brain fuel."

"Caffeine detox."

"Since when?"

He shot her the bird. "Why are *you* here on a Monday morning and not at work?" If Helena wasn't out of town on an op, she usually spent weekdays at MCS headquarters, her law office, or in court. Occasionally, she'd hang out at her girlfriend's auto garage, but Celia more often than not cried "distraction" and chased Helena away. This morning, however, she'd left the city to hunt him down at the fixer-upper he'd bought and was renovating in Pacifica. A prickle of unease tickled his fingertips. "Something's wrong."

"You could say that." She dug her phone out of her pocket, and after a couple quick taps, handed it to him.

His fingers seized, almost dropping the phone. "What the fuck is this?" Or maybe he should throw it. The news-paper headline was *that* incomprehensible. And *that* anger inducing.

"Story broke a couple hours ago." Helena lifted Lily

and settled her on a hip. "We got a heads-up, but no one could reach you."

He reread the headline: *Police Chief Implicated in Bribery Scandal.*

Below it were two pictures. The first was Brax's professional headshot from SFPD's website—uniform, badge, cap, awkward smile. The second picture was fuzzier, but even in plainclothes, Brax was unmistakable. Tall and lean like a pine tree with broad shoulders and long legs, his brown hair clipped short and his nose and chin sharp. Not as sharp as Holt's siblings' but cut enough that Holt had always drawn the contrast to his own more rounded features. But it was the tattoo on Brax's right forearm that was a dead giveaway. The inked pattern—a tribute to his mother—was exposed by his rolled-up shirt sleeves and visible just above the hand Brax had extended to the other man in the picture, unidentified, who was holding out a stack of bills.

Two fingers to the screen, Holt spread them to zoom in. Didn't help. "Can we get a cleaner shot?"

"Jax is working on it."

"That's not one of our people, is it?" He didn't think so, but Helena had been recruiting, and she and Hawes had more day-to-day contact with the operatives than he did.

She cocked a hip, the one with Lily on it, and his daughter giggled at Helena's death glare. She wasn't old enough to fear it yet. "One, what the fu"—Holt shot her a look—"dge would we need to pay Brax for? Two, our operatives know better than to approach him directly." She flicked a finger between them. "You, me, Hawes, and Chris are the points of contact."

"And three, Brax wouldn't take a bribe."

"It's been a rough year for him, and he's been pushing us away. How sure are you?"

She wasn't wrong on either count. Between their grandmother's failed coup last summer, and the drive-by shooting at Celia's garage this past winter, their family had made life tough on Brax. Add to that a busy end of year that had kept the chief working around the clock at the station, missing their first holiday together in six years.

The second one with Lily, who'd been asking for her "Ba-Ba"—the second "name" she'd learned—and used more and more insistently.

Holt's confusion and rising panic over the growing distance had gotten the better of him at Hawes and Chris's wedding. Helena hadn't mentioned his blowup with Brax, but it had to be on her mind as it was frequently on Holt's. It was half the reason he'd made so much progress on the house. He hadn't gotten a decent night's sleep in months. He couldn't get the look on Brax's face that day out of his head—a potent, devastating cocktail of frustration, betrayal, fear, and loneliness—and his even more devastating words, "*I don't know if I can do this anymore.*" His voice had been weary, resigned, and Holt's heart had withered on the spot.

All he'd wanted to do was help his friend, understand what was going on with him, return all the favors Brax had ever done for him, and fix whatever needed fixing—he had the tools now—and Brax wouldn't let him. Because Brax no longer trusted him? Or because Holt and his family were the problem? Had the professional conflicts finally become insurmountable? A part of Holt had always feared the day would come when he asked too much of Brax, but Holt didn't think that was all it was. This weird, awful tension between them had landed about the same time Chris, a former ATF agent, had hurled a verbal grenade into his and Brax's path last summer.

"Because if she hurt you, Holt would either fall apart or kill her himself."

One sentence, one uttered truth that Holt hadn't denied then and still couldn't deny now. Said aloud, it had felt like one of those earthquakes that periodically jolted San Francisco. Not the big rolling ones like Loma Prieta, but the sharp quick hits that were like a pile driver ramming the earth's surface from underneath.

The tremor had knocked Holt off-balance, but he'd recovered. Brax, though, seemed to have been permanently shifted. Holt had tried to ask about that too at the wedding, but Brax had cut him off. Because Holt wouldn't like the answer? Was he losing his closest friend and Lily's godfather? After a year when Holt had already lost so much, he couldn't lose Brax too. Couldn't lose the connection that had been a pillar of his life for over a decade. Outside of Lily and his siblings, Brax was the most important person in his life. The person who'd saved him, figuratively and literally, those last few years in the army, and after too, making sure he had the support to handle his PTSD once he'd discharged. Who had still, despite whatever was going on with them, answered

Holt's late-night phone call last month when the night-mares woke him.

Because Brax kept his word. And *that* Braxton Kane—a man who valued his honor, his reputation, his job, and the difference he made in others' lives—wouldn't risk all that, his word, for a bribe. "I'm sure."

Holt scrolled to the video embedded in the news bulletin, pressed play, and watched as the assistant chief issued brief remarks, stating that an investigation was ongoing, and that Chief Kane was on administrative leave.

Suspension, effectively.

"Fuck." He handed the phone back to Helena before he gave in to the earlier urge to chuck it across the room. He reached for his daughter, needing the comfort she provided. When his thoughts were a tornado, there had only ever been a few things that could quiet the storm: hacking; Amelia, for a time; Lily; and Brax. "Did you call him?"

"Tried," Helena said. "So did Hawes and Chris. No answer."

Not a good sign. "I have to go to him."

"Yeah, you do." Reading his intent, Helena was already packing Lily's go bag. Holt scrambled around the room, Lily still on his hip, as he packed up the rest of her things one-handed. When he turned back to Helena, she held out the toddler carrier to him. "Bike or Beemer?"

He took the carrier, rolled it, and tucked it under his other arm. "Beemer. I want to take Lily." She had the same calming effect on Brax as she did on him. Another reason this distance was absurd. Why not at least let him drop off

Lily for some time with her godfather? They hadn't had a proper visit in months. "She'll make him feel better."

Helena's face transformed from mission critical into the soft expression Holt had seen more often lately, thanks to Celia.

"What's that smile for?" he asked.

She grinned wider. "Nothin'. Don't let him push you away. This is too serious for whatever stick he has up his ass."

Nodding, he readjusted Lily and added her go bag to the same shoulder his laptop bag hung from. "Can you close up here?"

"Sure thing. Keys?"

"There's a spare set in the top kitchen drawer." They were supposed to be for Brax. "And—"

"I'll round up Hawes and Chris for a debrief this afternoon. House or MCS?"

"House," he said, following her down the stairs. "Let's get a handle on this privately before involving others. But do put Oak on alert."

She opened the door for him. "Already did."

He leaned down and kissed her cheek. "Thank you."

"Good luck!" she shouted after him as he hustled down the steps and along the short path to the driveway.

He popped the SUV's trunk, tossed the bags on top of the folded stroller in back, then carried Lily around to her car seat, fighting the tremble of his hands as he fastened her in.

Her little hands patted his arm excitedly. "Go?"

"Yeah, baby girl, we go." He smoothed her wild auburn

curls and kissed her forehead, letting the warmth and smell of her calm his nerves. "To see your Uncle Brax."

She clapped. "Ba-Ba!"

Holt hoped Brax would be as happy to see them.

"What the fuck are you doing here?"

Holt glanced up from where Lily was crawling after the multi-colored sensory balls on Brax's carpeted office floor. Holt had been heartened to find the toys still stashed in Brax's bottom desk drawer. Brax stood in the doorway, just back from a meeting that, by the hard set of his jaw, the deep crease between his brows, and his overly wrinkled shirt sleeves, had turned his already bad day to worse. Guilt racked Holt; he should have been here sooner.

Shouldn't have let three months go by with only a single phone call.

"I just saw the news. I'm so—"

Brax slammed the door shut. "You can't be here." He crossed the room to the interior bullpen window and peeked through the slatted blinds. Blinds Holt had called ahead to Jax about, to make sure they were closed. The usual protocol. That and some hijacked electronic locks and surveillance cameras. "No one saw us come in."

"I'm sure no one did." Brax snatched his fingers out of the blinds and turned, hands on his hips. "But it's grand fucking central around here. Anyone could come in at any—"

Holt stood, picked up Lily, and thrust her at Brax,

giving him no choice but to take his excited goddaughter. "Ba-Ba!"

As Holt expected, Brax crushed her to his chest. The maneuver muffled her squeals of joy, but the peace that swept over Brax's face—the fluttering closed of his eyelids, the flattening of the divot between his brows, the loosening of the muscle at the corner of his jaw—was indication enough that concealing their presence hadn't been his only motive. "Hey, princess," he whispered and dropped a kiss in her curls.

Lily shoved an arm between them, lifting a toy, almost ramming it into his nose. "Yes!"

Brax chuckled. "Your wish is my command." He took the toy and tossed it in the air a couple times, catching it easily.

Lily clapped and Brax held her closer, rubbing a hand over her back and shushing her.

"Better?" Holt asked once she settled.

"Yes, but I'm serious, Holt." He rested back against the credenza under the bullpen window. "The hot water is rising, IA is already on my case, and the state attorney general is asking questions now too."

"Internal Affairs? Since when? We didn't get any flags."

Brax tossed the ball again, ignoring him.

Ignoring him.

"Is that why you've been pushing us away? An IA investigation? We can take care—"

"I can't answer that, and you can't get involved. This can't lead back to you."

The implication stung, but it was reality. Holt's family ran a criminal empire—*he* was a criminal. Whose best friend was the chief of police. Conflicts of interest were bound to catch up to them eventually. But it hadn't stopped Holt from telling Brax to take the job with SFPD. He would've done anything to have Brax in the same place with him again. And he'd do anything to make sure Brax was happy, his job secure, even if that meant backing off. But he didn't think that's what Brax needed either.

"You're worried about being connected to us," he said. "Don't be, Cap. I covered—"

Hazel eyes, made more green than brown today by the darkening circles beneath them, shot to his. "I'm not worried about *me*. I'm worried about them using me to get to *you* and your family. You can't be involved."

Holt should've known. Sacrifice, thy name is Braxton Kane. Well, fuck that. Brax had sacrificed enough already.

"*Our* family, and they won't get to us." He leaned a hip against the credenza next to Brax's. "And I won't let them take this from you either. I can handle IA." He and Hawes regularly reviewed SFPD's roster and updated data and leverage points. He knew what levers to pull, which keys to strike.

"Don't," Brax bit out. "It's too risky." He patted Lily's back. "For both of you."

It was riskier to do nothing, but Holt didn't say that. Arguing wasn't what Brax needed. He'd already had enough of that today by the look of him.

Brax inhaled deep, seeming to accept Holt's silence for acceptance. Or just falling under Lily's comforting spell.

She was humming a wordless tune and tapping out an uncoordinated rhythm on his chest. He listened for another minute before lifting his gaze. "You're not going to ask about the picture?"

"I don't need to." Holt shifted closer, one hand on Lily's back, the other braced behind Brax, caging him in for what Holt had to say next, expecting a protest. "And besides, Helena and Oak will ask enough for all of us."

Sure enough, Brax tried to push off the credenza and failed. His words shook with the growled brunt of his distress. "What part of *can't be involved* didn't you understand?"

"What part of *family* didn't you understand?"

Lily ended the debate for them, placing a tiny hand on the side of Brax's face. "Yes, Ba-Ba."

The innocent gesture knocked the wind right out of Brax. Deflating, he wobbled, and Holt lifted the arm behind him, curling it around Brax's shoulders and curling him into them. Holding him up with Lily between them. For the first time in months, he had Brax in his arms again, and the threads that tied them together didn't feel so frayed. "I've got you," he said, lending his physical weight. "I'll make this right," he added, lending the full weight of his heart, his skills, and their family's influence to back up the promise.

CHAPTER TEN

Holt opened the front door to his family's Victorian monster and was blasted with a wave of enticing aromas: braised beef, carrots and onions, garlic and herbs, red wine gravy. Not the first time he'd had the pleasure lately, and Holt was grateful for the food and the company. At the end of last year, with Hawes moved into Chris's renovated condo and Helena out of town for work, it had just been him, Lily, and the cats knocking around the house. They'd lost so many people—to betrayal, to jail, to death, to whatever the fuck was keeping Brax away—that the big empty house had felt like a giant cavern of loneliness and regrets. But it wasn't only the added company that had chased those ghosts away. This place was finally starting to feel like a home again.

Thanks in no small part to the Perri invasion. Celia and her two kids had practically moved in, and because Chris wanted to spend time with his sister and niblings, he was around more often, bringing Hawes with him. Gloria, the Perri matriarch, frequently visited too, and that woman was so full of energy she could power an electrical grid. A part of Holt felt disconnected still, outside their circle, but overall, it was a welcome counterbalance to the darkness that had surrounded the Madigans for too long.

Darkness that Holt couldn't handle at eighteen, so his grandfather had suggested he join the army. He'd needed the escape, and while there'd been darkness in the desert too, it had been a different sort. And there had been Brax. It had been a relief, a simpler life for a time, until he'd been needed back home. He'd been afraid to return, to the darkness and everything his family was, and it sure as fuck had gotten darker than he'd ever imagined, but the bright spots —his siblings, Lily, Brax—had carried him through to now when their family was expanding and life had finally begun to brighten again. Except that brightness had somehow skirted around Brax, and those same gray clouds were threatening Holt's daylight too.

Motion from across the dining room snapped Holt out of his thoughts. Celia tossed her apron on a chair, set an empty mason jar on the table, and grabbed her oversized leather purse off the floor, disturbing the snowy white Siberian who'd nested on it. She scratched the cat behind her ears. "Sorry, Daisy," she cooed. "Momma will give you a treat for your trouble." The tabby Tulip *meowed* in agreement. Grinning, Celia straightened and stepped to Helena's side. "Treat the cats."

"You fucking set me up."

"I did, and that's a dollar for you in the swear jar. The shelter kids are gonna have a bumper year at this rate."

Celia had been warning them since Lily started talking that *fuck* would be one of her first words if they didn't all cut back on using it. Holt tended to think Lily should learn when and when not to use it, but Celia had correctly noted that a toddler wasn't exactly the master of a well-timed *fuck*. So the swear jar had been introduced, with all proceeds going to their shelters. "Beef stew should be done in a few hours," she said. "I'm gonna swing by the shop, make sure all is under control, then pick up the kids and head to Ma's." She pecked Helena's cheek. "Call me when you get a break."

Helena gave her a longer smooch on the lips. "Thanks, baby."

Across the table, Chris averted his gaze, hilariously scandalized, while Hawes and Jax snickered. Holt laughed too, letting the warmth settle after an unsettled night and crazier day. He was happy his sister had found a partner so perfectly suited for her. Said partner approached him where he stood over the threshold of the room. Celia's dark eyes and easy smile were kind as she ruffled a sleeping Lily's hair. "You need anything, you let me know, okay?"

"Thanks, Cee."

He stepped back into the foyer and opened the door for her, waiting to hear her SUV crank before sneaking back inside. He didn't immediately return to the dining room, instead tucking Lily into her pack and play in the living room and diverting through the kitchen for a ginger ale and another whiff of goodness. "Someone's challenging you for best chef, Big H."

Hawes shot him the bird.

Helena preened. "I fucking scored."

Chris pointed at the swear jar. "That's my sister you're talking about."

Helena snickered as she shoved a wad of cash into the jar. "Your point, Mr. Hair?"

Definitely starting to feel like a home again, sibling teasing turned up to twenty.

"How'd it go with the chief?" Jax asked, bringing everyone back to the grim reality of why they were gathered there. His hacker protégé ran a hand over their head, flattening their pink-streaked Mohawk, the gesture strikingly similar to Brax's nervous tick. They were picking up both their habits—Holt's skills and Brax's behaviors. Not surprising. While Holt had been their mentor in hacker mayhem, Brax had been their mentor in law-abiding citizenry, taking Jax under his wing and giving them a post-shelter gig as an IT specialist with SFPD.

"This is going to be harder than we thought." Holt set his can of soda on the buffet table that ran along one wall, away from the dining table covered in photos and printouts. He repressed his twitch at all the paper; Chris's doing no doubt. "Brax is pulling away. Doesn't want our help."

"That's ridiculous," Helena said. "He's family."

"He doesn't want his family hurt," Chris correctly surmised.

Holt nodded. "Gold star for Mr. Hair." He lowered himself into a chair. "IA's all over his ass, and he's worried they'll use him to get to us. I got the impression IA wasn't only looking at this latest scandal."

"That's why he's been pulling away," Helena said.

"Makes sense," Hawes said. "Do we know what IA is after?"

Holt shook his head. "Brax wouldn't tell me."

All three Madigan heads swung to Jax, who lifted their hands. "Today was the first I heard IA was involved. I'll see if I can find out more." They gestured at the photos on the table. "Can we focus on these for now?"

Hawes rolled up his shirt sleeves and braced one hand on the table. With the other, he pushed three photos across to Holt. "Jax brought these over."

"These are from the news report?"

"Yes," Jax said. "I cleaned up the resolution on the original then split it in two, so we've also got solo close-ups of the chief and the other person."

Holt moved Brax's photo aside—that was clearly him—and examined the picture of the unidentified man. White, male, dark hair, dark suit. Late thirties or early forties if Holt had to guess. Still didn't recognize him.

He swapped the solo photo for the wide frame shot. Noticed something off. He pushed it out of the way and grabbed the solo shot of Brax. The same something was off there too, only it was clearer. "The photo's been doctored."

"I thought so too," Chris said. "Missing shadow." The former ATF agent was sharp. Good thing he was officially on their side now. "You wouldn't be able to tell in the fuzzy picture that's all over the news."

"Explain," Helena said.

Holt slid the photo of the two men in front of his sister. "It's not even that noticeable here because Brax's shadow eclipses most of it." The sun was slicing down the alley where they'd stood, between buildings and over roofs, casting long shadows on the pavement and up the walls. "But look here..." He tapped the spot where their shadows almost connected at the lower corner of the building.

Almost.

Helena bent and squinted, her blue eyes going wide, her brows racing high, when she also realized what was missing. "There's no shadow of the bills."

Holt nudged over the solo picture of Brax. "The missing shadow's more obvious in this one. Just two hands reaching toward each other. No straight line that would indicate a solid object between them."

"But he was there." Helena claimed the chair next to him. "Only the money wasn't." She wasn't wrong and that was a problem for them.

"Who got the photo first?" Hawes asked Jax. "Department or reporters?"

"Department."

Holt jerked in surprise, then briefly mentally applauded himself for setting his soda can aside before his anger—and worry—burned away the praise. "We have a leak to deal with too?"

"Which makes no sense," Jax said. "Everyone loves the chief."

"Except IA." Hawes, both hands on the table now, drummed his thumbs against the lacquered wood. "Leverage. Everyone has a weak spot."

And Holt, in his role for the organization, was a master at finding those, but first he had to find the leak. "Can you get me into the system?" he asked Jax.

"Yep," they replied. "Anything I can do to help."

"Did the photo come into IA?"

"No, it was sent to Assistant Chief Thompson." Jax scrounged around in their messenger bag, produced a tablet, and after a few quick taps, laid the tablet face up in the middle of the table, an email displayed. "She received it and turned it over to Internal Affairs like she's supposed to."

"What do we know about Thompson?" Chris asked.

"She gave the press conference earlier today," Helena said.

"Yep, that's her." Jax brightened for the first time since they'd started the debrief. "Maya's awesome."

"Maya Ann Thompson," Hawes added. "Promoted to assistant chief earlier this year."

"She's a former teacher who went into law enforcement," Holt continued, rattling off the facts from their most recent review of SFPD's roster. "Proponent of de-escalation and community policing."

"Possible she's the leak?" Chris asked.

"I'd be surprised." Jax reclaimed their tablet. "Maya worships the ground the chief walks on. They've been making a lot of headway in the department together. They actually met with the mayor last week on plans for reallocating police funds to more community efforts."

"Did she warn Kane?"

"In a way. She forwarded this to me." They gestured with the tablet. "Knew it would get to the chief."

"She told Avery too," Helena said. "Knew it would get to us."

Their top lieutenant was tight with SFPD brass? "How's Avery know her?"

"They grew up together. Reconnected recently."

Holt scratched a mental note to add that to Thompson's file. Across from him, Hawes appeared to be scratching a similar note. Until Helena shot him an icy glare. The operatives were under her command now, a decision they'd all made together. Hawes grinned and held up his hands.

"They just had an entire conversation, didn't they?" Jax said.

Chris chuckled. "Freaky, isn't it?"

Freaky and wonderful. The three of them had always been tight, the bond strengthened more after their parents had passed and made hard as steel last year when it had only been each other they could trust.

Each other and Brax.

Holt drew the wide shot photo closer again, contemplating the stranger once more. "We get an ID yet on the other guy?"

"You didn't ask Brax?" Helena said.

"Didn't get a chance to before he was called into another meeting, and the last thing he needed today was me interrogating him."

"Wasn't necessary. Mel came through with the ID." Chris shuffled through his messy stack of papers and produced a DMV printout, a mugshot, and a short rap sheet. "George Swanson. Accountant. Couple of white-collar convictions in connection with the 2008 market crash. Made getting a job hard to come by after."

"That suit"—Helena tapped the solo picture of Swanson—"is a Brioni."

"Camino cartel pays well."

Holt jerked again, hard enough to shake the table. "He's a cartel banker?" What the—

"What the fuck is Brax doing meeting with a cartel banker?" Hawes said, stealing the words right out of his head.

And on the heels of that question, Holt had another that sent tingles of anxiety racing through him and out toward his fingers. "Do the cops have this ID yet?"

Jax shook their head. "They've got a computer running the image cleanup. I might have tapped in and given it a bug. Should slow down recognition a bit."

"Even when they do get an ID," Chris said, "they're not going to want to broadcast this. That buys us some time."

Precious little to get Brax out of a mess that was getting messier by the second. "Might need a favor," Holt said to Jax. "Rush setup."

They cracked their knuckles. "Wouldn't mind a build."

And Jax was one of only a handful of people Holt would trust to do it, and of that handful, the only one he'd trust with the location.

"Back to the original question," Helena said. "Why the fuck was Brax meeting with Swanson?"

Holt shifted in his chair toward her. "That's what you and Oak need to find out."

"He gonna let me help him?"

"Don't give him a fucking choice. Like you said, he's

family." He jutted his chin at the swear jar. "Now, everyone pay up."

———

"You copy?" Helena's voice rang loud and clear through the speakers of Holt's digital surveillance wall at MCS headquarters.

He'd come into the office with Chris and Hawes, the former needing access to his detective setup, the latter needing to keep the family's legitimate enterprise on track. That morning, Hawes was closing on an acquisition that would bring MCS tools to make their operations more environmentally sustainable.

"Copy audio," Holt returned. "Hold still while I focus the video."

Video that was streaming in through the bi-pride pin Helena frequently wore on the lapel of her suit coat. Several keystrokes later and the view from Oakland Ashe's downtown law office began to resolve.

"Nice view."

"Right?" Helena said. "One of the best in the city. Big H has been holding out on us."

Holt chuckled as he made adjustments, using Alcatraz as a focal point, the island visible outside Oak's floor to ceiling windows overlooking the Bay. "Okay, we're good."

As she moved away from the window, the camera panned across Oak's desk. Large, polished, uncluttered. Laptop, desk phone, one of those fancy pen and clock combos, and a single framed picture. From some time ago, judging by Oak's appearance in it, no gray flecks dotting his dark hair. He was dressed in a tux, as was the younger man in his arms, matching wedding bands on their left hands. Oak's husband, then. They knew Oak was queer, but the attorney rarely spoke of his own family, even as he continued to be dragged into theirs—from Amelia's case last year to the drive-by a few months ago.

Speaking of, Oak came into view as Helena approached the round meeting table in the far corner of the room. Dressed in a sharp suit, Oak tapped his silver pen against a file folder atop a legal pad on the table. "You know *that*"—he pointed right at the pin, wise to their methods by now—"jeopardizes client confidentiality."

"Don't worry." The tips of Helena's fingers fluttered across the camera's lens like she was waving Oak off. "He and Brax are practically married. They can just make it official."

Holt's fingers froze on the mouse he was using to control the camera. Unbidden, a picture of himself and Brax jumped to mind. Him in a tux, Brax in his uniform, posed like Oak and his husband, matching bands on their fingers. And on the heels of that make-believe picture, a flurry of other mental pictures followed, only these were real, memories of the single night he'd spent wrapped in Brax's arms.

He strived to keep those memories in check, strived to look on them fondly and not contemplate missed opportunities. Not obsess over whether he should have said or done more that night, on so many levels. He'd had a wonderful first time, had lost his virginity to his best friend, who he loved and shared a mutual attraction with. But their lives had been headed in opposite directions then—Brax back to the desert, Holt to San Francisco.

Had Holt said or done more that night, had he asked Brax if it was more than mere attraction on his end, Holt might have missed learning more about his own sexuality, missed the good years with Amelia, never had their daughter. He didn't regret those experiences, not in the slightest, but he couldn't help but wonder about the experiences lost too. He'd had to let Brax go. But had he? Was that why they were in this situation now? Why someone was coming after Brax? Because Holt had never really let go of the other man, same as he'd never completely let go of those memories.

"At which point this becomes a conflict of interest since I represent Holt's ex-wife," Oak said as if he could see through the camera too, right into Holt's rattled brain.

"You okay?" Hawes asked from behind him.

Apparently more than just mentally rattled. Holt gave his head a sharp shake and glanced over his shoulder. "Fine. Deal closed?"

"Done. Checked on Lily in the daycare too." Another company perk they'd recently instituted—on-site childcare. "She's good. Still in love with jelly. Discovering the joys of combining it with peanut butter. Astronomical dry-cleaning bills, here we come."

Holt laughed. "Maybe wear less wool and silk."

Hawes shoved his shoulder as he dropped into the seat next to him. "Fuck your flannel." The playful banter faded, though, as Hawes's gaze drifted to the monitors. "If Kane finds out you're spying on him, he's gonna be pissed."

Holt shrugged. "He's gonna be pissed anyway."

Confirmed when Brax walked through the door and saw Helena sitting at the table. Holt would recognize the pinched brow, hard jaw, and ramrod straight posture anywhere. Brax was mad. He waited until after the door was shut, until after exchanging pleasantries with Oak, before lighting into Helena. "What are you doing here? I told Holt you needed to stay out of this."

"We didn't listen. Family. Also, you look terrible. When's the last time you slept?"

Brax ran a hand over his head, half turned toward the table, half turned toward the door, the ends of his sports coat flapping with his indecision. "Fuckin' family."

"Sorry. You're stuck with us."

Holt zoomed in for a closer look at Brax while Oak continued to try to mediate the situation in his office.

"Why don't you have a seat, Chief," he said. "And if you want Ms. Madigan to leave, I can make her do so."

"I'd like to see you try." Brax moved toward the chair across from Oak, then claimed the one across from Helena that was pushed out toward him. No doubt by her foot, aiming to keep him in clear view of the illicit surveillance.

Brax didn't argue, and that, along with the dark bags under his eyes, the sunken cheeks, and the duller than usual skin, worried Holt. Yes, Brax had been pissed when he'd first entered, but he had too little energy to keep it going. Not a good sign.

"It's fine," Brax said. "Though I don't know why I'm here. I have a union rep to handle these things."

"Your union rep is there to protect you as a member of SFPD and the union," Oak said. "Mediation and damage control. My job is to make sure there's no damage to you, personally, to mitigate."

Brax nodded. "Okay, thank you."

Oak opened the file folder and withdrew the photo that had been all over the news. "I need to know what happened here."

"I didn't take his money. There wasn't even any money offered."

"We know," Helena said. From her briefcase, she retrieved a separate folder with the photos Jax had brought them yesterday. "The news photo was doctored. There's no actual stack of bills being exchanged as you can see from the missing shadow in this cleaned-up version." She slid the photos in front of Oak. "We're working that angle."

Brax braced his forearms on the table and leaned forward. "Do not take action."

"Details." Helena waved him off too. "We're just looking for names."

By the narrowing of Brax's eyes, he'd heard her unspoken *for now*.

Oak forged into the staredown. "Tell us about the meeting, then. That's actually you in the picture, correct?"

"Yes. This was taken in January, last time I met with him."

"Who 'him'?" Helena asked.

Brax's gaze cut her direction, either surprised she

didn't know already or surprised she hadn't told Oak. When she didn't reply, he shifted his attention back to the other attorney. "George Swanson. He's a cartel accountant. He first made contact last fall, after his prior employer—"

He cut himself off, eyes darting back to Helena.

Hawes put it together the rest of the way. "After we dismantled his prior employer's network. He must have worked for Reno."

"Fuck," Holt cursed. "So this is connected to us?"

"Maybe." Hawes mirrored Brax's position, leaning forward, forearms on either side of a keyboard next to Holt's, and watched the monitors intently.

"After some shifts in the organization he used to work for," Brax diplomatically finished. "Those who were left were recruited by the rival Camino cartel, including Swanson. He was asked to do more, though. More than he was comfortable with."

"He wanted to turn informant?" Oak asked.

Brax nodded. "With his old employer, he was just moving money around inside the organization. But Camino was making deals with outside parties that, if discovered, would get Swanson pinched for significant jail time."

"Felonies."

"Arguably felony murder in at least one instance."

"Fuck," Hawes said. "That means they were contracting killers."

"Not us," Holt said. There was nothing about the Camino cartel's objectives that aligned with theirs, and they certainly didn't operate by the same rules—no indiscriminate killing, no unvetted targets, no collateral damage. Rules Hawes had put in place when he'd taken over, and that they'd fought off an attempted coup by their grandmother to uphold. "But it does give us another road to investigate."

"I'll get Chris started on it."

Holt nodded. While he could find a lot through digital means, Holt couldn't deny that having an old-fashioned detective on their team, one with a decade plus of law enforcement connections, helped too.

"Why didn't you go through the usual CI process?" Oak asked.

Brax slumped in his chair, running a hand over his head again.

"Brax..." Helena half coaxed, half chided.

"He wasn't ready, and I didn't want to risk his family."

Typical Brax. Always trying to protect someone.

"Is that why IA is investigating?" Oak asked.

Brax bolted upright in his chair, glaring at Helena. "You told him?"

She shrugged. "Of course I told him. He needs to know that too."

"They got wind of this?" Oak said, trying to draw Brax back to his question.

One Holt was eager for the answer to as well. He didn't get it, exactly.

"I'm not having that conversation with Ms. Madigan in the room."

But it was enough. "They were looking into him earlier," Holt said to his brother. "So again, this could be about us."

"Agree," Hawes said. "On both counts."

"All right," Oak said. "We'll discuss that when she leaves." Helena started to protest, but Oak cut her off, returning to his earlier line of questioning. "How many times did you meet with Swanson?"

"Three. He reached out the first time on Halloween."

"Good cover," Hawes muttered. "Camino throws a big Día de Muertos celebration. They wouldn't have noticed Swanson missing."

Halloween, just before Lily's birthday party at which Brax had barely said two words to him. Because of his meeting with Swanson? Was he trying to protect them from Camino too?

The door swung open behind them, and Chris ducked into the room.

In the room onscreen, Oak asked, "Any useful information?"

"Yes, we made two intercepts on tips he provided."

"How did you explain those," Helena said, "if Swanson wasn't a registered CI?"

"Attributed them to the tip-line."

"When's the last time you heard from him?" Oak asked.

Brax pointed at the picture. "That day in late January. I remember because it was unseasonably warm that weekend."

"That was the weekend we got married," Chris said.

Holt hung his head as pieces slotted together. That was

the same weekend he and Brax had gotten into the one and only fight of their fourteen-year friendship.

"I told him he needed to come in and do the CI paperwork," Brax said. "Make it official. I had the feds lined up to offer witness protection and everything, but he never showed."

Holt spun in his chair. "Is that how Mel got the ID?"

"I didn't ask," Chris replied. "But likely."

"Did you follow-up?" Oak asked Brax.

"I've been trying to make contact," he replied, "but all roads lead to nowhere. It's not uncommon for CIs to go dark, but I'm worried."

"With good reason," Chris said. He strode forward and shoved his phone under Holt's nose. Onscreen was an encrypted message from Mel:

George Swanson is dead.

CHAPTER ELEVEN

By midafternoon, Holt was back at the house, sitting on the floor of his lair with Lily between his legs, helping her fit textured shape toys into a bin while keeping an eye on the wall of monitors. Internal Affairs was conducting the latest SFPD press conference. No questions. Just an announcement that Chief Kane had been formally suspended, pending further investigation.

No mention of the cartel at least, though reports from Oak and Helena confirmed SFPD had identified Swanson. SFPD didn't want that news to break while they were still searching for his whereabouts, so they'd kept the details of the investigation quiet. That was the only positive Holt could discern in this whole shitstorm of a day, and it wasn't enough of a win to quell the nearly overwhelming urge to hurl.

Or to crawl under a fucking bed, an urge he hadn't felt since before Lily was born. She kept him grounded. Lily and Brax and his hacking, which Brax would tell him to go do. And Holt had been, all last night and today to the point his fingers ached. And his head. And his heart.

Lily managed to push the squishy blue cube through the elastic strings of the bin. "Yes!" she squealed, tiny arms raised in victory.

Holt plastered on a smile and clapped. "Good job!" He picked up the ribbed yellow ball next. "Now, try the sphere."

The task would also keep her busy for whatever Hawes was coming up the stairs to tell him, his twin's tread as familiar as his own. But Holt had a question—a quandary—for him first, because nothing they did would matter if they couldn't answer it with a *yes*. "Even if we clear him," Holt said as soon as Hawes cleared the baby gate at the top of the stairs, "will he ever get his good name back?"

"Depends on what happens with IA."

Holt appreciated the truth, even if it did cause his gut to roil.

Hawes tossed his suit jacket at the corner rocker, then lowered himself onto the floor. He hauled an excited Lily into his lap and helped her out by pushing the sphere through the bands. They cheered and clapped, then Hawes picked up the ridged green triangle for her to work on next. "If it were up to the rest of the officers, no question. He's well liked in the department and his predecessor was an ass—awful."

"I vaguely remember Williams."

"You didn't have to deal with him much. He hated me because I was gay and hated Rose because she was a woman. And he was corrupt as hell. We didn't even need to dig too deep to find the dirt on him."

Like someone was now digging for dirt on Brax. Holt covered his shiver by tilting forward to offer Lily the purple diamond instead; the triangle always gave her trouble. "When Brax told me he was joining SFPD, a part of me was scared."

"Because he would come into direct conflict with us?"

Holt nodded. "I didn't know what to say at first." He remembered that day like it was yesterday. He'd been sitting in front of his command setup, monitoring an op, when the message had come in from Brax. Tremors had rippled through him and dread had settled like a brick in his gut. But fast on its heels had been so much elation, so much happiness spilling from his heart, that it had chased the apprehension away. "I wanted him here. So freaking much."

Hawes's icy blues softened. "Of course you did. He's your best friend."

"Yes!" Lily interrupted, the diamond slipping through.

They cheered with her, then Hawes encouraged her to try the triangle again. "I'm glad Kane is here," he said. "He's helped us."

And that right there was the rub. "But I never wanted to put him in that position." Except it was impossible not to, by virtue of who they were. "If he's compromised because of us..."

Hawes pointed at the monitors on which the local news was replaying bits of the press conference. "One, we didn't do this. Two, it's not a state secret that Brax is connected to us nor are we and what we do unknown to SFPD. It's a miracle IA hasn't come after him before now."

"But his connection to us has never appeared to adversely affect his job." It had come close last year when Chris had been working against them, but Chris had come around to their side before Brax was implicated. Holt never wanted to come that close to compromising Brax again. "We can't let it now. If someone connects us to the cartel hits last year—"

"Double-check." Hawes shifted to accommodate a waning Lily, who teetered back against her uncle, triangle slipping from her hand. "Make sure our tracks are covered."

"Already did, and we are, but—"

"We'll get him out of this."

"With his reputation intact." It was the least Holt could do after Brax had saved his multiple times over, starting with the night Holt had first heard the raid sirens at Camp Casey. Brax could have reported him for insubordination, but instead he'd talked Holt out from under the bed and set him on the path to promotion. Hell, to where he was today. Not to mention every time he'd kept his distance those three years in the desert, building a friendship while still respecting their ranks and positions. "His honor means everything to him, and people need him. Like I did. Like I still do. He's a natural leader, he draws people to him, and there aren't enough of those people in the world. Even CIs seek him out. You think Swanson would have gone to anyone else?"

"Not likely," Chris said, appearing at the top of the

stairs. He slung his denim-clad legs over the baby gate one after the other. Jax, in pressed slacks, a button-down, and a goofy tie— their standard work attire—followed behind him. "Especially since someone sent him to Brax."

"What?" Holt and Hawes gasped together.

"Jax tracked the email to Thompson to an email address that Swanson used."

"But Swanson's dead," Hawes said. "He didn't send it from the great beyond."

"No, that must have been someone else," Jax said. "Maybe the same person who sent Swanson this a week before he first reached out to Brax."

Chris held a sheet of paper out to Hawes, who scanned it over, then cursed. "Someone was watching him the entire time."

Hawes passed it to Holt.

Take your concerns to Chief BK.

One line, that's all it said. And sure "Chief BK" could be someone else, but in this situation, Holt was ninety-nine-point-nine percent sure Chief BK was Chief Braxton Kane. He scanned down the page. No prior email. Scanned up the page. Subject line indicated this was a new email, not a reply or forward. He checked the sender's email address. "Hold a sec. This email address is different than the one that sent the photo to Thompson."

"But similar enough IP addresses," Jax said as Chris handed a second sheet to Holt, a list of IP addresses, with two highlighted. "I think they originated from the same network or source."

Maybe the same network or source where the photo was altered too. "Any idea where?"

They shook their head. "I couldn't go farther on SFPD's system without raising flags."

Holt climbed off the floor and gestured to the computers. "Care to join me?"

"Ooh, more projects!"

The gleam in Jax's eyes almost made Holt laugh, until Hawes sucked the tiny bit of joy out of the room. "Back to the first project, did you find out who's leading the IA charge?"

Jax nodded. "Detective Isiah Fletcher."

"Fuck," Holt cursed. "He transferred here at the end of last summer."

"The timing lines up," Hawes said as if reading his mind.

"The chief recruited him," Jax added. "Keeps to himself."

Par for the IA course and consistent with the thin file Holt had on him. There wasn't a lot to go on there. "I'll get to building out his profile," he said.

Hawes shook his head. "You stay on this," he pointed at the computer wall where Jax was already seated. "Chris and Mel can work the Fletcher angle. The less we touch that, the better for Brax." He turned to his husband. "On the other matter, how long until SFPD and the press get wind of Swanson's death?"

"They didn't know who they were looking for before," Chris said. "Now that they do, it's only a matter of time before they ID the John Doe Mel found in Bakersfield as

Swanson. And if the leak finds out, it stands to reason the press will shortly after."

"I did find out who that was," Holt said. "The leak came from a homicide detective. Dustin Packard."

Jax swiveled in their chair. "I would not have expected that. Dustin's a good cop, by the book, former vet too."

"Leverage, remember," Hawes said. "Same thing we'll be looking for on Fletcher."

"Jax is right," Holt said. "At least with respect to Packard. He's got no immediately obvious pain points, but I'm still digging. In the meantime, all his emails—to and from—get routed through me. I'll divert any more leaks."

"You got a physical address for him?" Hawes stood, a sleeping Lily still in his arms. "Avery's on her way over. We'll pay Packard a visit."

"I should go with you." No one had said it, but the Madigan organization would not be fighting this hard for Brax—for an LEO—if it weren't for Holt's connection to him. He'd brought Brax into this family; he needed to be on the front line.

"No, someone else needs you"—Hawes patted Lily's back—"and her tonight. Work with Jax, get things going here, then go to Brax. Calm him down. Make sure he doesn't go and do something honorable before we can get our arms around the situation."

While said with an eye roll and a teasing grin, Hawes's words were no less true. Given Brax's resistance to letting them help, to his push back at Helena's and Oak's legal involvement, to that damn savior complex Holt knew all too well, Brax needed managing too. More than that, he needed comfort. Brax had looked wrung out yesterday during their brief visit, and he'd looked worse at the one with Oak and Helena that morning. The day couldn't have improved, same as it hadn't for Holt, and fuck if that didn't remind Holt how much he needed comfort too. He'd done the hacking, he'd spent time with Lily, now he needed time with his other touchstone.

"All right," he conceded, "but remember what I said. Brax has to be able to go back to work with these people when it's all over. He has to be able to lead them as much for himself as for them and others. That's who he is. We can't take that away from him."

"Cap, you here?" Holt called into Brax's condo.

No response.

Same as there'd been no response to Holt's two knocks on the front door. He'd let himself in with his key and found the condo quiet and dim, the only light in the long entry hall filtering in through the windows of Brax's adjacent bedroom and the home office that doubled as Lily's playroom. Like the toys in his desk drawer, Brax hadn't disassembled Lily's setup here either, and Holt breathed a measure easier.

Lily, strapped to Holt's back, patted his shoulders. "Ba-Ba!"

"I know, baby girl, but I don't think he's back yet."

Holt had texted earlier that he was bringing Lily and dinner over. Brax had replied, **Going for a run. Let**

yourself in. Apparently, they'd beaten him home, which was fine with Holt. It would give him time to heat things up. Except when Holt reached the open living area at the back of the unit, the door to the tiny balcony was open, and through the window, he spied Brax at the table there, beer tipped up to his lips.

Holt flipped on the kitchen lights and hefted two bags of food onto the counter. "Hey! You didn't answer."

Brax didn't bother to turn or put any inflection in his reply. "You have a key."

"I brought dinner."

"Not hungry."

"Have you eaten today? At all?"

No answer.

Answer enough.

Holt glanced over his shoulder at his daughter. "We've got our work cut out for us." He wiped his hands, unhooked one strap of the carrier, and slid Lily around to his hip. Lowering her to the ground, he aimed her the direction of the balcony. "Go give Ba-Ba a hug. He needs it."

She toddled toward the door, arms spread. "Ba-Ba! Yes!"

That did the trick. Brax set aside his bottle and turned sideways in his chair, catching Lily as she stepped outside. He'd covered the area with rugs and added extra slats to the railing as soon as Lily had become mobile, but he was always extra cautious with her, three floors up as they were. Lily threw her arms around his neck, hugging him tight, and Brax smiled. Not as big a grin as Holt would've liked, but given the day, Holt counted it a win.

As Lily babbled with the seven or so words she knew and Brax gamely pretended to understand her, Holt put together a salad and heated up the leftover beef stew he'd brought from home. Once the food was plated and on the table, along with fresh beers and twin stacks of cards, he went to retrieve his two favorite people.

"And what shape is that?" Brax stretched out an arm and pointed at the Transamerica Building.

She couldn't say the word yet, but Lily formed her hands into a triangle.

"That's right!" They clapped together, and Lily demanded, "More!" Another of her recent favorites.

Holt smiled. "Maybe after dinner," he said, alerting them to his presence. Lily shifted on Brax's knees, bottom lip stuck out. "Gravy veggies," he promised her, and her bottom lip quickly unjutted. Ever since Celia's son Marco had dredged a baby carrot of hers through the gravy on her plate, Lily had been a veggie eating machine. Holt would be forever in the teen's debt for getting Lily to try new foods. She held out her arms and Holt plucked her off Brax's lap.

Brax, however, didn't move to stand. "She can have mine too."

"Then at least come play cards with me. It's been too long."

Something flashed across Brax's eyes, too quick for Holt to discern but powerful enough to tickle the base of his spine, a feeling he'd almost forgotten.

Almost.

Brax rose and tickled Lily's dangling foot. "Your daddy is the worst card player I've ever known."

Holt let him have that dodge. "Traitor."

"It's true." He skirted past them and threw a smile over his shoulder. A little wider than the one before, even if it didn't quite reach his eyes. Still, another win as far as Holt was concerned. As was every carrot Lily dredged through the stew and held up for Brax to share. He was as bad at saying no to her as Holt was at playing cards. He ate half the beef on his plate, and the whole side salad Holt had dressed in his favorite sumac vinaigrette, all while handily beating him at cards. Lily cheered Brax on, first bouncing in her booster seat, then in his lap until after several games when she fell asleep sprawled across Brax's chest. Holt conceded another defeat and stood to clear the dishes.

Brax grasped his wrist as he passed on the way to the sink. "Thank you for this."

Holt reversed the grip and squeezed Brax's hand. "Thought you might need a distraction."

"You thought right. Thank you." He released Holt's hand to rub Lily's back, his eyes drifting closed as he hummed an off-key lullaby.

Holt stepped the rest of the way to the sink before Brax noticed his blush, blood rushing to his face and heating his skin. The anxious tingles that usually rushed out to his fingers were tripping inward, causing ripples in his stomach that joined the tickle at the base of his spine. Holt remembered those ripples. Recalled the first time he'd felt them, sitting at an unconscious Brax's infirmary bedside.

He'd dismissed the feeling then, written it off as fear of losing his friend, the person who mattered the most to him out there in the desert a world away from the rest of his family. But he'd felt it again a year later, on a DC dance floor, every time Brax's body had brushed against his. A spark. He hadn't dismissed the feeling then. He'd acted on it, still not exactly understanding what it was but not willing to let it go without drowning in it for a night. He had Amelia to thank for the understanding part. He'd felt the same sort of ripples in his belly when trust had grown into more with her. Then he'd feared it had disappeared for good for him when the trust had disappeared between himself and Amelia. But there was no mistaking that feeling again now, for Brax, amplified to twenty with Lily in his arms. Sparks and more. And fuck, Holt's reawakening desire was the last thing Brax needed to deal with on top of everything else.

"I need to know what's going on with the case," Brax said as if Holt needed the reminder. But the bucket of ice water was well timed. "What else have you found out?"

Holt grabbed two more beers out of the fridge and handed one to Brax as he returned to the table. "You're not gonna like it."

Brax's beer disappeared, gulp by gulp, with each detail Holt relayed. By the time Holt was done talking, Brax's beer bottle was empty and he was clutching Lily, his face buried in her auburn curls. Several deep breaths later, he lifted his face and pinned Holt with hard, hazel eyes. "You need to stop. You've done enough."

"We're still—"

"No. I've got to handle this on my own."

Holt expected some push back but not with this degree of vehemence. The fire in Brax's words, in his eyes, was a welcome sign of life but not if it was going to destroy Brax in the process. "What else is going on, Cap?"

"This has to be by the book."

"I know. That's what I told Hawes."

"And will you tell me everything you're doing?"

"You know I can't."

Brax rose, Lily in his arms. "Exactly." On his way to the study, he swung past the couch to snag her favorite blanket, a match to the one on the rocker at home.

Holt sat glued to his chair, listening to Brax tuck Lily into the portable crib, afraid that if he moved, if he followed Brax back there and continued this argument, his life would unravel. The inevitable conflict they'd been dancing around for six fucking years would finally come to a head and he'd lose someone else. Had Holt really thought, less than two minutes ago, about dancing around something else?

"Fuck," he cursed low and pushed out of the chair. No matter the risk to his heart, this was too important. Brax's future and the job he loved and the good he did for others were too important not to plead the case.

He made it as far as the end of the overlong couch when Brax reemerged from the hallway. He stopped in front of Holt, hands on his hips and head hung, his chest rising and falling at uneven intervals. Holt sank back on the arm of the sofa, de-escalating and inviting Brax to go first. "Talk to me, please."

"This is my life, Holt. My career on the line. A trumped-up bribery scandal, a dead CI, and IA crawling up my ass. I can't be kept in the dark, but with you and your family, I can't know everything either. I don't know how to square that. I don't know if I can take that risk, especially when it puts you and Lily at risk too."

"Is this why you were upset at the wedding?"

Brax quickly averted his gaze, looking past Holt and out the window. "Some of it."

"You wanna tell me the rest? Whatever it is, we can fix it."

Resignation streaked across his face, too reminiscent of that January afternoon. "I can't protect you if I don't know what's going on. It's safer for all of us—"

"Fuck that." Holt reached out and grabbed both of Brax's wrists, dislodging them from his hips and dragging him closer between his spread legs. "We're safer together than apart. I'm not going to hang you out to dry, Brax. You didn't leave me in that building when it was my job, my life, on the line. The walls were coming down around us, literally, and you saved me."

"That was war." Brax stared past him, out the windows again, and Holt suspected it wasn't San Francisco's twinkling skyline he was seeing. But fuck, it needed to be. Hell, the field of focus needed to be even more narrow than that.

"So is this." Holt lifted a hand, grasping Brax's chin and bringing his gaze back to his. "Someone attacked our family, attacked you."

"Because if she hurt you, Holt would either fall apart or kill her himself."

Still true, nine months later, except Holt was past falling apart now. It was his turn to be the strong one. He released Brax's chin but not his face, gliding his hand up to frame his cheek. "I won't let anything happen to you either."

Brax couldn't stop the flare of his eyes, his own words no doubt familiar, before he closed them and turned his face into Holt's hand. "I'm sorry," he murmured, lips tickling Holt's palm, sending a blast of heat racing from the point of contact straight to Holt's center where it collided with the lightning zipping up his spine and the ripples in his belly that had morphed into giant waves echoing in his ears, his pulse so loud he almost missed Brax's next words. "I can't let you get hurt."

He curled his hand around Brax's neck, drawing him down, forehead resting against his own. "I can't let you get hurt either. Let me help you, Brax."

And fuck if in that moment Holt didn't mean more than just hacking, more than just getting Brax out of this jam, more than just protecting him. He wanted to comfort him, wanted to hold him close and erase the breath of distance between their—

Holt's phone on the table rang, startling them apart.

They stared at each other, a long awkward two rings, before Lily cried "Ba-Ba!" and Holt snatched the phone off the table.

"Hey, Jax," he answered, having glimpsed their name onscreen. "What've you got?"

"You're not gonna like it," they said, and Holt had a feeling he was going to like it a whole lot less than anything else he'd told Brax earlier. He wasn't wrong. "I tracked Swanson's emails back through the IP addresses," Jax said. "You were right. They were rerouted, same as the photo. I found the same digital fingerprint on both."

"Whose?"

"I don't have a who exactly, but I have a where, and that might be good enough to get us to who."

Brax rounded the corner, Lily on his hip, dozing with her thumb in her mouth and her head on his shoulder, blanket wrapped around her. Holt held on to that vision, to the sense of home and joy it sparked, and used it as a buffer. "Spill, Jax. From where?"

"FCI Dublin."

"You've got to be kidding me." He lowered the phone and ran his other hand down his face, groaning in anger and frustrated exhaustion.

Brax caught his wrist. "What is it?"

"Amelia."

CHAPTER TWELVE

The door to the visitation room opened, and Lily spun on Holt's lap, her little body vibrating with excitement. Amelia appeared from behind the guard who'd opened the door, and Lily squealed with delight. "Ma-Ma! Ma-Ma!"

The guard met Holt's gaze, and Holt nodded, giving him the go ahead to remove Amelia's cuffs. They always asked; he always conceded. Was it a risk? Yes. Amelia was almost as good as Helena at hand-to-hand combat, and she had a particular skill with pressure points. If she got a hand on Holt's neck, squeezed in just the right spot, he would fall like a giant redwood tree. But while there was a lot Holt no longer trusted about his ex-wife, he did trust the adoring look in her eyes whenever they landed on Lily. Over the past nine months, she had proven, at least in this setting, she wouldn't do anything that might risk Lily or the limited time she got to spend with her.

Holt wouldn't begrudge their daughter that either.

"Give her just a minute," he said to Lily, holding her around the waist as the guard removed Amelia's cuffs.

Holt looked Amelia over as they waited. Not the vibrant, confident presence she'd once been—even at her over-mom'ed and overworked worst—but she looked the best she had since being incarcerated. Her long dark hair was pulled into a neat ponytail, her green eyes were sharp and alert, and the bags under them weren't so pronounced. One might even say she looked settled. Because she thought she might have found a way out? Because revenge was on the horizon? Except the genuine joy in her eyes and her wide smile as she wrapped Lily in her arms belied the ill will Holt suspected. But he hadn't suspected before either. For years, Amelia had lied to him, had used him to manipulate others, like Max Bailey, and had watched over his shoulder as a means to later betray him. Was she doing that now? *Fuck.* He was so tired of being turned around. Of not knowing which end was up. Of not trusting his own fucking instincts.

"This is a pleasant surprise," Amelia said, snapping him out of the mental merry-go-round.

"Belated Easter," he replied. "I'm sorry we missed swinging by."

"Probably for the best." She tickled Lily's tummy, eliciting a peal of giggles that also made Holt smile. "Between visitors and a food poisoning incident, it was a madhouse here. I got to help out in the infirmary. Didn't even mind the overtime."

Maybe that was the reason for the light in her eyes. She was getting back to the work she loved, able to apply her training as a nurse. Holt hoped that was it, but he still had to find out, for his and Brax's sake.

"How was yours?" she asked.

"No food poisoning, thankfully." He retrieved the soft feely box out of Lily's go bag and dumped the animal toys inside it out on the table for Lily. "A bit nontraditional, for us. The lamb was familiar, but the spaghetti pie thing, carrot tart, and Italian Easter bread were new additions." The house had smelled amazing, and they'd had leftovers for days. And leftover Perris for days too, but he hadn't minded. It had been the first big family holiday they'd all shared together, and the sense of home had been welcome.

Amelia smiled. "Perri?"

"Both of them."

"Ah, that's right. Helena's girlfriend."

"More," Lily said, adding her review.

"I bet you did want more," Amelia replied. "Especially when it's homemade. Just wait until Christmas. They'll feed you like you've never been fed before."

A mix of sadness and fondness swirled in Amelia's eyes, and Holt wondered if she was remembering her own family. She wasn't in touch with them any longer. They'd turned their backs on her when she'd come out as queer. Holt still kept tabs on them in case any tried to make a play for custody of Lily. Thinking further on it now, he wondered also if maybe someone—the cartel—was leveraging them against Amelia, forcing her to help them go after Brax. "You miss your family?" he asked.

She hugged Lily closer. "Of course I miss all of you."

"No, I meant your biological family."

Her eyes took on a faraway look, but only for a split second before returning to the present and catching a falling lion Lily had knocked off the table. "I miss certain memories from my childhood, but them, no. I didn't really know family until I met you Madigans." She brushed a hand over Lily's head. "And this little girl." Kissed her crown.

Lily *muah*-ed a kiss back to her and continued to play with her toys.

Amelia laughed, and Holt too, even as his anger and frustration bubbled again. He didn't think this was an act, but how could he be sure? And if he were wrong, it wasn't just his life on the line. Brax's was too. "You still feel that way about us?" he asked.

"Stop beating around the bush, babe. Your siblings are better at it than you."

"Did you ever respect me?"

She lifted her face to the ceiling and laughed, rueful almost. Her gaze was soft, though, when it landed back on him. "Fuck, baby. I feared you. Still do. You were always just one click away from destroying me. You're the smartest of them all."

"But I didn't catch on to you."

"That's because you also have the biggest heart of the lot. Got me right here." She tapped her own chest. "But I know whatever it is you're trying to ask, and doing a terrible job of, can't be about us. There's no magical reunion in our future. I know that's not how you work. The trust is broken, and I"—she tapped her chest again—"did that. That's on me, not you. But family?" She hugged Lily again with one arm and used the other to help their daughter push the lion inside the opening at the top of the box. "We're still that because of her, so tell me what's really going on."

He carefully parsed her words—through everything she'd said and everything he'd already been over with his own therapist and with the child psychologist they'd agreed on for Lily. Amelia was listening too. She got it—seemed at peace with it even—but then again, she'd always gotten relationship dynamics better than him. Except one thing she'd said was wrong. "It's not all on you. My grandmother manipulated you too. That's on her. And it's on me that I was so wrapped up in Lily, and in my own head, that I didn't have an inkling of what was going on in yours, and I'm sorry for that."

Amelia's shoulders lowered, and she released a long slow breath, and with it some of the tension eased from the room. "Thank you for that." The sentiment was genuine. Holt didn't question that. And no longer questioned putting his cards on the table when she prodded, "Now, tell me what's going on for real."

"Someone framed Brax for a crime he didn't commit."

"Ba-Ba!"

"Yeah, baby, we're talking about your Uncle Brax." She picked up the blue car and handed it to Lily. "And you think it's me?"

Holt rested his forearms on the table. "The supposed evidence came from an email and IP address that traced back to here."

"I didn't do it."

From the conversation so far, he tended to believe her, but he'd learned enough from watching Hawes and Helena to know not to give that away yet.

"Say what you will about me," Amelia continued. "Yes, I let Rose turn me around. Yes, I fell for promises of a better, more secure life for my daughter. Yes, my notions of power got twisted up in my head. But I'm not a total fool. There's a reason I never went after Brax. Never tried to get between you two even though I felt like the third wheel half the time, and I was the one married to you."

Holt rocked back, her words a punch to the gut. "What?"

She adjusted Lily in her lap, their daughter done with her toys and just happy to cuddle with her mother. "There's a bond there," Amelia said, her tone matter-of-fact, not cruel or angry. "One you don't share with anyone else, one I'm not sure anyone else could ever comprehend. You should have seen the light in your eyes the day he arrived in San Francisco. I honestly thought I'd lost you, and I would have been okay with that because you were that goddamn happy, even though the man you were hugging was the assistant chief of police."

"But you didn't lose me."

"No, I didn't. Until I severed what was between us." She lowered her chin, nuzzling it into Lily's curls. "But she still ties us together, and because of your bond to Brax, there's a bond with her too. I can't be out there to protect her, but he's protecting both of you. That man would throw himself in front of a bus for either of you. I'm not about to risk that."

He didn't doubt the truth of her words. Brax would do whatever it took to protect him and Lily. Fuck, he'd proven that multiple times over. He wouldn't think twice. Had Amelia recognized that as well? Was she telling the truth? Could he trust her? That she wasn't the one who'd moved against Brax, against their family again? "Are you being real with me?"

"I have lied about a lot, Holt Madigan, but this"—she patted Lily's back—"a good, safe life for her, has always been my primary objective. I understand I went about securing that the wrong way for too long. I won't make that mistake again, and threatening Brax..." She widened her eyes, flashed both hands in the air, and emphasized her words. "Big. Mistake."

The *Pretty Woman* impression made Holt laugh. It had always been her favorite movie.

The lighter mood evaporated, however, with her next words. "Honestly, Holt, it sounds like something your grandmother would pull."

"She made a deal with Hawes."

"You think that still holds?" She shot him an unamused smirk. "If I didn't have our kid in my lap, I'd reach across the table and thump your head."

He chuckled darkly and lifted a hand in acknowledgement. "You're right, and the thought did cross my mind." He didn't want it to, but it had been impossible not to lie in bed last night and run through the gamut of possibilities, including the possibility that this was all tied to Rose somehow.

"Let me see what I can find out for you," Amelia said.

"You'll help us?"

She patted Lily's back again, in time with their daughter's light snores. "For her, of course. And I learned a thing or two watching you. I can get into the system here and find out who really sent that email. If it's tied to Rose, I'll spot it. I learned a few of her tricks as well."

Was it possible Amelia was still working for Rose? That Rose was behind this? Yes, on both counts. Yes, maybe he was wrong again, but his instincts—*fuck*, his instincts had been too often wrong where Amelia was concerned. And if she was working with Rose, if she told Rose they were coming after her, and if Rose escalated the campaign against Brax...

"Because if she hurt you, Holt would either fall apart or kill her himself."

A cool hand landed on his fist, which he hadn't realized he'd formed. "Bottle that anger, babe," Amelia said. "Hold it for when you really need it. In the meantime, let me help. Let me start to make up for the hurt I caused my family."

Even if his instincts were wrong, instincts that were telling him he could trust Amelia in this instance, could he afford not to take the chance if this could possibly clear Brax's name? Fuck, for Brax, he'd risk it all.

He relaxed his fist and nodded. "Okay, but please, Amelia, if you ever loved me, if you love our daughter, don't make me regret this."

Lily dozed the entire drive back from FCI Dublin to MCS. Holt parked his SUV in the spot between Hawes's Benz and Chris's Hog, gathered Lily's go bag and his laptop from the back, and carefully extracted his daughter from her car seat. Situating her on his hip, he encouraged her to go back to sleep. He and her mother had work to do. He carried her inside, past the main reception area and into the executive-level elevator. Exiting on the third floor, he silently nodded to Victoria, their lieutenant who manned the executive-level reception desk, walked by the glassed-in conference room where Helena was meeting with several other captains, and headed toward the row of executive offices. Hawes was on the phone in his corner suite and in the office next door, Chris and Avery were riffling through papers strewn across the investigator's desk.

"Fuc—freaking menace," Holt muttered as he continued on to his office. He lowered the bags off his shoulder, then carried Lily to her pack and play in the corner, another thing she was about to outgrow. When he straightened, Avery and Hawes were standing outside his office door.

He waved them in and plopped into a chair. Midday and it felt like midnight already. "It's not Amelia," he said.

Avery tucked a folder under her arm and leaned against the wall. "How can you be sure?" Her voice was neutral, her stance casual, but her dark eyes were a sea of anger and skepticism. Both warranted. Amelia had used her as a decoy during the attempted coup.

"I can't be," Holt admitted. "Not one hundred percent, but she made a convincing argument."

"Holt—" Hawes started.

He lifted a hand. "Look, I know she fooled me for years. I know that now, so does she, and I don't think *this* is *that* situation."

Chris entered the room, a steaming mug of coffee in hand, which bless his paper-loving heart, he offered to Holt. "Why's that?"

Holt took the mug and savored a long swallow of the strong brew. So much for his caffeine detox. But he needed it—probably a whole pot full—for the hours ahead. He turned half around, getting things running on his computers while also explaining. "She derives no benefit from going after Brax. It won't win us back, and it risks one of Lily's best protectors."

"Okay," Hawes said. "Say we believe her." He pulled out the chair next to Holt, spun it around, and straddled it backward. "How did that email get routed through FCI Dublin?"

Holt nodded at the monitors flickering to life. "That's what she's working on." An incoming encrypted message *dinged*, and Holt rotated back to the console.

I'm in. Amelia's message read. **Opening door for you.**

He'd been impressed as he and Amelia had devised their plan. While her hacking skills had originated in mimicry—observing him and using her eidetic memory to repeat his steps—she'd expanded her knowledge and learned the how and why behind certain digital maneuvers. She was a more than capable partner for this back trace.

A terminal box appeared—the door, courtesy of Amelia—and a few commands later, Holt was inside FCI Dublin's system. A much faster process than if he'd had to hack in himself. **Got it**, he typed back. **I'll pull histories.**

I've got the actives.

While she pinged all the current IP addresses that registered to FCI Dublin terminals, Holt pulled the histories of all IP addresses associated with FCI Dublin terminals the week before, of, and after the date the email about Brax had been sent to Assistant Chief Thompson. He'd compare the two lists, looking for two things. First, any one-time hits, which could indicate someone outside FCI Dublin using its IP addresses as a smokescreen to cover or divert. Second, IP addresses in use on the same dates, and then with Amelia's help, the terminals and users attached to them. From that narrowed list, his team would then search for the connection to someone who wanted to frame Brax.

Someone like their grandmother.

"Amelia thinks it could be Rose," Holt said to the audience still in the room.

"I considered it," Hawes replied. "Brax is a loose end."

Chris moved to stand behind him, hands on his husband's shoulders. "By that token, we all are."

Holt lifted his fingers off the keyboard and curled them into fists. Last year, when Papa Cal had died, when Amelia had been exposed along with Rose and the other traitors in their organization, all within short order, it had felt terrifyingly like that early morning in the desert when the floor had crumbled and the walls had come tumbling down around him and Brax. A dark, chaotic free fall. The only way he'd survived was by hacking his tail off and holding Lily close, making sure his family's new empire succeeded and his daughter had everything she needed to weather the storm. He'd grieved the losses, but he'd never let himself get angry. But now... Now someone was coming after the person who'd kept him safe during that first free fall, the one person who'd been his port of calm in last year's storm, and Holt was fucking furious, all the tamped down anger rushing to the surface. He glanced up, meeting Chris's eyes, the detective's words ringing in his ears.

"If she's behind this—"

Hawes rolled out from under Chris's hands and closer to him, stretching an arm across the back of Holt's chair. "We won't let anything happen to him."

"There's another possibility we have to consider," came Helena's voice from behind them.

Hawes lowered his arm and Holt swiveled, knocking knees with his twin as they both turned the same direction toward their sister. "Who?" Holt asked.

"Jax."

Holt clenched his fists again, even as Helena raised her hands, palms out. "I don't want to think it either, Little H, but they have the expertise and the SFPD connections. It'd be easy enough for them to slip that photo in."

"No way," Chris said, beating Holt to a retort. "I watched them interact with Kane a lot last year and since then too. Jax wouldn't turn on him."

"Or on me," Holt added. Helena opened her mouth, no doubt to play lawyer, but Holt was already a step ahead of her. "But I never thought my own wife would betray me either, so I'll run the checks." He jutted a thumb at a secondary window he had open onscreen. "Same as I'm running a piggyback on Amelia's work in case she tries to redirect or copy it elsewhere."

Helena lowered her hands. "Okay, so, who's that leave us with?"

"Detectives Packard and Fletcher," Avery answered. "That's what we were going over in Chris's office when you came in," she said to Holt.

"What'd you find out?" he asked.

"Packard is a nonfactor. Dude is scared shitless. Saw me and Hawes coming last night and spilled his guts."

"We didn't even have to press," Hawes said. "He didn't want to leak that report. He looks up to Kane like a mentor, and he's a fellow vet, but he got a series of texts the other night."

Avery stepped forward, removed the folder from under her arm, and handed it to Holt.

Holt flipped through the pictures inside it. A smiling woman with two preteen kids bearing a striking resemblance to her and Packard. The woman and kids were dressed differently in each, and the backgrounds varied as well. Fuck. "Someone was on his family?"

Hawes nodded. "For a few months, he thinks."

"They recently reconciled," Avery said. "He's terrified to lose them again."

"You get the details on the text?"

Hawes stuck a hand in his jacket pocket and produced a flash drive. "Thought you might ask."

Holt closed his fingers around the small piece of plastic. "And what about Fletcher? If I had to guess, he's Brax's bigger worry right now."

"I made some calls," Chris said. "Everyone I talked to confirmed the loner bit. Prefers to work solo, some say he's aloof, others say he's arrogant. They all say he works hard, closes cases, is fair and above-board. A natural at internal affairs as much as one can be."

"Personal details?" Helena asked.

"Forty, unmarried, no kids, cut off his family in college. Rents a condo in The Montgomery."

"Why'd he cut them off?" Hawes asked at the same time Helena squawked, "How the hell does he afford The Montgomery on a detective's salary?"

"Unclear," Chris answered. "On both."

Two good questions. "I'll dig into those," Holt said. "Any other leverage points?"

"None that I could find."

Just because Chris couldn't find anything on the surface didn't mean there weren't skeletons buried in the web somewhere. And now Holt had more to go on. His fingers itched with the anticipation of the hunt.

"He and Kane crossed paths in Boston," Chris continued. "Worked a few cases together. I suspect that's why Kane recruited him. Good cop and a known factor."

And for the kill. "Who's betraying him now," Holt fumed.

"Not exactly how it works," Chris replied. "Yes, IA can

initiate its own investigations, but the more likely course is that someone brought the matter to IA."

"That's what we need to figure out," Hawes said.

"You've got two days," Helena interjected. "Brax's IA hearing is set for Friday."

"Fuck." Holt swung back around to the computers, shoved in the flash drive, and stretched out his fingers, dispersing the tingles.

Hawes stood and squeezed his shoulder. "What do you need?"

"Who," Holt said. "Get me Crystal and Monroe from my team. I need extra hands on this," he said, gesturing at the lists of IP addresses populating his screen. "And field operatives on standby to run down leads once we narrow the list."

"Alice and Malik just left on an op," Helena said, "I can free up Connor and Elisabeth. Victoria too."

"That'll work."

"On it, boss," Avery said and disappeared out the door.

"I'll take Lily duty when she wakes," Hawes said.

"Once I get going here, she'll stay out for a while." Much to their relief, his rapid-fire typing still seemed to keep his daughter in a deep slumber, teething fits aside.

"More coffee, then?" Chris said, retrieving Holt's empty mug.

"Hey!" Helena squawked again, and in the reflection of the monitors, Holt could see her face scrunched in mock outrage. "What happened to detoxing?"

He smiled, improbably, then leaned his head back and blew her an upside-down kiss. "If you love me, you'll get

me some of that Turkish rocket fuel you guzzle when
you're in trial."

Bending, she kissed his forehead. "You're lucky I love
you."

"I know." He was lucky. Lucky to have the love and
support of all of them and their skills when he needed
them most, to help save the man he'd brought into their
family, who mattered most to him.

CHAPTER THIRTEEN

Holt held his tablet in one hand and knocked on Brax's door with the other. Sure, he could have used his key, but he could scroll through data just as well out here while waiting for Brax to open the door. Besides, letting himself into the condo in the middle of the night seemed rude. Unannounced no less, because in his excitement at finally having a lead, Holt had forgotten to call first. What if Brax had company? What if Holt was interrupting—

That half-formed thought settled like a brick in his stomach, heavier than it had any right to be. He didn't expect Brax had been a monk all these years, but in the time since Brax had been in San Francisco, he'd never brought anyone around for Holt to meet. Why was that? Had he made Brax feel like he couldn't?

Fuck.

And fuck, why had he had so much coffee? His thoughts were pinging all around like a pinball in one of those machines with too many flashing lights and levers.

Like that night he'd shown up in Brax's officer quarters. Only then it had been a never-ending string of fears and what-ifs. His own life, those of his teammates, the entire operation. Brax had been the only person he could talk to freely. The only person who could make the storm stop. Was this any different? Yes, the storm was swirling around Brax this time, he was the center of it, but what was it they said about hurricanes? The center—the eye—was the calm of the storm. Holt was in control of the information this time—he had a lead—but that didn't make the storm, what was at risk, any less terrifying.

He raised his fist to knock again but stopped just shy of his knuckles hitting wood. Light flickered on in the hallway on the other side of the door, and through the gauzy curtain that covered the inset window, Holt watched as Brax—alone—approached the door. He opened it, and Holt bit back a wince.

Fuck, he should have waited until morning. Should have ignored his own needs, his own terrified excitement, and put Brax's needs first. He'd definitely been asleep—had the pillow crease on his cheek to prove it—but he also had the bags under his eyes to prove he hadn't been out for enough hours. He looked tired, drained of energy, a look Holt couldn't remember seeing on Brax before the past nine months, during which he'd worn it entirely too often.

"Holt," Brax greeted on a yawn. He stood over the threshold, flannel-clad hip and T-shirted shoulder leaning against the door frame. "It's two in the morning."

"Blame Helena's coffee. Fuck. No, blame me. I'm

sorry." He tucked the tablet under his arm and turned to go. "I'll come back in the morning."

A hand clutched the back of his jacket. "Get inside."

He let himself be tugged back into the condo, turned, and shoved forward, down the hallway in front of Brax. "Where's Lily?"

"Asleep at home."

"Where you should be."

"I had a pot of that rocket fuel Helena drinks."

Brax chuckled. "No more for you, then." He gave Holt another shove toward the couch and continued to the kitchen. "What can I get you instead?"

Holt tossed the tablet onto the coffee table, feeling all kinds of guilty at the way Brax swayed on his feet as he stared into the open fridge. "Seriously, I'll go." He stood again. "I'll come back in the morning."

"Sit, Private."

Holt obeyed, then shot Brax the bird when the other man turned around, a smirk turning up one corner of his mouth. He knew Holt would react on instinct to the barked order. "Not fair."

Brax shrugged. "Worked, didn't it?" He held out a can of ginger ale. "Now, tell me what was so important you rushed over here."

He popped open the can, took a sip, and waited for Brax to get situated on the sofa. He angled toward Holt, one leg hitched up on the seat, an arm braced on top of the cushions, a hint of ink Holt didn't recognize peeking out from under his short sleeve. Overall, Brax looked mostly awake. He looked determined to stay that way, more than anything. Damage done, Holt took one more sip then traded his can of soda for his tablet. A couple of taps and he handed the tablet to Brax, open to a profile photo of a young woman with purple hair, delicate features, and tattoos—sunflowers—that ran the length of her arm, exposed by a sleeveless sundress. "Do you know a Samantha Pritchard?"

"This is her?"

"We think so."

Brax handed the tablet back. "Name doesn't ring a bell. Picture doesn't either. Who is she?"

"I'm working with Amelia—"

Brax bolted halfway to standing, shaking off the last vestiges of sleep. "You're *what?*"

Holt caught him by the wrist and tugged him back down. Then tugged the soda can out of his hand before Brax crushed it. "She got me into FCI Dublin's mainframe." He set the can next to his on the table. "I piggybacked all her maneuvers. She didn't pull any shit. She's helping for real. I think she actually likes you."

"Debate for another day." He propped his elbow on the sofa cushion again and rested his head in his hand. "Tell me the rest."

"We think Samantha Pritchard"—he gestured with the tablet—"is the person who altered the photo of you and Swanson and sent it to Thompson. We linked an IP address to her, and that same IP address pinged two other cartel contacts."

"Shit. They found out Swanson met with me."

"Seems like it. They took him out the cartel way, but it's harder to kill a police chief."

"So they're trying to get rid of me another way."

Holt nodded. "They hired Samantha to doctor the photo and send it to SFPD."

"Fuck." Brax shifted, putting both feet on the floor and slumping back into the sofa, head tipped back, eyes closed. "Camino's been trying to get a foothold ever since you guys took out Reno's crew. There's a power vacuum."

"And you're gumming up the works." In some ways, it was a relief. Yes, the Madigans had created the vacuum, but Brax had unwittingly stepped into the middle of a cartel grab for power. Any police chief who had a potential CI in that crime circle would do the same. This wasn't someone—wasn't Rose—coming after Brax as revenge or as a way to get at them.

"Is she at Dublin?"

"No, but we think she might have been. The spoof was too good. I don't think physical forgery is her only specialty. There were three pings from that IP address in the history, so she was there, or is tight enough with someone there to walk them through the process."

Brax rotated his head and lifted his eyelids, looking at Holt with tired hazel eyes. "But she's not a registered prisoner there?"

Holt shook his head. "Nor is Samantha Pritchard an alias of anyone there."

"Fuck." He shifted forward on the couch, grabbing his soda and taking another long swallow.

Holt reached out and laid a hand on his back, digging

his fingers into the knot between his shoulder blades. "Who do you want to take it to?" he asked softly.

Brax's gaze whipped to his. "I'm sorry, what?"

Holt stopped the motion of his fingers and flattened his hand. "I heard you last night. This is your job, your decision. Helena can call the warden in the morning, see if she recognizes Pritchard. Or you can take this info to your assistant chief or to IA. Or we can take this to the feds, which was Hawes's suggestion. In any case, it's your call."

Brax held his gaze a moment longer, then retreated back to staring at the floor. But elbows braced on his knees, he rolled his back for more of the massage and Holt picked up where he'd left off. "I trust Maya," Brax said, "but I don't want to put her in that position. IA... Fletch is a good cop, but it's bigger than just this matter."

Some of the shine wore off Holt's excitement. He was still hitting roadblocks where Fletcher was concerned. He was sure something was there. Personally, it didn't all add up, but professionally, the detective's IA career and investigations seemed to be in order. For now, they had to go with the lead they did have. "But this can be a start, yeah? Take this matter off the stack? Get you reinstated."

"Maybe, but we need it nailed down better before we take it to Fletch. That's the only way I get reinstated." Brax straightened and scooted to the end of the couch cushion. "Tell Helena not to call the warden yet. I agree with Hawes. We take this to the feds. They've been building a case against the cartel."

"Since Hawes turned over Reno's guy last year?"

Brax nodded. "But we take this to them through a

broker. This may help them but not without helping us too." Holt liked the sound of *us*.

"Mel?"

"She's our best bet." Brax leaned forward and retrieved the tablet. "Send me the picture of Pritchard." He handed the tablet to Holt and stood with a barely muffled groan. "I need to make a call. Phone's charging in my room."

"This late?" Holt said.

"Cruz sleeps less than I do. I'll be right back."

Brax tossed him a half smile over his shoulder. Tired, but real, and reaching his eyes for the first time in days. Weeks maybe. Months even. Definitely a win. Smiling himself, Holt forwarded the collected info, then tossed his tablet on the table and leaned back. He'd made the right decision convincing his family this was Brax's choice. Brax had needed that control, needed to know and trust that they could help him without compromising his job or how he wanted to handle things. He needed an active role in the chaos. Holt could appreciate that, having felt like a bystander to his own hurricane more than once last year. More than that, Holt needed to start rebuilding the trust that had been crumbling between them. Satisfied things were moving the right direction, Holt closed his eyes, resting them for just a minute.

"Come on, let's get your feet up." Brax's words came at him as if from far away, muffled and quiet. Familiar hands shifted him on the couch, lifting his legs and gently lowering his torso. Eyes still closed, his lids too heavy to lift, the caffeine high finally worn off, Holt nestled into the cushions that smelled like all the good things he associated with Brax—caramel, fabric starch, and his daughter. He stretched his legs out and smiled sleepily, a question he'd always wondered flitting through his fuzzy head. "Why's it so long?"

A calloused hand, then soft warm lips, brushed his forehead. "In case you ever needed to fit."

Brax's breath was gone before Holt could fight through the fog of sleep to chase after it, and then he didn't want to when warm, knitted wool was spread over him. Lily loved this blanket. Brax covered her with it all the time like he had the other night. Like Brax had used its match to cover both of them the night Holt had learned of Amelia's betrayal. Holt had cried and cradled Lily close while Brax had stood guard over them, his hands on the top of the rocker or on Holt's shoulders. If Holt had had the legs to stand on that night, he would have been in Brax's arms. He didn't doubt that Brax would have held him all night if that's what he'd needed.

What he needed.

Holt pushed through his own drowsiness, enough to open his eyes and flail out a hand, catching Brax's wrist. "You can fit too."

"You should be comfortable."

"And you should sleep. I can make sure you do that." He scooted back and eyed the room he'd made. "Here."

Holt tugged on his wrist again, and Brax put up a token resistance. "Private."

"Captain."

A long stare later, Brax gave in and lowered himself onto the couch, his back to Holt. He tossed his phone onto the coffee table, then glanced over his shoulder. "Are you gonna get any sleep this way?"

"I'm exhausted, Cap."

"What happened to that caffeine high?"

"Used it all up." He held up the end of the blanket, inviting him under. "I'll sleep. Just making sure you do too. Feel guilty I interrupted."

Brax glided a hand over his head, took a couple deep breaths, then finally swung his legs up and stretched out, his back to Holt's front. He took the end of the blanket from Holt, pulling it tight around them, and when Holt curled an arm over his waist, Brax, after a few tense seconds when Holt feared he'd gone too far, exhaled a long slow breath and relaxed, letting himself be held. Desire rippled again, but Holt's own exhaustion muted the effect, as did his contentment at having Brax in his arms and giving him something he needed. During moments like this, Holt thought maybe he could give back an ounce of everything Brax had given him over the years. Maybe... if he had a lifetime with the man in his arms.

CHAPTER FOURTEEN

Helena worried a nick in the scuffed and scratched conference room table, deepening the groove with her manicured nail. "You ever hear the joke about the three assassins, a PI, and a cop who walked into the FBI?"

"Hena," Hawes chided from one side of Holt.

"Christ," Brax cursed from the other.

Helena aimed a side-eye at Chris, who declined to comment from the corner where he doctored his second cup of coffee.

"Killer story," she snickered.

Hawes angled his chair toward Holt and away from their sister. "You shouldn't be here." His brother's gaze skipped past him. "Neither should you," he said to Brax. "We shouldn't all be here."

"I'm not sitting this one out," Holt said.

"And this is my career we're talking about." Brax leaned forward, his right arm brushing Holt's left. "Not to mention, I called this meeting."

The weird distance that had been between them didn't seem so vast, so frightening, after last night, furthering Holt's conviction that he'd done the right thing, letting Brax make this call and making sure he slept. Even if, despite those wins, Holt also couldn't shake the feeling they were sitting ducks. Hawes was right to a degree. Where possible, he and his siblings avoided all being in the same dangerous pond at once. Holt was usually the one at home or at MCS, running comms for operations. Today, though, he wasn't the duck out of place.

"Helena is here as Brax's attorney," Holt said. "I'm here as his best friend. What are you doing here?"

"He's right, Big H," Helena said. "We've got Mr. Hair as your proxy."

Chris made a show of flipping them all off. Probably not a good idea, then, to ask him for a cup of what smelled distinctly like Dunkin' goodness. Holt was about to get up and pour himself a cup when the door opened.

Mel entered first, statuesque and dressed to the professional nines for a morning back in her old office. On her heels were two men Holt recognized, though he'd never met them in person. The redhead in a three-piece suit was FBI San Francisco's Special Agent in Charge, Aidan Talley. They'd kept an eye on the Irish ex-pat—Mel's brother-in-law and best friend—as he'd climbed the FBI's ranks. Holt respected the company he kept and the way he did business. The man beside him, a hand resting on Aidan's lower back, would be recognizable to anyone who paid the least bit of attention to sports. Jameson "Whiskey" Walker was a former star basketball player who'd made headlines several years back, coming out as gay and leaving the FBI to return to basketball as an assistant coach at St. Mary's. And so he could marry his Bureau partner, Aidan. He was also, Holt grudgingly admitted, the best hacker he knew. Holt wouldn't, however, begrudge Jamie the fact that he and his husband looked like they belonged in a menswear catalog or on the cover of *OUT* magazine, both so gorgeous and both so obviously in love it made his own chest ache.

"Oh," Helena drawled in an exaggerated whisper. "Now I get it."

Chris leaned back in his chair, reaching behind her to nudge Hawes's shoulder. "I ain't even mad, boo. Think they'd go for a quad?"

Helena coughed, poorly hiding her laugh. "Wrong Talley."

Mel replied with a wink.

Hawes shot to his feet so fast Holt failed to muffle his laugh. Beside him, Brax chuckled too, and Holt was glad for the amusing start to what was going to be another long day. Brax shot him a grin, and for a moment, Holt forgot about everyone else, his world revolving around a pair of smiling hazel eyes. Objectively, he couldn't deny the other hotness in the room, but as far as he was concerned, a rested and suited Braxton Kane, smiling just for him, was the only hotness that mattered.

"Mel," Hawes said, "Good to see you."

Brax rose too, popping their bubble, but Holt internalized the warm, soft feelings and let them buoy him through the round of introductions.

"Nice to finally meet you in person," Jamie said as he shook Holt's hand. After Jamie had helped them last year, he and Holt had struck up a friendship, frequently chatting online or by video, trading hacker tips and tricks.

"There a reason we needed to meet here?" Hawes asked. "I know Brax called this meeting, and we're on board with cooperation, but the setting is—"

"Pretend it's Switzerland," Mel said. "At least for today."

"And we have a common target," Aidan said, his friendly Irish brogue fading as he shifted into work mode. He stepped forward, a stack of files in hand. He dropped the first on the table. "Samantha Pritchard." Dropped another. "Aka Sam Gilbert." And another. "Aka Sammy Wallace." Then the rest. "She's got a half dozen other aliases too. She's a master forger"—he cut a glance to Holt —"real and digital"—then reverted to addressing the room at large—"and she's the target of an active federal investigation."

"Any idea how she got tangled up in this?" Chris asked.

Aidan pushed the folder labeled Sam Gilbert toward him. "She's done work for the Camino cartel before."

"So then, what? This is revenge?" Holt said, picking up the thread he and Brax had speculated about yesterday. He angled toward him. "The cartel getting back at you?"

"Guess they're tired of me gumming up the works."

"You turned their accountant," Mel said. "Which led to two busted deals and multiple arrests." She shifted her attention to Hawes. "And you fucked up their rivals last year, real good. They don't want to be next."

Hawes pressed his lips into a thin line.

"They're sending a message," Aidan said. "To all of us."

Guilt reformed in Holt's gut. Not quite a brick but weighty and jagged enough. He clasped his hands, stilling them before they started air-typing. The cartel had their own reasons for going after Brax—it wasn't only his connections to the Madigans that had made him a target— but they were all tangled up in this together.

Brax's hand landed on Holt's bouncing knee beneath the table. With his hands clasped, Holt had displaced the nervous energy, and Brax aimed to calm him. But the divot between Brax's brows and the worry in his eyes did not project calm.

"Sorry to break up the fun with lawyer-speak," Helena said. "But—"

"But this isn't enough to clear Chief Kane," the other lawyer in the room, Aidan, finished. "And it's not enough for me to catch my suspect either."

"Which is where I come in," Jamie said. His gaze landed on Holt. "How do you feel about setting a trap with me and a friend?"

Holt unclenched his hands and stretched his fingers, letting the trapped energy flow back into them. "Thought you'd never ask."

They had all just stood when the door at the opposite end of the conference room opened. A dark-haired, dark-eyed man Holt recognized from their FBI files as Aidan's

ASAC, Cameron Byrne, poked his head inside the room. "I'm patching through a video call." He pointed at the wall-mounted screen flickering to life. "You want to take it."

Agent Byrne closed the door, and a moment later, the image onscreen resolved. Holt bit back a gasp at the man he knew but hardly recognized. ATF agent Scotty Wheeler's suit was days wrinkled, his dark blond hair was greasy and long past regulation, and his brown eyes were red-rimmed and bloodshot. It wasn't I'm-hiding-and-recovering-from-a-gunshot or your-grandmother-kidnapped-and-tortured-me bad, but it was the look of a man on the verge of losing everything.

Scotty didn't bother with pleasantries, cutting right to the chase instead. "You're investigating Samantha Pritchard?"

"And her other aliases," Chris said. "Scotty, what the hell—"

"You're missing a few names," he said. "Samantha Smith was the alias she used with Remy Pak. Her real name is Savannah Grace Ryan, and I've known her since we were kids." No one managed to hold in their gasp at that unexpected revelation. Or at the next, more shocking one. "That trap you're setting, it's for my ex."

"Fuck, Scotty," Chris cursed as Aidan ducked out of the room. "Does the ATF know about this? Are you flying solo on it?"

Scotty's answering laugh was just this side of hysterical. "I can't believe *you're* asking me that."

"Aww," Helena drawled, mocking the Georgia lilt in

Scotty's voice, the more pronounced accent evidence of his weariness. "We missed you, Agent Salty."

"Leave him alone," Hawes chided gently.

Holt lowered his chin to hide his smile. Despite married bliss, Hawes still projected cold efficiency to the outside world. He hadn't earned his moniker, Prince of Killers, for nothing. He did less of the killing these days, leaving that to Helena and their operatives, while he focused instead on their social and political connections and running their legitimate business, but he was still the too serious oldest sibling, the patriarch of the family. Except Hawes's marshmallow center had leaked out more often the past year, most surprisingly where the federal agent who'd tried to bring them down was concerned. Hawes had developed a soft spot for Scotty Wheeler, one that included keeping tabs on the agent. Holt had attributed Scotty's wild travel patterns to cases—he was the ATF's best undercover wrangler—but by the look of him, he was the one who needed wrangling.

"This is the Sam you wouldn't tell us about?" Hawes said.

"For obvious reasons. When I found out you'd pinged one of her aliases, I caught the next flight out there but missed my connection in Vegas."

"Rewind," Chris said. "You said her real name is Savannah, but you call her Sam. Why?"

"She was named for the place we grew up, and she wanted the hell out of there. She started calling herself Sam when we were twelve. She wouldn't answer to her real name anymore, so we all got in line. That was her way."

"Why *didn't* you tell us about her?" Brax asked.

"I didn't expect her to cross SFPD's path," he said to Brax, then to Hawes, "And I wasn't going to put her in yours."

"Fair enough," Hawes replied.

"You were looking for her," Chris said. "When you came back to town in November?"

Holt recalled seeing the rumpled agent slip into the restaurant where they'd held Lily's birthday party. Chris and Hawes had spoken with him. Holt hadn't joined them, too caught up in keeping Lily distracted from her mother's absence and too caught up in whatever odd distance was building between him and Brax. In any event, *that* rumpled Scotty looked prim and pressed compared to the Scotty onscreen now.

Another bitter chuckle confirmed how much the agent's world had darkened. "I've been looking for Sam since we were teens and she made herself a fake ID and skipped town. I thought I saw her one of the times I was at FCI Dublin to meet with Amelia after her arrest."

"You did," Aidan said, reentering the room with a folder in hand. "Didn't take long to find her once we knew who we were looking for. She was bonded out. Skipped bail."

"Who paid the bond?" Scotty asked.

"Hyokkose LLC."

"Remy Pak," Holt said, recognizing the entity name.

As had Scotty, who scrubbed a hand over his face and mumbled a weary, "Fuck."

Pak was tight with the Russian mob. The ATF had busted and turned her too, and in so doing, discovered a trust fund she'd set up for Samantha Smith.

"I met with Remy in December," Helena said. "And she helped us out earlier this year. Sam wasn't with her either of those times."

Scotty lowered his hand. "She's running from both of us."

"This is how she spoofed the IP addresses for FCI Dublin," Holt said, reminding them of the primary matter at hand, the one involving the man beside him. "She knew the system." He turned to Jamie. "You got a trap in mind?"

Jamie nodded. "We make it look like the cartel is contacting her to fabricate more evidence. Emails in Chief Kane's SFPD mailbox. If the trap works and she produces the emails, it'll support the manufactured evidence theory to clear Chief Kane. And hopefully we can also get a location on Sam and anyone else she's using to route the email traffic or money."

"And if Sam takes the bait?" Scotty said.

"I'm willing to cooperate if she does," Aidan said. "The FBI isn't after her so much as her various employers and contacts."

Holt caught the exchange of looks between Hawes and Mel, Hawes and Scotty, then Scotty and Aidan. Nods all around.

"All right," Holt said. "Let's do this."

Holt and company followed Jamie past the lobby elevators, down the hallway, and into a large interior space. A converted boardroom by the look of it, no windows and AC blasting. Single file, their group wove through stacks of servers, and Holt slowed his steps, desperate for a peek. Behind him, Brax chuckled low and put a hand to his back, shoving him forward. Holt wanted to be angry about it, but the fact Brax knew him so well sent a gentle wave of warmth sluicing through him. They emerged from the stacks into a sort of mini-bullpen, several rows of desks comprising SF-FBI's cyber division. A petite brunet, hair in a wobbly pencil bun, stood in front of a line of three workstations. Holt recognized her from their files as Agent Lauren Hall.

Arms spread, Jamie strode forward. "Mini-Me."

Lauren dodged the baller who was clearly playing at obnoxious older brother, though said files indicated he wasn't older by much and he wasn't blood related. But that was the vibe Holt picked up, the two of them acting much the way he and Helena teased each other sometimes.

"Ohmigod," Lauren huffed. "You act like it's been ten years. You saw me last weekend at Gravity, for fuck's sake."

Laughing, Jamie moved to her side, an arm slung over her shoulders. "Holt Madigan, Agent Lauren Hall," he said. "Lauren, this is the other hacker we run into from time to time."

"Barb—"

Helena backhanded his gut, then rose on her toes and whispered, "Brax might like your balls too someday."

Holt blushed and prayed to all that was holy that only he'd heard Helena's words, a callback to a conversation over cards last year.

Lauren slipped out from under Jamie's arm, stepped forward, and held out her hand, her manicured nails painted alternating blue and red. "Agent Lauren Hall. Nice to meet you."

"Same," Holt said.

"You get the protocols I sent over?" Jamie asked.

"Yep, we're all set." She pointed at the middle computer first. "This one will spoof the target's cartel contact." Then the one to the left. "This one is for Holt to back trace and for you"—she looked to Brax—"to log into your email account. We need before and after screenshots so we can show the forged email traffic." She gestured to the last computer. "And this one will make the bank transfer." She circled behind the computers. "We just need the relevant IPs to ping. See if we can get her attention."

"And that's where you come in," Jamie said to Holt.

Helena withdrew Holt's tablet from her briefcase and handed it to him. Holt followed Jamie behind the desks and pulled up the necessary IP addresses and permissions, courtesy of Amelia.

"And we think Sam will respond right away?" Helena asked.

"Chances are good," Holt said. "She responded to each of the other relevant communications within five minutes."

Helena nodded and rejoined the ongoing legal discussion with Scotty via a video call on Chris's phone.

"I'm good here," Jamie said from behind the middle unit.

"All set here too." Lauren bounced on her toes behind the far unit. "Game time!"

The same excitement coursed through Holt, tingles radiating out to his fingers and toes. He forced them calm, using the memory of that earlier wave of warmth as he familiarized himself with the new computer, which was already logged into SFPD's mainframe. He called the source of warmth closer, and Brax sank into the spare chair next to him.

"Log in, please," Holt said, sliding over to make room for Brax in front of the keyboard. "We need to get the before screenshots of your inbox and outbox."

Brax entered his username and password, and his desktop appeared onscreen.

"We're in," Holt told the others. "Dates for the screenshot?"

"Aim for the period between the second and last meeting with Swanson," Helena said, an ear on both conversations. "That'll be most convincing to her and for our case."

Brax provided the date range, and Holt, rolling back in front of the computer, quickly took the needed screenshots. Brax, however, didn't get up to rejoin the others. "Thank you for doing this," he said. "For working with them and for coming to me last night."

"This was your call to make." His gaze drifted to where

the others were still arguing with Scotty. "And we owe Agent Salty a favor," Holt added. "If we can help him with this too…"

"Do you realize what an incredible man you are?"

Holt's gaze snapped to Brax's, and the emotions in his hazel eyes—warmth, admiration, affection—set off an ocean of ripples again. And a blush that by the heat of Holt's face, Brax had to notice. "I—"

"We've got a hit," Lauren nearly shouted.

Smiling, Brax patted Holt's knee, then rolled to make more space between them. "Do your thing, Private."

Distance was good. He needed it to concentrate, including on the incoming messages from Sam that were lighting up Jamie's screen. Holt was supposed to be back tracing them, trying to get a lock on Sam's location, while Jamie kept the negotiation going.

Need more, Jamie typed after some initial back and forth, "confirming" identities.

The photo wasn't enough? Sam replied.

There's some doubt. Lawyers.

Price has doubled.

Fine, time is tighter.

Two days, Sam offered.

Two hours, Jamie countered. "Gamble," he said aloud to the others who had gathered around them. "But we don't have time to waste."

They waited—the longest five minutes of Holt's life—for Sam's response. **Photo or email?**

Email to/from BK.

Other party?

"Okay, I need that email address," Jamie said to Lauren, then to the group. "This is the other gamble. Do we think she'll check it?"

"Whose is it?" Hawes asked.

"Reno's guy you gave us last year," Aidan replied. "We turned him. Planted him in Camino."

Chris flipped through Sam's file. "Her rap sheet doesn't indicate she's deep in the organization."

"She wouldn't be," Scotty said. "I would have found her by now if she were. I haven't because she's stayed on the move, never tying herself to one party."

"Until she caught Remy's eye," Helena said.

"Seems so," Scotty replied. "In any event, chances are good she won't know or look that closely. That's not her business."

"The less she knows the better," Hawes said.

"Exactly."

"Do it," Brax said, and Jamie sent the address through.

Give me an hour, Sam replied. **Price just tripled.**

Lauren glanced up, blue eyes wide. "That's more than we're authorized for."

"We'll cover the difference," Hawes said, stepping to Lauren's side. "Just tell me where the money needs to go."

"You can't—" Brax started.

Helena cut him off. "You're family, Brax. We can and we will."

"We square?" Jamie asked.

Holt rolled to Brax's side. "Come on, Cap, let us do this. We're *this* close."

After another long moment, Brax nodded.

Account number? Jamie typed back.

An encrypted link appeared, and Lauren went to work, finalizing the wire transfers on the third computer. "It's rerouting through a cartel account we seized," she explained. "And the money is on its way."

Sam's acknowledgement came fast. **Received. Give me an hour.**

It only took her fifteen minutes. Two emails appeared in Brax's mailbox, arranging the meeting and discussing the payment that was supposedly evidenced in the photo. Holt snapped the after pictures.

"Bingo!" Helena said, looking over Jamie's shoulder. "That's it."

"Did we get a lock on her location?" Scotty asked.

"We did," Holt said, zeroing in on the location. "Looks like a rental. Mussel Shoals area, between Santa Barbara and Ventura."

"Give me a head start, Talley," Scotty said, his accent thicker, taking on an edge of desperation. "I'll catch the next flight out of here. Let me convince her to cooperate."

"And if she bolts?"

Mel snatched the Savannah Ryan folder out of Chris's hand. "Seems I have a bounty to catch."

Holt glanced to Helena, then to Hawes. This was enough to clear Brax, who had Holt and Helena at his back. Someone else needed Hawes and Chris.

"We've got this covered," Helena said, reading Holt loud and clear.

Hawes had too. "Chris and I will back them up."

Aidan had that same stunned look on his face like Jax had the other day.

"Shake it off, hermano," Mel said with a laugh. "You and Daniel do the same."

The redhead laughed, then smoothed down his jacket and tie. "It'll take me a few hours to get the warrants and coordinate with the LA field office. That's your head start."

Scotty hung up, and Hawes and Chris bolted for the door, Mel on their heels.

"We'll need the records of the conversation," Helena said. "And those screenshots of Brax's mailbox."

"Yep," Lauren said with a nod, her bun wobbling precariously. She blew an errant strand out of her face. "Let me get everything into evidentiary format."

Jamie stood and stretched. "I can help with that. Just like the good ol' days."

"All the data's transferred to my office," Lauren said. "Let's go."

The three of them left, catching Aidan up in their wake and leaving Holt and Brax still in their chairs. Even Holt was half in awe at how fast that had all gone down. Brax too, judging by his dazed, "Did that just happen?"

Holt rolled over and pulled him into a hug. "You're almost clear, Cap."

They held each other, silent as the computers whirred around them. When Brax's body began to tremble, Holt thought he might be crying, until a bubble of laughter escaped from between them. "Did those fools just leave *you*, Holt Madigan, in the FBI cyber cave?"

Holt drew back enough to appreciate the easy smile stretched across Brax's face. "Guess they figured it was safe with the chief of police."

Brax smiled wider. "If I still am, it's because of you." The tears did appear then, Brax's eyes going glassy. He hid the tears before they fell, burying his face in Holt's neck. "Thank you."

"You're welcome." Holt hugged him tighter, not the least bit tempted by direct access to the FBI servers, not when he had Braxton Kane wrapped in his arms instead.

CHAPTER FIFTEEN

Holt sat in the passenger seat of the X5, knee bouncing, fingers tapping the open window frame. Sunny and sixty-five, a perfect spring day in San Francisco. He hoped the news they were waiting for didn't dampen the mood.

"I'm about two seconds from ejecting your ass out of this car," Avery said, not taking her eyes off the building across the street from the lot where they were parked. "That or putting on some music so I can at least pretend the fidgeting is in rhythm."

"I've got rhythm."

Avery flicked him a side-eye. "Okay, white boy."

"Hawes and Helena both do."

"*They* do."

"I went to a club once. Had people all over me."

"It wasn't your rhythm they were all over." Her gaze slid forward again, and the corner of her mouth twitched. "I've seen you dance with Lily in your arms while Brax tries to sing. Two wrongs don't make a right."

Chuckling, he dropped his elbow from the open window and shifted in his seat, trying and failing to ignore the memories that wouldn't stay locked down. Brax could move, even if he couldn't sing, and those moves had been getting all kinds of attention that night in DC. Same as Holt acknowledged Aidan's and Jamie's objective good looks, he wasn't blind to Brax's. Tall, leanly muscled, a way of carrying himself that spoke of authority but not the fear-me kind. Hair, eyes, and features that all complemented. But that night in DC, attraction had flared, a new appreciation for Brax's handsome qualities stoked by years of friendship and trust and amplified to twenty by how free and at peace Brax had been on that dance floor. So much of Brax had been hidden, even from Holt, by virtue of the army, DADT, and their ranks, but that night, the uniform and insignia had come off, and Holt had seen more of Brax than he ever had before. Than he had since. And fuck if Holt didn't want to see more of the free and real Brax again. Holt had briefly glimpsed that Brax yesterday morning at the FBI, a layer of the ever-present exhaustion peeled back, more of those threads of trust between them stitched back together. Now, if they could just navigate the latest obstacle—

"Showtime," Avery said.

Across the south and northbound lanes of Third, on the sidewalk near the entrance to SFPD headquarters, the gathered press surged forward. The glass doors opened, Assistant Chief Thompson emerging first. Behind her exited Brax and Oak, the former's chin down, the latter's face carefully blank. No sign of Fletcher. Helena and Jax were last through the door, hanging back and stepping the opposite direction of the cameras.

Holt leaned forward, elbows on his knees, chin resting on his clasped hands, using his own weight and strength to suppress the nervous energy that wanted to bounce every part of him. What had IA decided? It drove him nuts that he couldn't hear what was being said, but it was too risky to bug Helena today. He contemplated grabbing his tablet from the door pocket, but he couldn't tear his attention from Brax. Standing beside Thompson, his posture was soldier perfect, always the consummate professional. He only shifted when Thompson stepped aside and stretched out a hand to him. He lifted his chin, smiling, and shook his deputy's hand, which she used to yank him into a crushing hug.

"Does that mean what I think it does?" Avery said.

Holt unclasped his hands, scrubbed them over his face, and peeked through his fingers, making sure the scene didn't morph into a nightmare. Nope, still the good kind of dream. Brax and Thompson separated, and she held his badge out to him, the sunlight glinting off the metal shield. Brax's expression eased but was still professional until he stepped forward and looked across the street, right at Holt. His smile broke free of its reins, and Holt's curved to match, splitting his face in two.

"Hell yeah!" Avery shouted with a fist pump.

Fuck, Holt didn't know it was possible to be this happy for someone else. Yes, he'd been in awe the day Lily had been born, and he'd been thrilled for Hawes at his wedding and for Helena when she'd finally accepted all the love

Celia had to offer, but this sort of joy was on a whole other level. This was his heart exploding, bumping against his rib cage and making way for a tsunami. Holt did not want to rein in those feelings either. Like that night in DC, he wanted to drown in the waves—happiness, desire... love—but unlike then, he wanted more than a single night. Holt shoved a hand in his pocket, an idea—an overdue celebration—coming to mind. He just needed his phone to order a few things.

He barely had the device out when *pings* sounded for real, the dream in front of him morphing into a nightmare. Only not as he expected and far more terrifying. The *pop, pop, pop* of AR fire rent the air, followed by the *crack* of shattered glass, spiderwebs fanning out from a bullet's impact against SFPD's bulletproof lobby wall—behind Brax, directly to the right of his head.

Those shots were meant for him. Bile, very real, churned in Holt's gut and surged up his throat, chasing away any joy. Another round of shots popped off—from the same direction—and the screaming, scattering crowd devolved into a panicked mob. And fuck if Brax didn't run forward, without cover, exposing himself more, so he could help Oak and Thompson corral everyone inside the building behind the bulletproof glass.

A call rang through the car's speakers, Helena's name flashing on the dash display. Holt slapped the answer button. "Get Jax inside and Brax the fuck out of there."

"Bike's in the garage. Meet us at the southside door."

"On our way." He yanked on his belt, Avery already doing the same. "Go!"

She careened out of the space, switching the X5 to manual and tapping the paddles. She gunned the engine, flying down the row toward the parking lot's exit. Another round of shots rang out, from a lower trajectory this time, due east, flying directly over the car. Heart in his throat, hands clutching the belt across his chest, Holt watched as Brax pushed Jax inside the lobby. Holt counted the seconds his brain calculated for the bullet to travel to its target. Two seconds to impact, a flash of blond hair sailed in a circle, Helena grabbing Brax by the arm and spinning him away from the door. Glass shattered, multiple bullets making impact. Holt's head spun, faster even than Helena had moved. Fuck, he'd been on ops before, had been there last year during the raid at MCS headquarters, coordinated more ops than he could count from command, but nothing had felt like this, nothing had prepared him for this. *This* was an earthquake like Loma Prieta, rolling and potentially devastating.

A second ringtone jerked Holt back inside the car, to the logistics of the emergency op they all needed to survive. "Converging on your position," Victoria said. The lieutenant and Connor, one of their captains, had been stationed a block over, just in case, Helena had said. His sister's instincts were usually right. "Shots coming from the west and northwest."

"Confirmed," Holt said. He grabbed his tablet from the door pocket and opened his chat window with Jax. "I'm texting Jax the location of the shooters. They'll get SFPD there. You and Connor keep coming this way. We may need a diversion."

Outside, car horns blared from both directions as Avery blasted across four lanes of traffic and the Muni tracks. "How you wanna play this, boss?" she said, once they were on the other side.

"Need to get Brax in the car and get him clear."

"Agree," Helena said, still on the open line. "Vic and I will divert."

"He safe?" Holt asked.

"Fine. Pissed as fuck I dragged him away."

"Cuff him if you have to." She was half his size, but only one person had ever bested Helena in hand-to-hand combat, and it wasn't Brax.

"Copy that."

She clicked off as Avery sped down the street alongside headquarters. Holt held his breath. The half-full parking lot to their left made him nervous. There would have been no advantage to setting up there to take a shot on Brax at the front of the building, and they were going fast enough to be ahead of either converging shooter. But for how long? He sat sideways in his seat, head on a swivel, rotating from the back window, to the parking lot, to the garage door ahead at the back of SFPD headquarters. They pulled to the curb outside the garage door, and the squeal of tires behind them made Holt's heart leap back into his throat. And almost lose it completely. Victoria's Wrangler drifted into a skid in front of the road they were on, blocking another vehicle's entry. Tires skidded, then, on the other side of the Wrangler, a dark SUV sped ahead, down Third toward the adjacent parking lot entrance.

Holt started counting seconds again.

An engine roared to the right, and Helena's Ducati barreled out of the garage, Brax on the seat behind her.

"Get in!" Holt shouted out the window.

Brax shook his head. "It's safer if—"

He slapped the outside of the car door. "I am not moving until you get in this car. What's safer? Me waiting here like a sitting fucking duck, or you in this car so we can get the fuck out of here?"

Properly motivated, Brax practically dove from the Duc and into the car through the door Helena had wrenched open. She slammed it shut behind him, and Holt clasped Brax's knee through the gap in the front seats, needing to lay a hand on him, to assure himself he was there. Brax's hand landed on his, squeezing hard, but that was all the time they had. The dark SUV was charging across the parking lot toward the back row, just on the other side of the fence from the X5.

"I'll cut a path," Helena shouted, then zoomed ahead.

"Victoria," Avery said. "Pull alongside." Avery hit the gas, but not all the way to the floor, giving Victoria and Connor time to catch up. And also giving the SUV time to careen around the corner and start down the row that would bring them even, only a fence and the odd car in the back row here and there between them.

Holt lost his grip on Brax as Avery gunned the X5, the vehicle lunging ahead. The first shot pinged off their back fender. The charging SUV didn't get off another before Victoria sped in between them. Through the Wrangler's open top, Connor lobbed flash bangs the direction of the dark SUV, creating a smoke screen for the X5 and Wrangler to hide behind as they zipped ahead. At the end of the street, Helena had blocked traffic, allowing Avery to shoot out and veer south down Terry Francois. Victoria took the turn with them and switched places with Helena, continuing to cut a path for them. As the smoke cleared behind them, the attack SUV zoomed through, probably thinking they'd caught up, only to find Helena waiting with her blades. Knives flying from both hands with a lightning-fast flick of her wrists, Helena lodged one in each front tire, then drew another and hurled it into the SUV's grill. They didn't need flash bangs for cover after that. The SUV careened out of control and plowed into the parked cars and fencing, setting off explosions and billowing smoke of its own.

Revving the Duc, Helena sped to catch up to them, then stayed on their six as Avery and Victoria continued to weave through Mission Bay. Holt only breathed easy, only signaled "All clear," once they hit 280.

Avery slowed, blending in with the other traffic. "Where to?"

"Teton," Holt said, using the code name for the house in Pacifica, a location only immediate family and their lieutenants knew about. And Jax, as of this week. It was the closest thing they had to a safe house within a short distance of the city, and it was at least minimally stocked. The cabin in Tahoe was an option, but not before Elisabeth, who was keeping watch over Lily at MCS daycare, another Helena precaution, brought him his daughter.

"Copy that," his sister said. "Victoria, Connor, good

work. Circle back to the scene. Shooters are probably gone by now, but the car may not be."

"Check on Jax too," Holt added.

"Will do." Victoria dropped off the call, and the Wrangler peeled away onto the next exit.

The Ducati did not.

"You sticking with us?" Holt asked his sister.

"Wouldn't mind seeing the ocean after that ordeal. You want me to have Elisabeth bring Lily down?"

"Please."

"I'll ring her now."

She clicked off, and he lifted a hand to wave his thanks, but his view of Helena through the rearview mirror was cut off by a pair of hard hazel eyes.

"What the fuck is Teton?" Brax growled.

Avery chuckled low, and Holt shifted in his seat, looking Brax over. Aside from the pinched brow and tightened jaw, he looked to be in one piece, despite the rough and tumble ride. Out of danger now, Holt wished Lily was in the car with them. He needed her to help keep Brax from exploding at the unintended surprise Holt was about to lay on him.

"Just pull the pin, boss," Avery said as if reading his thoughts.

Detonation in three, two, one... "Cap, there's something I haven't told you."

CHAPTER SIXTEEN

Brax stood frozen on the foyer landing, gaze darting up and down the split-level stairs. "How did I not know about this place?"

Holt shifted on his feet. "I... We... It's not..."

Last inside, Helena closed the front door and shoved her way between them, following Avery up the stairs. "I believe you're familiar with the concept of a safe house. We were keeping it off SFPD's radar. I buried it in shell companies."

Brax didn't handle that news any better, rotating half-around like he was about to leave. Holt grasped his shoulder. "And it wasn't done yet."

Avery jiggled the loose stair rail. "Still isn't."

Brax's brows snapped together, the divot between them deepening as his eyes cut from the rail to the baby gate and back. Great, overprotective Brax added to surly Brax. Holt squeezed his shoulder. "Come on up. Let me get things ready for Lily, then I'll show you around."

"He doesn't have a coffeemaker here," Helena said from up top. "So it's definitely not finished yet."

"Hena," Holt warned, afraid her sarcasm would push Brax over the edge.

"What?" She shrugged. "Just trying to help." Leaving the baby gate open, she disappeared around the corner into the kitchen.

Holt inhaled deep and sent up a silent prayer for patience, his own and Brax's, before looking over at the other man, expecting the worst. Instead, one corner of Brax's mouth twitched like he was fighting a smile. "There's no coffee?"

"I'll order some, and a press like the one you have at home."

His almost grin vanished. "We're going to be here that long?"

Holt hated resurrecting the tension, but he wouldn't lie to Brax after the very real attack they'd just survived. "Possibly. Here or the cabin in Tahoe." Brax did know about the latter, but they'd only ever visited in the summer when the ice pack was well and truly gone.

"I'd rather stay closer. And out of the snow."

"Figured you would." He gave Brax a gentle push to start him up the stairs. "That's why I came here. We've got a small stash already, including diapers, baby food, and essentials. If we need more, there's civilization around."

"There are neighbors around too."

"I've met and background checked them all. They're used to seeing us come and go as we renovated. Good a place as any to hide in plain sight."

Brax halted midclimb, and Holt didn't need to see his face to read his reaction. The slump of his shoulders, the tilt of his head, the wobble in his step. The reality of their situation, the events of the morning, were hitting Brax hard.

Holt climbed a step, directly behind Brax, offering him more than just a hand to the back for balance. He lowered his voice and aimed to keep it steady, comforting. "We need to find out what's going on. The entire picture. While we do that, this is the safest place for us."

Brax eyed him over his shoulder. "Us?"

"Not leaving you, especially not after this morning."

Brax's breath caught, gaze locked with Holt's. So many emotions flashed through his eyes. Surprise—*Why was he still?* Fear—*Of what or for whom?* Confusion—*Over what?* Adoration—*Did Holt's eyes reflect the same?* Did they reflect the love—*the vital necessity*—that dictated he not let anything happen to this man?

Holt leaned in to get a closer look, to taste the breath that puffed over his lips, to find out if the tremors under his hand, against his body, would extend to Brax's—

"No time for that." Helena's voice jolted them apart. Her raised brow said she knew what she'd just interrupted. Her raised phone gave good reason for doing so. An incoming call from Victoria. "Let's see this fancy setup Jax built for you."

Brax created more distance between them, and Holt didn't think it was only to make room for Helena and Avery to pass. "Jax knows about this place?"

"Only as of Monday. I needed their help with something."

Holt reached for him, and Brax dodged, a hand raised to keep him back. "I need a minute." He headed down the stairs and opened the front door. "I'm gonna call the station and Oak. Make sure everyone's okay."

"Brax—" Holt didn't want him to be angry, but more than that, he couldn't let him leave. Together was the only safe bet. "You can't—"

"I'm not gonna leave." His broken smile was as painful to witness as it must have been to force. "Go. I'll be there in a minute."

The door slammed shut, and Holt cursed the seventies sidelight again for being opaque. He fisted his hand once, twice, debating whether to go after him. His insides were pulled that direction, always in Brax's wake, but the instincts attached to his brain told him to trust Brax. Told him Brax wouldn't lie, wouldn't put them at risk. And unlike his instincts regarding Amelia, his instincts about Brax were usually right. Stretching out his clenched fingers, he gave the door one last lingering look, then climbed the stairs. He made sure everything was ready in Lily's newly completed room, including the convertible crib/toddler bed that had also been delivered that week, grabbed two ginger ales from the kitchen, then hustled down the stairs to the lower level.

Helena was waiting for him, leaning against the doorjamb between the unfinished den and the lair Jax had been tasked with outfitting. "He'll come around," she said. "He always does."

Holt spared a second to kneel and check the spot on the floor from the spill Monday morning. All smooth. "What if this was a push too far?"

She grinned. "Not how it works."

Standing, he glanced back toward the stairs, wishing he could see through the sidelight to the patio where Brax paced. Apprehension bubbled until Brax's shadow passed in front of the textured glass. Holding the cold soda cans in one hand, Holt cupped the back of his neck with the freed one, hoping the radiant chill would ease the lingering dizziness from the head-spinning morning. "Jesus, I could have lost him today."

His sister's smile widened. "*That's* how it works."

The front door opened and Brax's steps started down the stairs.

"See?" Helena pushed off the jamb and patted his chest. "That man moved here for you. Stayed here for you. He's not leaving you." Truth bomb lobbed, she ducked into the lair, leaving Holt shell-shocked as Brax cleared the den threshold.

"Everything okay?" he asked.

Holt cleared his throat. "Yeah." He held out a can of soda to Brax. "You?"

"Maya has it under control. Jax and Oak are safe."

"Good."

Brax opened the soda can and took a long swallow as he surveyed the room. Holt cringed, considering the sight through his overprotective eyes. The wires, ducting, and insulation in the still open ceiling, the sheetrock and plaster walls, the exposed electrical outlets, the plastic on the sliding glass doors, the hard floor, which, while anti-slip coated, still needed rugs for Lily's safety.

Holt gestured around them. "Like I said, unfinished."

"But I can see where it's going." Brax turned back to him. "It's a good direction, good bones. I can see why you bought the place. I like it."

The simple praise shouldn't have felt so good, but it was a testament to the work Holt had put into the remodel and to the fact Brax also recognized the potential in it. Unlike his sister, who, on the closing walk-through back when it was a dilapidated seventies relic, had shivered and mumbled "murder house" under her breath.

"This is not unfinished," Avery said from inside the adjacent room.

Brax raised a brow, and Holt tilted his head, encouraging him to take a look. Brax crossed the room in front of him, peeked around the jamb, and whistled low. "From the attic to the basement, Private?"

Holt jutted a thumb toward the outdoor patio. "Closer to the hot tub."

Brax laughed, a real one that deflated the lingering tension from earlier and set off a pool of ripples in Holt's belly. "This is why you needed Jax?"

Holt nodded. "When things started to go sideways Monday, I wanted to have this part of the house ready too."

"So get in here and show us how to use it," Helena said.

He and Brax shared another laugh, then stepped the rest of the way into the lair. Brax took up position on the wall next to Avery, while Holt claimed the chair beside

Helena. He handed his soda can to his sister and powered on the system. All systems were a go, faster than he expected. Jax had done a stellar job and had added some additional bells and whistles.

He put the call through to Victoria, and her face appeared onscreen after a couple rings. She was using a tablet, judging by her window size, and behind her, in the distance, a cargo ship passed, cutting through the sunlight reflecting off the Bay. Closer, two flags flapped in the breeze off the aft of the boat—Irish and American.

Helena peered at the screen. "Are you on Mel's yacht?" she asked, clearly having recognized the same clues as Holt.

"You look a little green, Vic," Avery teased.

"Yes, and I do not have the sea legs for this shit," the lieutenant said. "I'm up here for a reason. I can still see land. Down there"—her gaze cut to where the lower deck door was—"*green* is an understatement."

Avery chuckled. "That's why you never want boat duty."

Victoria's raised middle finger lowered when Helena prompted her for an update.

"No shooters arrested," she told them. "And no one in the car once SFPD got to it."

"Plates?" Holt asked as he opened search windows.

Victoria shifted to the side, and Jax appeared next to her. "Stolen," they said. "But we were able to pull a partial VIN, which Mel traced. Several layers deep we got to a company. Mercs. You're not gonna like the answer."

Brax pushed off the wall, stepping next to Holt. "Local?"

She nodded. "Frank Ferriello."

"Christ," Brax cursed as Holt uttered a "Fuck." Holt reached for his hand, but the chief was already pacing out of reach. Holt focused on his sister instead. "So we're back to this being a revenge hit?"

They'd taken out Frank's brother, Nicky, last summer, when he'd tried to kill Hawes on a bounty from Rose. Then earlier this year, they'd suspected Frank might have been involved in the drive-by shooting at Celia's garage. The rogue Ferriello brother, August, had mediated, confirming Frank wasn't involved, but maybe they'd ruffled Frank's feathers in the process.

"I don't think so," Helena said. "We left things on good terms with Frank. But if the money was good enough, Frank would take the contract. Business is business."

"Why would the cartel hire mercs?" Avery said.

"We're gonna have to go below deck for that answer," Victoria said, grimacing. "We'll call back in."

When she did, Mel had joined them. "The cartel didn't hire those mercs," Mel said. "In fact, I think the whole bribery-cartel frame-up was either a failed first attempt or a smoke screen. Or both."

"But Swanson came to me," Brax said.

"That much is true. But someone sent him there."

"The email," Holt said. A few quick keystrokes, and he opened it on an adjacent screen. **Take your concerns to Chief BK.**

"I'd wager a guess," Mel said, "that the same person

who sent that email, that put Swanson on a path to Brax, also put a contract out on the chief's life."

Holt lurched forward. "A what?"

Brax's, "Fucking hell" echoed on one side of him, Helena's conclusion on the other, "Frank picked it up."

"How did we not see it first?" Avery chimed in.

"It wasn't by name," Jax said. "Not even 'Chief BK.'"

"Which I had flagged," Holt added.

"It was buried on the dark web," Jax said. "But we're pretty sure it's him."

Holt opened the portal to their secure server. "Send it through."

The post appeared a moment later, and if it hadn't been in digital, if it had been a physical piece of paper, Holt would have ripped it up or set it on fire. It didn't call Brax by name, but the string of demeaning and offensive slurs—homophobic, anti-Semitic, anti-law enforcement—accompanied by the description of Brax's forearm tattoo made the hit's target clear.

"Let me see," Brax said.

Holt spun in his chair, attempting to cut him off. "You don't want—"

Too late. Brax's gaze had flickered over his shoulder, his eyes roving left to right as he read the post. His face fell, and tension visibly tightened his body with each word read, each insult that had to hit right at the heart of his identity. At the end, his eyelids fluttered closed, his expression pained. "I need..."

Two cracked words that cracked through the heart of Holt too.

Brax turned on his heel and fled the room, fighting with the patio door in the den a few curse-filled seconds before he managed to wrench it open. Holt rose, ignoring the voices behind him and following the only voice that mattered.

Outside, Brax stood beside the hot tub, his arms spread and hands braced on its edge, his head hung between his heaving shoulders. Holt didn't hesitate, letting his instincts —his heart—guide him. Trusting both. He laid his hands on Brax's back, and when Brax didn't startle or object, wrapped his arms around his middle, hugging him from behind. "Give me an hour. Lily will be here by then. I'll get her packed up and get Victoria down here too with everything we need to run. Go bags, fake papers and passports, everything we need."

Brax did startle at that, straightening in Holt's arms. "For me too?"

"They've been ready since you set foot in San Francisco." He nuzzled the back of Brax's shoulder. "We'll just go. Leave the country. Anywhere you want."

"You'd leave your family?"

"You are my family, and yes, as long as I have you and Lily, I'd leave the rest of them if it keeps you safe."

Brax shifted, and Holt loosened his hold enough for Brax to rotate in his arms. "Who the fuck is coming for me, Holt? Like this?" He lowered his forehead to Holt's shoulder. "You two are the most important people in my life. I won't be the reason—" He swallowed hard, hard enough for Holt to hear. "You're all I have left. I couldn't save my mom, but I can save you and Lily. You need to go, or I'll go. Alone."

Holt lifted his hands between them, cradling Brax's face. "Is this why you've been pushing me away? The rest of the story?"

Brax looked anywhere but at him. "Most of it."

Holt wondered what part of it there still was, but this was more of the story, more of the truth and trust stitching itself back together. He'd sort the other later. He had enough to go on for now, enough to make his argument and win. "Did you leave me alone in that building in Afghanistan? Did you abandon me when I came home? When I struggled to find a place in my own family? Still struggle." Glassy eyes shot to his. "I've said it before, and I'll say it again. You didn't leave me, and I'm not leaving you. You are the most important person to us too—we fit with you—and there's no one else I trust more to keep me and Lily safe."

The staredown continued, and Brax curled his fingers around Holt's wrists. Holt's heart skipped a beat, afraid Brax would use the grip to push him away. Instead, he held Holt tighter, resolve flowing into his hold and his gaze. "Then we stop running. You've got everything here you need to work?"

Fucking finally. Holt bit back his smile and nodded.

"And you'll let me help?"

"You can start by making a list of any particularly difficult or violent arrests you've made or suspects that got away. The more racist, homophobic, anti-Semitic the better. It's an ugly avenue, but we have to consider it."

"It's a lead." Brax nodded. "I can do that."

He loosened his grip, and Holt coasted his hands down the pressed lines of Brax's uniform, coming to rest on his firm chest. "Good. You do that, then you take a nap since I'm guessing you didn't sleep last night."

Brax's grin broke free. "Why are you obsessed with how much I sleep?"

The words rumbled under Holt's fingertips, sending gentle ripples of desire inward. "How *little* you sleep." He patted Brax's chest, then stepped back before those gentle ripples became great big waves. "And I have a toddler. My life has revolved around sleeping patterns the past seventeen months. Hard habit to break."

Brax caught him by the flannel shirttail. "When did *you* last sleep?"

"Don't ask those questions."

Brax's smile softened, and Holt couldn't resist cupping his cheek again, thumb skirting the upturned corner of his mouth, pleased he was able to do that. Less pleased he had to cut short the moment, but if they wanted more of them, they had work to do. "I need to get back in there. You coming?"

"I need a minute more."

"Take your time." He lowered his hand, clasping Brax's in a quick squeeze before heading back inside.

"He okay?" Helena asked.

Holt teetered his hand. Better in the moment? Yes. In the grand scheme of things? Eh. He reclaimed his chair and directed his attention to Mel. "If the frame-up was a diversion, we have to find out who's behind it. The answer must be somewhere in all the shit we have. I'm going to download and go back through everything."

"Do you need me there?" Jax asked.

"No, go back to the station and stay on top of things. See if anyone else there is connected."

"Hawes and Chris are due back this afternoon," Helena said. "We'll brief them."

"MCS?" Mel asked.

"Southside slip will be open for you."

Once she'd clicked off, Helena rotated toward him. "Family debrief tonight?"

Holt started to nod, then glanced again at the advertised contract. "Morning," he said instead. He'd secured Brax's physical safety as best he could. But more than that needed protecting, needed shoring up... and cherishing. "Something else I need to take care of first, and I need your help."

CHAPTER SEVENTEEN

"Any hits on the list I—"

Brax rounded the corner into the kitchen, and Holt wished his hands weren't covered in potato goop so he could grab his phone and snap a picture. He had countless memories of Brax, but he would have loved to have this moment in hard copy, framed and hanging on a wall somewhere. Wide-eyed, brows chasing his hairline, mouth hanging open, Brax had worn a similar expression the first time Holt had pulled off this particular surprise. Now, though, twelve years later, there was a teensy bit of horror in his expression too, probably because of the potato-goop-covered munchkin at Holt's side.

"Ba-Ba! Ba-Ba!" Lily clapped, flinging more of the latke batter around the kitchen and onto Holt. He'd brought her high chair into the kitchen, next to him at the island, and within seconds, she'd been elbow-deep in the bowl of potato, egg, and onion mixture. And before they'd started on the latkes, she'd also "helped" him hang the blue and silver streamers that crisscrossed the dining and living rooms in no discernible order. It worked, though, in their way, as did the twinkling blue and white lights and the softly glowing menorah with its rainbow candles in the center of the table. He'd only asked Helena to arrange for groceries, a few things from Brax's place, including his French press, and their go bags, but she and the lieutenants had outdone themselves.

"What is this?" Brax said.

Holt flicked a glob of batter at him. Why the hell not? The shit was everywhere already, including covering his sacrificed flannel in the corner. "What's it look like?"

"More!" Lily giggled.

Holt kissed her head. "Hanukkah is a tad advanced for toddler speak."

Shaking off his surprise, and the batter Holt had landed squarely on his T-shirt-covered chest, a dressed-down, barefoot Brax unstuck himself and joined them at the island. "I imagine so," he said as he wiped batter off Lily's face.

Holt covered the swells of warmth rippling through him with a splash of sarcasm. "But you notice she knows the word *more*."

"More!" Lily proved.

"*More* latkes are never a bad thing." Brax laughed, gaze flicking to Holt. "But *you* might have missed a couple of courses."

"In the fridge, just need to heat them up. I wanted to make these, though, and those doughnut things you love." He tilted his head back, toward the ingredients stacked on the countertop next to the stove. "There's a bag of candies in there to tide you over."

A touch of worry, of indecision, pinched Brax's features. "Don't we need to—"

"We need to celebrate the fact we survived today—hell, the last nine months—and I know it's months late, but we missed this in December, and I didn't—"

Brax's thumb over his lips silenced Holt's words while amplifying the desire roaring in his ears. It was all Holt could do not to part his lips and suck Brax's finger into his mouth. The idea both embarrassed and excited him, and he had no doubt Brax felt the outward inferno of Holt's inner conflict beneath his fingertips. The blush intensified as Brax's gaze drifted to his mouth, as his trembling thumb skated over his cheek and removed a glop of batter. He flicked it off but didn't tear his gaze from Holt's. "Thank you," he said, voice gravelly.

Holt was still searching for his words when a Lily-created *splat*—a handful of latke mixture hitting parchment paper—forced them out of the moment.

Brax cleared his throat and shifted his attention to Lily. "Okay, put me to work, Chef."

She slapped another ball of mush into his hand, and Brax laughed out loud, free and easy, and the sound soothed the hard edge of desire Holt was riding, making it more manageable, more livable. Peace settled in Holt's belly and chest, and together with the joyful mood, carried him through the rest of dinner prep and dinner itself. He happily played host, serving courses, pouring wine, and removing dishes while Brax played storyteller, sharing with them the origins of each dish, its relevance in Jewish culture and holidays, and why it was special to him. Lily was too young to absorb much, but Holt soaked up every detail Brax dropped, tucking them away for future use.

Lily was still hit or miss with certain foods, but she'd loved the latkes and loved the caramel-filled sufganiyot most of all. "More," she begged, but any more sugar was a recipe for disaster. Holt sipped his coffee as Brax appeased her by rattling off all the fillings he'd ever had. The mention of *strawberry* did the distracting trick, Lily begging for her toys instead. Holt cleared dishes while Brax ferried over a few of her plush fruit toys. On his way back to the table, Holt slipped Brax one more doughnut, then filled their mugs up with the rest of the coffee.

"You've done a good job with the house," Brax said.

"There's still a ways to go. Need to finish the den and bathroom downstairs, the third bedroom up here, and get furniture that matches instead of the leftovers from Hawes's old condo. But it's a long way from the falling down wreck it was when we bought it, for a song if I might add."

"I bet. You do all the work?"

"We had contractors do the structural and plumbing. Some of the mechanical. Same crew who did Chris and Hawes's reno. I wired the electrical and did most of the interior. It's been an oasis when I needed it."

"That why you bought out here?"

He remembered Hawes and Helena—and Rose—being surprised at the location. It was only a half hour to MCS or to the family fort in Pacific Heights, closer even to other parts of the city, but that seemed too far for them. Amelia, however, had backed his play. "In part. I loved growing up in the city, but we wanted something else for Lily." He glanced toward the west-facing windows. He couldn't see the ocean from out here in the canyon, but knowing it was right there, on the other side of the fog-shrouded hills, seeing it every time he came and went from the neighborhood, was a sort of peace too, one that even MCS's waterfront headquarters couldn't provide. "Living near the water, it meant more—"

"After you got home from the desert."

Holt's gaze drifted back and locked with Brax's. Of course he would get it. Of anyone, Brax understood what it was like to look in every direction and see nothing but miles of sun-hued sand. And like Holt, he'd grown up in a place where you didn't have to go far in either direction to hit blue-green water.

"I like it," Brax said.

The pride Holt had felt at Brax's same words earlier in the day were infused now with the rising wave of peace, of home, of family that had built over the evening, setting off underwater volcanos in his belly and threatening to shake the surface. In a good way. "I'm glad."

"Yes!" Lily said, palms smacking the tabletop for emphasis. "More!"

"I'll show you more," Holt said, pushing to his feet. "More of your new room"—he booped Lily's nose—"and new bed." He picked another dried bit of potato goop out of her curls. "But I think you need a bath first."

She stuck out her bottom lip. "No."

Brax chuckled. "Good luck, princess. Your daddy is obsessed with making sure we sleep."

"Hey!" Holt grumbled in mock protest. "No fair."

"No!" Lily repeated. She tilted back her head and blew a raspberry up at him.

And then so did Brax, and a fucking tsunami crashed into Holt, hard enough he had to grasp the back of Brax's chair for balance. He'd never been so in love as he was with Braxton Kane in that moment.

———

"Out like a light," Holt said as he returned to the kitchen. "Between daycare and the great latke-making party, she was zonked."

Brax glanced over his shoulder from where he was washing dishes at the sink. His eyes cut to the flannel he'd picked up off the floor and hung on the back of Holt's chair. "Sorry if it killed your flannel."

Holt squinted playfully. "Are you really?"

Brax cocked a brow before turning back to the sink, his shoulders shaking with quiet laughter. Holt set the baby monitor on the island and slid in beside him, knocking his hip out of the way of the dishtowel drawer. They worked in tandem, Brax washing and Holt drying, and the simple domestic comfort of it did nothing to quiet the storm raging inside Holt. If anything, it made the hurricane that much worse, made the realization of how much Holt wanted this and the man beside him inescapable. Also inescapable, the realization of how close he'd come to losing it all earlier in the day.

"Something I've been meaning to ask you," Brax said, jarring Holt from his spiraling thoughts.

"What's that?"

He stepped closer, his left arm jostling Holt's tattooed right one. "Tell me about this. I've wondered ever since you showed me the design, but I never asked."

"I wouldn't have told you then. Fuck, I couldn't." Holt wrapped his fist in the towel and shoved it into the mixing bowl, drying the stainless steel. "It's how I felt about my family then. To some extent, still do. Like, no matter what life I try to lead, no matter if it's in camo or flannel, the family obligations are always there, clawing at me, peeling back the disguise and exposing what's underneath. What we really are. Who I really am. We're trying to do right now, I know, but..."

A warm, sudsy hand landed on his biceps. "This isn't all you are, Holt."

"I know." He pulled down the collar of his tank, exposing the lotus tattoo on his left pec. Lily was the purest part of him.

Brax removed his other hand from the water, gave it a shake, then nudged Holt's fingers out of the way, covering the lotus tattoo. "She's not all either." He moved his hand to the center of Holt's chest and another realization tore through Holt. *That* was exactly where Brax existed in his world, straddling the light and the dark, understanding and accepting both parts of him—all of him—better than anyone.

"You're a good man, Holt Madigan. Twelve years ago, you recognized I was hurting, and you did something like this for me." He released his biceps and gestured around the room. "Same as you have in the years since and today."

"I missed last year."

Brax took the bowl, set it aside, and stole Holt's towel to dry his hands. "Last year was…"

Holt's chuckle was almost as dark as Scotty's yesterday. "A clusterfuck of epic proportions. I still shouldn't have let this slip by."

Brax pitched the towel onto the counter. "First one since I moved here. After a clusterfuck of a year. Not holding it against you."

"I didn't expect you would, but…" With nothing in his hands, Holt flailed, ripples of energy firing in all directions, and into his words, which he couldn't stop, the storm billowing outward. "I was excited, especially when you came out of the station earlier and smiled, and I thought we had something else to celebrate too, that it would make up for last year, and then you almost got shot, and—"

Brax lightly grasped his outer shoulders. "Breathe, Private."

Holt hung his head. "That was too close, Brax. After we missed it last year—I missed it—and if that had been the last—"

"Hey, I'm here." Brax trailed his hands up and over his shoulders, a trail of fire and goosebumps in their wake. His hold around Holt's neck was gentle but firm enough to force his gaze. "I'm right here, Holt. I'm fine."

"It was too close to missing this for good, Cap." He

covered Brax's hands and drew them up to his cheeks, needing to feel their warmth, needing to feel the trembles that were quaking through Brax too. "I don't want to miss any more of these with you." He angled his face, kissed one palm then the other, before bringing his gaze back to Brax's, finding the hazel there on fire. "I don't want to miss anything else with you."

Brax's fingers stilled, his grip on Holt's face firm. "What are you saying?"

Holt stepped closer, erasing the distance between their bodies. "If you still want—"

Brax erased the distance between their lips, answering Holt's unfinished question with a strong, sure hold and a tongue demanding entrance. Fuck yeah, he still wanted, and Holt wanted even more. Opening his mouth on a groan, he wrapped his arms around Brax's torso and curled his fingers into the back of his T-shirt, trust, love and desire knotting tight, cresting, and making his head spin, in that good way. He rotated and rested back against the counter, hauling Brax against his front, everything he wanted in his arms, flooding his senses. Ripples of pleasure zoomed inward, making his heart race and his cock harden.

Fuck, he wanted, like he had at twenty-three, except not, another decade of trust and friendship—*of love*—sharpening and deepening his feelings, making his need for Brax an imperative, a necessity.

"Fuck, I need you." He shoved a knee between Brax's thighs and rocked his hips. "Please, Brax."

Panting, Brax shifted his legs wider, bringing their bodies impossibly closer.

"Fuck."

They froze. Neither of them had spoken the word.

"Fuck," it came again, through the baby monitor, and their lust bubble dissolved with a Lily-sized pop.

What could he do but laugh? And when Brax's body against his shook with laughter too, Holt's chest filled to bursting—with happiness, family, and belonging. Feelings he needed to share with Brax before they went any further. He wanted this, these moments, even more than he wanted their ones in bed together, in the past and hopefully to come. Holt was pretty certain Brax was on the same page, but he needed to be sure. He pressed a kiss to Brax's temple. "I think I need to go handle that."

Brax pushed off his chest. "Probably a good idea." He reached around Holt for the towel, muffling another laugh in his shoulder. "I'll finish cleaning up here."

Holt lightly grasped his wrist before he moved away. "I want to finish what we started."

Brax shifted their hands, giving his a squeeze. "Don't worry, Private. So do I."

"One other thing," Holt said. "We don't tell anyone about this." His eyes cut to the baby monitor. "Celia will never let me hear the end of it."

Brax chuckled. "My lips are sealed. Now go see about your daughter's."

He blew a raspberry at Brax, Brax blew one back, and Holt laughed all the way to Lily's room, eager to get her back to sleep so he could get on with the conversation that would hopefully win them many more dinners, many more family nights to come.

CHAPTER EIGHTEEN

"She good?" Brax asked as Holt pulled shut Lily's bedroom door.

He held up the strawberry plushie. "For the swear jar." He shook his head in chastened defeat. "I just hope she gets it."

Brax, propped against the hallway wall, chuckled, and Holt leaned a shoulder next to his. Their *I'm sorry*s collided, setting off another round of soft laughter.

"I—" Brax started.

"We need to talk."

"That's usually not a good thing."

"But it always has been with us. And we haven't done enough of it lately."

Brax dipped his chin. "I'm sorry."

"Me too." Holt pushed off the wall and snagged Brax's hand. "But we're gonna talk now, Cap. We need to so we can get back to fu—what we were doing."

Brax glanced up through his lashes, one corner of his lips twitching. "Nice save."

"Better late than never."

Brax lifted his face the rest of the way, eyes clashing with Holt's. He understood the double meaning of Holt's words, and he didn't resist as Holt tugged him along to the master suite at the end of the hall. Holt closed the door, set the monitor on the side table swiped from Hawes's condo, added his phone and keys to the pile, and flicked on the likewise rehomed lamp. Again considering the surroundings from Brax's point of view, Holt cursed himself for not doing more with it. A single table and double-stacked foam mattresses seemed rather pitiful, but as Brax sat on the end of the bed without so much as a creak of wood or squeak of springs, Holt thought maybe inertia had worked in his favor for a change.

"I owe you the rest of the story," Brax said, snapping him from his thoughts.

He rounded the end of the bed and knelt in front of Brax, between his bent legs. "The reason you were pushing me away?"

Brax nodded. "It wasn't just Swanson, or the cartel, or IA."

"Was it about what Chris said last summer?"

Brax stared over his shoulder, toward the window, like he'd stared out the window of his condo the other night. "I didn't know what to do with that."

"Because it was true."

He swung his gaze back to Holt's. "Because it was true, because I'd do the same, because I didn't know where that put us as far as my job, your family, us. I didn't know where that put us after—"

The last piece slotted into place. "After Amelia."

Brax lifted a hand, fingers lightly cupping his neck, thumb skirting his jaw. "The last thing I want to do is pressure you, Holt. To rush you, and if all you want is to be friends—"

"I think what just happened in the kitchen proves otherwise."

"The moment—"

The *moment* was here to lay it all on the line; the moment the past fourteen years had been leading to. "I love you."

Holt had expected surprise, not the immediate "I love you too" in return. Instinct, he supposed, except... "It's more now, Cap. Different."

"Different how?"

"I'm *in* love with you, Brax."

There was the jolt he expected. "Holt—"

"Let me say this first, please." Holt shifted, moving to sit on the bed beside him, needing all the nearness he could get. "I meant what I said yesterday. Besides Lily, you are the most important person in my world. Chris was right last summer. If something happened to you, I'd either fall apart or destroy the person who hurt you. I'd burn the world down for you, Braxton Kane." Brax cast his gaze aside and dipped his chin, but Holt wouldn't let him— wouldn't let either of them—hide from the blinding truth of the bond between them. Brax needed to see the commitment in his eyes, needed to understand how deep Holt's emotions ran. "I didn't know what to do with that either, but over these past months, the past week, the answer resolved. Hell, it was always there, but now it's in focus, and I can't look away, Cap. I don't want to."

"What are you saying?" Brax's words were so soft, so tentative, so full of barely restrained hope they shook.

Holt wanted to pry the reins loose for good. Scooting closer, he laid a hand on Brax's thigh and cupped the nape of his neck with the other, teasing the short hairs there. "I felt it in DC all those years ago, felt it before that even, sitting at your bedside in the infirmary. I didn't know what it was then, but I know now." He kissed Brax's shoulder and reveled in Brax's answering gasp and the shifting of the denim beneath his hand. "Feel it like I never have before." He lifted his eyes, and they clashed with heated hazel. Hope was there too, so overwhelming, so fragile, it roughened Holt's next words. "I'm in love with you, Braxton Kane, and I want you so much. If you still want me too."

"Christ, Holt." Apprehension and agony scared off the hope, and Holt wanted to rail. "You know I do, but it's only been nine months."

"No, Brax, it's been fourteen years."

Brax swallowed hard, Adam's apple bobbing, and his eyes flicked away, then back. "How does this work? I'm a cop. You're—"

Holt pressed a hand to Brax's chest, over his heart, which was pounding almost as fast and hard as Holt's. "Does what my family and I do change how you feel here?" He slid his hand lower, to where he'd intended it to go before, over Brax's dick, which was hard as a rock. "Or here?"

Brax bit his bottom lip, failing to stifle a growl and the thrust of his hips. "Of course it doesn't." The flare of anger, of frustration in his voice matched the same in Holt's. "I wanted you—loved you—before I ever knew about your family, and despite that tattoo on your arm, it doesn't change who you are. You are a good man, but while I know that, while I know the changes your family is making, and that in all of it you've been kept mostly clean, to the rest of the world—"

"The rest of the world can fuck right off." Shifting, Holt slung a leg over Brax's lap and straddled him. On the end of the bed as they were, Brax was forced to grab hold, and his hands on Holt's ass were almost too distracting.

Almost.

"This is between you and me." He framed Brax's face, thumbs sweeping his cheeks. "But I know how much your reputation means to you, so if I need to leave the family business for you to keep it, then so be it. I will."

Brax inhaled sharply. "You'd do that?"

"Did you miss the flee the country together offer earlier?" Holt rolled his eyes hard, and Brax released his breath on a chuckle. Holt lowered his forehead, resting it against Brax's. "Same principle applies. We fit, Cap, we always have, better even than I fit in my own damn family, and as much as I love them, if it comes down to a choice between them or you, I choose you. With you is where I belong."

Brax straightened and hauled Holt closer. Leaving one hand on his ass, he glided the other up his spine, under his tank, and fuck if Holt didn't want to melt right there. Brax's words didn't make his insides any more solid. "I can't have this piece of you and walk away again. I can't, baby."

Holt groaned and rocked his hips, recalling Brax's slip of the endearment in DC and drowning in it all over again. Groaned more as Brax's lips coasted over his cheek, along his jaw, and down his neck.

"I need more," Brax whispered into the hollow at the base of his throat.

"I can't give you everything," Holt said. Brax tensed beneath him, and Holt drew back, but only far enough to look Brax in the eyes, to make sure he could see and hear the truth of his words, the depth of his love, and the desperation of his own plea. "Lily will always have a huge piece of me. My family will have a part of my heart, Jax and my other kids at the shelter too. Amelia, even, as the mother of my child. But everything else, all the rest of me, it's yours, Brax. I'm yours. Is that enough?"

Agony faded and hope rushed back into Brax's eyes, and the grin that split his face was the biggest Holt had ever seen on his best friend. "More than enough." He stretched up, slamming his smile against Holt's, claiming his mouth and his heart, and fuck if Holt didn't want him to claim every other part of him too.

After several long, plundering kisses, Holt skated his lips off Brax's mouth and trailed kisses along his jaw, stubble prickling his lips and stoking his senses. "So can we get back to what we started in the kitchen?" He nipped a path to Brax's ear and ran his hands down his torso. "I remember this body. Wanna feel it against mine again."

Brax rolled his hips. "Yeah, baby, nothing I want more." Holt moaned in pleasure, then in protest when Brax removed his hand from his ass. "I remember things too," Brax said. "Vividly." Then brought his hand back down to spank Holt's ass.

Holt's jeans muffled the sound, not loud enough to wake Lily, but the smack was hard enough to send sparks firing through him, making his head spin with unbridled desire. Brax swallowed his wanton groan in a kiss, muffling the needy sound. He was on fire, every part of him burning, hottest where Brax's lips and hands roamed. Brax delivered another spank as his other hand quested under Holt's tank, bunching it up and forcing Holt to break their kiss to shuck it off. Totally worth it for the feel of Brax's lips and tongue dragging across his chest, of Brax's long thin fingers spreading over his torso.

"I didn't get enough time before, with this body or with you." Brax captured a nipple between his teeth and sucked.

"Jesus, Brax, that feels..." Fuck, he was almost thirty-four, not twenty-three, but fucking hell, he was right there at the edge already. He reached between them, needing to adjust, to shove a hand down his pants and grab his balls and beg them to please fucking wait, but Brax smacked his hand aside.

"Nuh-uh, that's mine tonight." He palmed Holt through his jeans.

Holt thrust up, chasing his touch. "Not helping."

Brax chuckled. "When's the last time you were tested?"

"After... Last summer..." He stuttered, heat rushing to his face again. "Hawes made me, just in case. I'm fine, and I haven't... There's been no one... I don't..."

"Shh, baby, I know, not how you work." He kissed some of the awkwardness away. "No issues here, and I haven't been with anyone since my last test either."

He made to move, and Holt stopped him, a hand around the side of his neck, thumb skirting over his hammering pulse. "Why didn't you ever bring anyone around?" he asked, apparently unable to let go of awkward.

Brax's pulse skipped and sadness raced across his hazel eyes. "Because they weren't you. I didn't need the direct comparison to know that."

"Fuck, I'm sorry I made you wait."

"No, baby, don't apologize for that." He drew back, the sadness in his eyes erased by conviction, fiery and absolute. "We're where we're supposed to be when we're supposed to be. And that little girl down the hall, the man you are today, both were worth the wait. I wouldn't trade either of you for anything." He brought their mouths back together, and the truth of Brax's words painted every swipe of his tongue, every press of his lips, every inch of Holt's skin his fingers traversed and seared. Muffled his startled gasp when Brax shoved to his feet, Holt in his arms, and flipped them, bringing Holt down on his back in the center of the bed. Holt parted his legs, feet braced on the mattress, and Brax lowered himself between them, on top of him.

They sighed together, the fit and torture perfect.

Surprise had taken enough of the edge off that Holt happily lingered in the kisses Brax demanded, enjoyed the coast of hands across his skin and the gentle roll of hips, relished Brax's hard cock grinding against his own.

He couldn't get enough of Brax's taste. He'd locked that memory away too, caramel, beer, and whisky the flavors he remembered most from that night in DC. Tonight, the taste of Brax was even better—caramel still, always, but add good coffee, braised brisket, and fried potatoes, and it was a Brax-wrapped delicacy—across his tongue and inside his mouth, imprinting a new memory beside the old one.

He wanted more of it. Same as he wanted more of the lean, strong body writhing against his. He glided his hands down Brax's sides and under the hem of his shirt. He grappled at the warm skin underneath, trailed his fingertips up Brax's spine, and laughed through a kiss as a shiver followed in their wake.

"My spine is not a keyboard," Brax grumbled around a smile.

Holt hooked his legs over Brax's hips, holding him with his knees and hands to help Brax balance as he levered up to pull off his shirt. "I know," Holt said. "My computers don't shimmy like—" His words died, choked by the heart-shaped lump in his throat that had materialized at seeing the ink on Brax's shoulders and arms. The tattoos that hadn't been there a decade ago and that Holt had only ever glimpsed the ends of under Brax's sleeves.

"Brax, what..." There were no words for everything

crashing around inside him, for this feeling like his heart was about to beat out of his chest.

Brax planted his hands back on the mattress, on either side of Holt's head, and hung his own, a blush sweeping across his cheeks. "You're my family too. You and Lily. I wanted you with me always."

Holt ran his hands over the clean and simple line work. Vines dotted with flowers. Poppies, like the ones that grew all around Camp Casey, like the one Holt had had etched into the crystal candy dish for Brax's desk, and... Holt's fingers trembled over the lilies.

"I added those last year," Brax said.

"The trip back to the East Coast?"

"Wynn's the best."

"Brax, I don't..."

Brax sank onto his forearms, thumbs teasing Holt's temples, and fuck, if the ink hadn't already robbed Holt of words, the adoration in Brax's eyes right then would have. "I've loved you since the moment you stepped off that transport, Private."

"I—" Holt cleared his throat; he did have words, words he needed to say. Words to put to feelings he understood better now than he had a decade ago. Words and feelings the past fourteen years had built. "I trusted you that same moment, Cap, and then the love came. I love you because you're my best friend, because I trust you. More than anyone."

Brax dotted his face with kisses—both cheeks, the jaw hinge on either side of his face, his forehead, the spot between his eyes, the tip of his nose, his lips, the chin dimple buried in his beard. "Do you trust me to make this good for you?"

Holt hitched his legs higher, rutting and keening. "Fuck yes." He raced his hands down Brax's back, beneath the waistband of his jeans, clenching the tops of his ass cheeks and toppling him off-balance so Holt could nip at the tendon of his neck. "You're mine, and I'm yours. Make love to me, Brax. Please."

Brax claimed his mouth, and after another thorough plundering, went to work systematically claiming the rest of him. Military efficiency put to wicked good use. Kissing, nipping, and licking every inch of Holt's torso, lighting fires with each possessive touch and sending ripples inward— desire the pinball now, tossed between two levers, Holt's heart and dick. Relief came in short quick bursts, Brax stroking his cock or levering up to steal a kiss. The torture, though, was brilliant. The slow slide of denim off his legs, the teasing snap of elastic before Brax yanked off his boxers too, the flex of Brax's muscles as he removed the rest of his own clothing. And then the perfect goddamn heat when there was nothing left between them, skin to skin, limbs and tongues tangled, the scratch of Brax's brown and gray chest hair revving him up as much as the bump and grind of their cocks.

Brax shifted as if to slide down Holt's body, and as much as Holt wanted Brax to suck his dick again, he wanted something else more. He grabbed Brax by the shoulders, stopping his descent. "You do that, and I'm gonna blow in about two seconds, and while that was forgivable at twenty-three, not so much at this age."

Brax laughed and buried his nose in Holt's armpit, the motion and affection so pleasantly distracting to Holt that Brax managed to sneak a hand down and around their cocks, holding them together. "I'm fairly certain you'll have no trouble with a repeat performance."

Eyes scrunched closed, Holt bowed his back off the bed and cursed through gritted teeth. Fuck, that felt better than he'd allowed himself to remember. He thrust into Brax's grip, driving against his cock, and smiled when Brax moaned.

"You want it like this?" Brax said. "Whatever you want, I'll give it to you, Holt. Always."

Fuck yes, he wanted this, for the rest of his life, but still, in this moment, there was something he wanted more. He clasped the side of Brax's neck, holding him close. "Suck me on round two. Pump us on round three. But for right now, fuck, Brax, just get inside me."

Brax's stroke faltered. "Keep talking like that and *I'm* gonna blow in about two seconds."

Holt flailed an arm out to the side, reaching for the bedside drawer where he'd put the condoms and lube that —bless his meddling sister's heart—she'd also included in the supply run. "I'm prepared this time."

Brax laughed, the noise so free and loud that Holt had to slap a hand over his mouth to muffle the sound. "I'm sorry," he mumbled behind Holt's hand, then proceeded to lick his palm, sending shivers and goosebumps racing across Holt's skin.

Holt snatched his hand away. "That's dirty," he playfully chided.

Grinning, Brax popped the cap on the lube and poured a generous amount in his hand. "I might have to play dirty to make this good for you. That okay?"

Nerves skidded in the wake of Holt's earlier goosebumps.

Brax soothed them with a gentle hand coasting over his thigh. "Trust me."

Easiest ask in the world.

Holt released his held breath, forced the tension out of his limbs, and laid himself out for the person he trusted and loved most in the world.

"That's it, baby." Brax cupped his balls with his slick hand, then slid it lower, over his taint, massaging and teasing as lube trickled down his fingers toward Holt's hole. Brax added more as he fingered his rim, the sensations so insane, so intense, Holt bowed off the bed again. He came back down to a pillow placed under his hips.

"This'll make it easier," Brax said.

Easier to bear down as Brax slowly slipped one, then two, lubed fingers inside him, coaching him through the unfamiliar pressure on the way to the blinding pleasure of fingers massaging his prostate. "Holy fuck."

"Feel good?"

"Fuck yeah." Heat rushed to Holt's skin as he fisted the sheets and rode Brax's fingers with abandon.

Kisses peppered his torso. "Do you have any idea how hot the blushing and the freckles"—he licked a path over the auburn trail bisecting Holt's pelvis—"and the red hair are to me?"

Oh, Holt had an idea all right, Brax's rock-hard dick

evidence aplenty. His own dick was a straining, leaking mess, and Brax playing dirty was pushing him closer and closer to the edge. "Need you to fuck me, please."

The rip of foil and the snap of the condom were a symphony to Holt's ears. A squirt more lube—Brax coating himself might have been the most erotic sight Holt had ever seen—and then Brax's cock was nudging his hole, pushing at his rim... and getting nowhere. Keening turned into whining that would crush Holt under a mountain of embarrassment if he weren't already being crushed by a mountain of turned-on frustrated impatience. Fuck, he just wanted...

"Hey, Private."

He opened his eyes, and Brax's hazel ones were right there, smiling and full of love and mischief. "I'm gonna have to play dirty."

"Whatev—"

Brax spanked his thigh harder than before. Holt tensed, the spike of stinging pain intense, then groaned as his muscles relaxed under the flood of pleasure. And Brax's cock eased in an inch. Eyes still locked, he gave Brax a nod. Brax snaked an arm under his knee, propping a leg against his shoulder and hitching his hip higher, shifting Holt so the next spank hit his ass, and fuck, Holt was gonna—

Brax closed his other hand around Holt's dick, stroked it, and holy fuck, there was that melting sensation again, distracting and relaxing him enough that Brax's cock slid in farther. One more spank and Brax thrust the rest of the way home. The pressure in Holt's ass was like nothing he'd ever felt but so was the pressure in his chest, in his heart, for the man connected to him in the most intimate way possible. He closed his eyes and dropped his head back onto his pillow. "I think I like dirty."

Brax stretched over him and kissed across his collarbone. "Figured you might."

"Think I might like to come sometime tonight too."

That earned him another pop and answering laughter against each other's lips.

"I love you, Holt Madigan, so fucking much."

Holt trailed his fingers across the ink again. "I know, baby." And fuck if speaking the endearment wasn't as much of a turn-on as hearing it. The reverse seemed to hold true for Brax, judging by his dick swelling in Holt's ass and his hand tightening around his cock. "Now, show me," Holt panted against Brax's cheek. "I trust you. I love you."

Brax kissed him, slow and deep, and drove into him the same way, his strokes sure and steady, his hand likewise keeping pace, only speeding up when Holt urged, "Faster." He ached for the heavenly pressure now, for the repeated punch against his prostate, and for the release gathering in his balls and dick.

"Make us come, Holt," Brax panted against his lips.

Past and present collided, and Holt covered Brax's hand with his, gripping him tight, shuttling up and down his cock as Brax pumped his hips in time. Holt erupted, stars exploding behind his eyes and come covering his hand, and his ass, fuck, his ass clenched around the solid length of Brax there, making them both shout into each other's mouths and making Brax come too, thrusting and burying himself one last time deep inside Holt.

Coming down from the high together, Holt wrapped himself around the man in his arms, around his world, and Brax buried his face in his neck, breathing hard. When Holt finally caught his own breath, he nuzzled Brax's temple and whispered in his ear, "How much do you think we owe the swear jar now?"

Thank fuck Brax's face was buried in his neck because his unchecked laughter was even louder than the shout when he came.

CHAPTER NINETEEN

Banging sounds jolted Holt awake, and the jolt to his well-used body was equally startling. On his belly, he shoved his head under his pillow and groaned. "Fuck, Cap, that third round might've been a bad idea."

He expected a laugh, maybe a slap to his ass or a protest. Round three hadn't been a bad idea at all. The thought alone—of him and Brax on their sides, chest to chest, Brax's leg thrown over his hip, their mouths inhaling each other's pants, their combined grip slowly stroking them to release—was enough to make Holt shift, his morning wood digging uncomfortably into the mattress.

Until the next thought registered.

Silence.

Unexpected.

He threw off the pillow and glanced to his side. Empty. No Brax. He ran a hand over the sheets and into the divot in the other pillow. Both cool.

An undertow of worry collected in the vicinity of his

stomach. He reached for his phone. Nine in the morning. Explained the sunlight sneaking in around the curtains, trying to blind him. Fuck, when was the last time he'd slept so late?

More banging. On the front door, by the sound of it.

And then the best sound in the world. "Coming!" Brax called.

Relieved, Holt sagged back into the mattress.

"Na-Na?" Lily asked.

"Don't know, princess. Let's go see."

Brax must have gotten up with her. Holt smiled into his pillow, letting warm contentment—*home*—wash over him. Fuck, he wanted this. So much. He wouldn't let anyone take this life from them, not now that he'd had a taste of it and knew how good it could be. On the heels of that thought, the realities of the last week came crashing back, and Holt pushed up in bed. "Check the peephole!" he hollered.

"Cop, rememb—" Brax's retort died, eaten up by a curse. "You've got to be fu—kidding me."

Not welcome, whomever it was. Holt scurried as much as his big, sore body allowed, tripping over clothes and almost killing the lamp in the process. He saved it from the floor at the last second—a near thing—then a good thing when, with no other weapons in sight, he realized he had a heavy, metal object in hand.

The whoosh of the door opening echoed down the hallway. "Where the fu—heck have you been?"

"Aww, come on now, Major Kane. I had my reasons."

Holt recognized that voice. Couldn't believe he was

hearing it for the first time in years. He righted the lamp on the table, yanked on his boxers and tank, and hurried down the hall. He had to make sure his ears weren't deceiving him. From the top of the stairs, he glimpsed the cowboy hat first. Brax, with Lily on his hip, stepped aside and revealed the man wearing it, the owner of that familiar Texas drawl.

"Major?" Holt said. "You're here?"

Emmitt Marshall's dark brown eyes bounced between him and Brax, brightening as his smirk deepened. "Oh good, y'all finally sorted your mess. Now the rest of us can move on with our lives." He swept inside and snagged Brax's coffee mug from his hand. "Thank you, Kane."

Lily giggled. "More!"

"Yeah, more," Brax said as he slammed shut the door. "More of an explanation for a chess game—and friend—you left hanging for over a year."

The major ignored him, drained the coffee, and took the stairs up to Holt. "Just Marshall or Marsh now." He set aside the mug, then yanked Holt into a back-slapping bro hug, like the one he'd given him on Holt's last night at Camp Casey. "How you doin', big guy?"

Brax stomped up the stairs, his steps heavy for bare feet. "Hello!" he barked. "Answer the question, Marsh."

Marsh drew back, eyeing both of them. "Y'all got your hands full."

"I haven't had an email, call, or postcard from you since your retirement," Brax said. "And now you just show up?"

Apparently, it hadn't been only Holt who Marsh had iced out. Holt hadn't taken it personally. Yes, Marsh had trained him, taken him under his wing, and helped refine his hacking skills, and in working together, they'd become friends, but Marsh had been his CO. Brax had been tight with him, though, ever since the raid gone sideways and even more so after Holt's discharge. Holt had been glad Brax had had someone to turn to. He wasn't sure he would have been able to leave Casey otherwise. Given their closeness, it surprised Holt that Marsh's radio silence had extended to Brax.

"We've all got our messes," Marsh said. "Mine happened to blow up at the same time as y'all's, but I'm here now."

Which brought up another question. "How did you find this place?" Holt asked.

Marsh's look rivaled one of Helena's are-you-serious glares. "You have tells, Oski, like every other hacker. And half those tells are ones you inherited from me, so I just followed the breadcrumbs."

"Fu—fudge, we should—"

"I scattered the breadcrumbs," Marsh said. "You're safe."

"More," Lily said again, her brown eyes wide and staring at Marsh like he was her new favorite toy.

"Me or the voice, sweetheart?"

Lily clapped. "Yes!"

He ruffled her curls. "I like this one."

Holt was still half-amused and half-bewildered at Marsh's presence. He understood the *how* of it now but was still missing the *why*. "We're happy to have the help, but we didn't put out an SOS. How'd you know we needed it?"

"Your searches last night set off one of my tripwires."

"You've been tracking our searches?" Brax said. "The searches on my collars? But you can't pick up a damn phone or send an email?"

Marsh dipped his chin, dark waves falling across his forehead. Flecks of gray that hadn't been there last time Holt had seen him caught the light. When he lifted his face again, the teasing glint was gone from his eyes. "I'm sorry I went AWOL, Kane, but you are one of the few people who will put up with me, so yes, you are on the short list of people I keep tabs on. So is Tessa St. James."

"The arsonist for hire I put away?"

Marsh nodded. "Fires ain't all she sets. She's a key witness on one of my collars."

"*Your* collars?"

"Don't ask. Neither of you have the clearance."

"Clearance?" Brax squawked. "What the... What's going on, Marsh?"

Marsh again pretended he hadn't heard Brax. "She's at FCI Dublin. Been routing things through there for her old cellmate."

"Let me guess," Holt said, connecting the dots. "Savannah Ryan."

"Bingo." Marsh withdrew several sheets of folded paper from his back pocket. He handed the first to Brax. "She routed this through late last night."

Holt stood close enough to Brax to read over his

shoulder and to offer support if needed. Which was a good thing. The post was from the same dark web channel as the last one concerning Brax. Same syntax and spacing too. But the words were even more disturbing than the last post.

A new contract with a new timeline, and it wasn't designed for a one party answer. It was open fucking season. On Brax. A hefty bounty to whichever party delivered him—tonight—half paid at proof of capture, half on delivery.

"There are additional comments of interest." Marsh handed them the other sheets of paper. "Tips on who Brax is most likely to be seen with."

Three pictures: Brax and Holt in the stands at a Warriors and Raptors game, Brax and Jax eating lunch on a bench outside the station, Brax on a stroll through Washington Square with Lily in her stroller.

Brax stood frozen one second and shoved Lily into Holt's arms the next. "You've got to get her out of here. Get Jax someplace secure too. Or I'll go."

Sensing their distress, Lily's face crumpled, and she opened her mouth, wail imminent. Until her new favorite toy swooped in. Marsh plucked her from Holt's arms like a natural. "How about we go get some more coffee?"

Hands free and with Lily distracted, Holt returned his attention to Brax, grabbing him by the shoulders before he could run off and play sacrificial lamb. Again. "Hey, Cap, calm down. No one knows we're here. We're safe."

Brax flung an arm toward where Marsh had disappeared into the kitchen. "He found us."

"Like the Major—" He cut himself off and corrected.

"Like Marsh said, all hackers have tells, and he knows mine better than anyone. That's the only reason he's here."

Brax didn't look convinced. "If something happens to them, to you, because of me..." His voice cracked, and Holt drew him into his arms, needing the comfort as much as Brax did. From the peak of happiness to the lowest low. "If something happens, Holt, I'll never forgive myself."

This needed to be over—today—so they could get back to happiness mountain for good. He held Brax tight and kissed his temple. "I'm not going to let that happen."

"Who's the new guy?"

Marsh spun in his chair next to Holt, eyeing Helena who stood over the basement lair's threshold dressed in cashmere, jeans, and riding leathers. He was out of his seat the next instant, smile bright, hand outstretched. "Emmitt Marshall, and you are even lovelier than your brother described."

"Helena Madigan," she said, shaking his hand. "You are certainly a charmer. Too bad I am very much taken."

Marsh grinned wider. "Good thing you're not my type." He tilted his head toward the screen where MCS HQ was on display, Avery, Chris, and Hawes standing in Holt's office there. "Your other brother, however..."

Chris stepped in front of Hawes. "He's very much taken too."

Marsh flopped back into his chair, his arms dangling over the armrests. "Well, that's just disappointing."

Brax chuckled as he entered the lair behind Helena. "He's an old friend." He set the baby monitor on the desk next to Holt's keyboard, then set his hands on Holt's shoulders. "And he was Holt's CO in Afghanistan."

"Where's Jax?" Holt asked, ready to skip over the introductions. It had been too long already, almost an hour since he'd texted Helena with a request to debrief and to secure Jax. He'd used the hour to calm Brax, detach Lily from her new best friend, and get Marsh up to speed. If Helena had chewed up half that hour driving, had there been time to also get Jax safe?

"Right here." Jax wheeled themself into view in front of the other three at MCS. Holt's shoulders ticked down a notch, the tension in Brax's hands with them. "What's with the fire drill?"

"Marsh came bearing more news. Not the good kind. I'm sending it through the secure server." Holt uploaded the pictures he'd taken of Marsh's printouts. "Further proof the bribery charge and cartel connection were part of a larger plan. A failed first attempt, like Mel suggested."

Their faces fell as they read and fell more as Marsh filled them in on St. James and the connection to his case. Behind Holt, Brax's breathing shortened and his fingers dug into Holt's shoulders. Holt covered a hand with his.

Jax finished reading first. "We have to take this to SFPD."

"Not yet," Brax said.

Holt whipped around in his chair so fast he nearly toppled both of them. "What?"

"We don't know who else might be a leak. I doubt

Packard was the only one. And the last thing I want to do is draw further attention and manpower away from the work they need to be doing."

"Like protecting you? You don't think that counts?"

"You said we're safe here. We work this for now."

Apparently, Holt's calming had worked a little too well. Or else he'd just transferred all Brax's worry and fear onto himself. He clutched the armrests on his chair and bit back his protest. He didn't want to turn this over to SFPD either, but fuck if Brax's sacrificial streak wasn't getting on his last nerve.

Which Hawes must have sensed, his twin jumping in before he could lash out. "It's consistent with everything floating around the periphery of this situation, except maybe what was on the outside edge before should be at the center now."

Brax nodded. "The email, the leak, the subsequent merc hit."

Holt rotated back around. "The forgeries. Any luck with Sam?"

Chris shook his head. "Gone again. We lost her outside Mussel Shoals. Last sighting of her was at a convenience store the night before last."

"Scotty?"

"Called back East on a case."

"You get any other hits on Brax's list?" Hawes asked. "Besides the one Marsh flagged?"

"Nothing else on the first and second passes."

"I can dig deeper," Jax said.

"Do that," Hawes said. "Holt, you find out everything you can on St. James. Marsh, can you get her to talk?"

"I can try," he replied. "See what else I can offer her, but I'll have to clear it with Justice first."

"We can help grease those wheels," Helena said.

Not fast enough. Not when Holt had a better idea. A more direct approach to getting St. James to talk. He stood with a mumbled, "Need to check on Lily."

"I didn't hear..."

Their voices faded as he took the stairs two at a time, dialing as he climbed. Holt understood now how each of his siblings had felt when their chaos had gone down. He did what he could behind the monitors, went into the field when it was required, but now, with Brax's life on the line, a relationship they'd danced around for more than a decade newly formed, he understood his sibling's drastic plays for love, Hawes bending the knee and Helena turning herself over to a rogue Bratva soldier.

The irony of who he was turning to in his chaos, the play he needed to make, was not lost on Holt.

"Federal Corrections Institute Dublin. How may I direct your call?"

"Warden Novak, please. This is Holt Madigan."

They'd met the warden several times, had her direct line, and they hadn't abused it. Holt was glad for that now.

"Mr. Madigan," the warden answered. "What can I do for you?"

"I need to speak with my ex-wife." Normal procedures required a call to the switchboard, a call time to be set, then a call back from Amelia from one of the prisoner lines. He didn't have time for that right now, nor did he want this conversation recorded. "It's a family emergency."

"One minute, please."

Holt played with Lily in her pack and play while he waited, trying and failing to stop his daughter from chewing around the brim of Marsh's hat. Would she forgive him one day for asking her mother to do this? Amelia had seemed happier this week, like she was getting back to her old self, working in the prison infirmary. Now he was dragging her back to the life that had landed her there, first with the hacking, and now—

The line clicked. "Hey, babe," Amelia answered. "I'm still working here."

Leaving Lily to her destruction, he ambled over to the balcony door and braced his elbow on the jamb, staring out over the canyon. He closed his eyes, breathed deep, and fought the clawing sensation working its way up his tattooed arm. "Could use your help on another angle. But it's your choice."

"Tell me."

He filled her in on the high-level details, enough for her to reason why he was calling. "You need me to find out who she's passing notes for."

"Only if—"

"It's what I'm best at, and it's what will keep you and Lily safe. That's all that matters."

"Amelia, thank you, and don't get caught."

"Please, babe." He could practically hear her eye roll, and he improbably chuckled. She laughed on her end too. "I'll get back to you."

Call ended, Holt dropped his arm, some of the guilt floating out on a wave of relief. That broke when he turned to meet a pair of hard hazel eyes.

Brax pitched a candy wrapper into the trash. "What did you just do?"

Holt expected this argument; he'd just hoped to have it after he already had the answers they needed. "She'll get us the information faster."

"At what cost?" Brax crossed the room to him. He lowered his voice, but it was no less gritted. "There has to be a line, Holt. One you won't step over."

"There is no line when it comes to you." He skated his fingertips over Brax's forehead, smoothing the lines there before cradling his cheek. "I will do anything to protect you."

Brax covered his hand, holding it against his face. "Then let me turn myself over. See who they take me to."

Holt snatched his hand away. "Hell no."

"It's not a bad idea," Helena interjected.

Holt glared around Brax to where his sister was trading Lily a plush banana for Marsh's cowboy hat. She straightened, and he intensified the death beams.

"Don't give me that look." She tossed Marsh's hat on the couch. "And it's not a bad idea, especially if we can control whose hands he winds up in."

"You're thinking Ferriello?" Brax said.

Holt saw red and barely stopped his voice from hitting five-alarm shrill. "He tried to kill Brax yesterday."

"When someone else was paying him."

Ignoring the blond traitor, he turned his full attention

to Brax, taking hold of both sides of his face. "This could go sideways a million different ways. If you go dark..." He swallowed around the knot in his throat. "If I lose you after I just got you..."

Brax clutched his waist and stepped closer, forehead against his. "You've always had me, Holt, and you know me better than anyone. I can't sit here and do nothing. I wouldn't be me if I didn't do everything I could, especially to protect the ones I love."

Holt closed his eyes before anyone could see the tears pooling there. Jesus, was this what Chris had felt like when Hawes had returned to their grandmother and pretended to bend the knee? What Celia had felt like when Helena had surrendered herself? Sucked being on the other side of this too, possibly worse. "Brax, please."

"I trust you too. More than anyone." Caramel-flavored lips brushed against his. "You'll find me. You always do."

CHAPTER TWENTY

Holt fidgeted in the passenger seat of Hawes's darkened Benz. Nerves on a rampage, stomach in knots, he needed a keyboard, his daughter, or Brax, none of which were currently available. The best he had was his tablet and even that was of limited use. Helena and Avery and Connor and Victoria were the only teams wearing trackers. Frank, who had a team of two with him, had flat out refused. Holt was surprised he'd agreed to the comm. Brax had forgone both, not wanting the person pulling the strings to find it on him and realize the setup too soon.

"Easy, Little H," Hawes said from the driver's seat. "We've got him covered."

"I don't trust Frank."

"None of us do, which is why Helena and Avery are a block closer on the Duc and Connor and Victoria are on foot a block the other direction."

Holt propped his elbow out the open window and

palmed his forehead, eyes scrunched closed. "Jesus, why did I think this was a good idea?"

Hawes chuckled. "I wasn't under the impression Brax gave you a choice."

No, he hadn't. Same as he hadn't that Christmas morning in Afghanistan, showing up kitted out for the mission Holt had come to him about. Except on that mission Brax had been protecting him. Fucking saved his life, almost at the cost of his own. And now, when Brax needed his protection, where was he? In the fucking car, the team farthest away.

"This is Brax," Hawes said. "He was going to do something like this regardless. At least this way we're controlling the variables."

Like the police cruiser that passed the alley they'd backed the Benz into. The cruiser headed down Grant toward Greenwich where it would drop Brax off in front of his building. There'd been three other exchanges before this one. Helena dropping Brax at the strip mall close to the house in Pacifica. Avery picking him up and dropping him a block from SFPD headquarters. Connor walking with him to the employee entrance at the back of the station. To no one the wiser, it would appear as if Brax had been at the station since the shooting yesterday morning and a patrol car was finally giving him a lift home.

"Eyes on Brooklyn," Helena radioed from her position.

Holt grabbed his tablet, opening the tracking app again. Something was better than nothing.

"Francis, you're up in two."

"Fuck you," Frank grumbled. None of the Ferriello

brothers seemed to like their given names. "We're in position," he said. "Inside Brooklyn's condo."

All was going according to plan. "Something feels off," Holt said. "We checked the surrounding areas?"

"Victoria and Connor did a walk through and around earlier," Hawes said. "Helena and Avery did another sweep on their way into position. All clear."

Except for the tingles radiating out from Holt's gut, instincts telling him it very much wasn't. "This is too easy."

"Queen, move to position two," Hawes said before casting Holt a sideways glance. "I agree." He cranked the Benz, kept the lights off, and inched to the mouth of the alley.

"Eyes on Brooklyn," Frank reported. "He's at the curb."

Holt took control of the security cameras in the building's stairwell, the feed redirected to his tablet. He watched with bated breath as Brax ascended the first set of stairs to the second-floor landing without incident. The second set to the third floor the same. In front of his door, Brax dug out his keys and snuck a peek at the closest camera, mouthing *I love you* around a small, secret smile.

Those three words rippled through Holt, smoothing some of his nervous edges with warmth and wonder. At how easy it was to say the quiet truth out loud now. At how much joy the truth brought Holt. The vision—the reality—of the life he and Brax could have together had solidified, as had Holt's desire to claim it, if they could just—

A *bang* blasted through the comms.

"Outside!" Frank yelled.

Outside, where Holt could no longer see Brax, an explosion whiting out the camera, then darkening it for good. Holt's stomach sank, then was literally slammed back against his seat—along with the rest of his body—as Hawes rocketed the Benz out of the alley.

"They're coming from the unit across the hall!" Frank shouted.

"Get him inside!" Helena replied over the roar of the Duc.

Glass shattered, wood splintered, and in Holt's mind, the sounds were accompanied by the whine of an incoming RPG and the crumbling of cement.

"Cap."

He was right back there, about to lose the most important person in his life. Except he and Brax weren't in the same room, and there wasn't a bed to dive under for cover or each other to hold on to as the world crumbled around them.

Hawes's hand clasped his thigh, bringing him back to the present. "When we get there, you do not get out of this car."

His voice shook. "Cap."

"We'll get him back." Hawes screeched to a halt at the curb behind the Duc and wrenched open the center console, retrieving his garrote. "You stay in the fucking car."

The car door slammed, locking Holt in, but there was no quiet. Between the pounding in his ears and the chaos over the comms, Holt was overwhelmed by noise. The sound of the future he so desperately wanted spinning wildly out of control, out of his grasp. And nowhere in all those sounds—Frank's "They've got him," Helena's "They're escaping," Avery's "Over the adjacent building" —did he hear Brax. Was he gagged? Unconscious? Still alive? Holt felt sick and dizzy and fucking helpless all at once. He couldn't just sit—

"Oski!" Hawes's bark cut through his misery. "They're in a black Jeep heading your way."

Holt tossed his tablet onto the floorboard, unfastened his seatbelt, and threw himself across the center console, thanking all that was holy that he and Hawes were about the same height now, the seat shoved back far enough for him to swing his legs around and under the wheel.

Lights flared ahead and tires squealed, the Jeep rocking around the corner on two wheels. It landed back on all fours and sped his direction.

Not enough time.

The best he could do was...

Fuck, he hoped Brax was belted in. He had no other choice.

He secured his own belt, slammed the Benz into reverse—enough to clear the Duc and gain momentum— then wrenched the wheel and jammed the gas pedal against the floor. The Benz lurched off the curb, aimed directly at the oncoming Jeep less than a car length away.

The Benz crashed into the side of the Jeep, metal grinding as they skidded across Grant into the cars parked on the opposite curb. Holt couldn't see over the airbag deployed in his face, but he kept his foot down, not letting up. Grinding gears joined the horrible screeching sounds, the Jeep trying to wrench free and shoot ahead. Holt eased off the gas only long enough to jam his foot back down and deliver another hit. It was the last the Benz had to give, the engine popping and dying. He batted down the airbag and squinted to see through the rising smoke. The Jeep was free, spinning across the lanes, tipping onto two tires.

Brax tossed around the back seat like a rag doll.

Bile rose, together with a knot in Holt's throat and tears in his eyes, not just from the smoke. Fuck, if it toppled over...

The Jeep landed on all fours and the driver hit the gas, speeding down the hill and out of sight.

Holt shoved open the door, heaving, losing what was left of his stomach, his heart falling with the tears he couldn't hold back any longer.

Brax was gone.

CHAPTER TWENTY-ONE

Back at the family fort in Pac Heights, Holt hit the stairs running. He made a quick pit stop on the third floor to check on Lily. His heart ached at seeing her favorite blanket clutched in her hands. Thank fuck she was young enough to sleep through this, and he'd be damned if he would let her lose someone else. He'd had his moment at the scene, had needed Hawes and Helena to drag him out of the car and back to reality. But now that he was there, he was determined his reality would be different by sunrise.

He crested the stairs to the lair, and Marsh spun his way. "Fuck, Specialist, I thought the setup at the other house was impressive."

"Shop talk later." Holt claimed the chair between him and Jax. "Update now."

Jax moved an image from their laptop monitor to one of the larger in-wall screens. "This just appeared on the same dark web channel as the contract."

A short video clip of Brax, the chief tied to and

slumped in a chair, cuts on his face, bumps and bruises rising, but his eyes were open and alert, his chest moving up and down at regular intervals.

Alive. For now.

Holt gulped back the fear that wanted to rise and grabbed hold of the anger. Anger that ratcheted up to fury as he read the accompanying post. Brax's captors had upped their price. According to them, the original party had refused to pay their higher price, so they were opening the auction wide.

Holt fisted his hands, collecting the anger, then spread his fingers, letting it power him as he began digitally digging. Marsh's fingers hit the keyboards a second later, Jax's a second after that, a chorus of furious keystrokes as they followed his leads. Behind them, the others strategized.

"We can outbid anyone," Hawes said.

"Yes," Helena replied, "but that won't stop the person who keeps coming after Brax."

"We can't keep SFPD in the dark," Jax said, multi-tasking as they accepted an airdrop from Holt. "Chris already told us they're on the scene. Fletcher has called me three times. If they find out someone's trying to ransom the chief..."

Fletcher. Holt pulled up the searches that had been running on the IA detective while Hawes and Helena continued to coordinate around him.

"SFPD won't negotiate," Hawes said.

"We don't need them to negotiate," Helena countered. "We just need them to stay out of the way. Any leverage?"

Holt quickly scrolled through the searches. "Nothing immediate."

"The apartment?" Helena asked.

"Someone died there. He's getting a steal on the rent," Holt answered. "He could afford full price, though. From his financial disclosures, it looks like he got in early on tech stocks."

"Let me talk to Maya," Avery interjected. "I'll bring her up to speed and try to buy us some time. She can take it to Fletcher."

"Go," Helena said. "Buy us until morning."

One of the screens blinked with an incoming video call from Chris. Holt clicked Accept, and Chris's worried face filled the screen, red and blue lights flashing around him where he stood on the curb in front of Brax's condo.

"What've you got?" Hawes asked, stepping closer behind Holt.

"Good news is that no one in the other unit was injured."

"Someone was there?"

Chris nodded. "Teenager hiding under a bed."

"They get video?" Holt asked.

"They're a teenager, of course they did, but unfortunately no faces."

"I can work with voices," Marsh said. "Send it through."

The file dropped into their secure server a moment later, and Holt clicked Play. Two men could be heard clearing the room, albeit poorly. When they were done, they'd rejoined their team in the hallway, too far away for more than muffled voices. Limited use, but Marsh was on it.

"Anything else from the scene?" Helena asked.

"Some evidence collected off the parked cars outside."

"Send that through too," Holt said. "Anything that might tell us who took Brax." Which in turn might tell them where they took him.

"Hand off," Hawes said to Chris. "Avery is on her way to run interference with SFPD. Get back here so you can check out the Benz for evidence." They'd managed to get it off the scene before the cops arrived. "Jax—"

"Already monitoring SFPD for further developments or evidence."

Holt finished typing in another search command, the last he could think of for now, and slumped in his chair. "This isn't how it was supposed to go."

Hawes clasped his shoulders, and Holt couldn't help but wish it was Brax behind him standing guard, and on that thought crested a wave of guilt. When it was supposed to be Holt standing guard, he'd failed.

"The original poster," Hawes said. "That's who we need to focus on. If that party can be pressured into paying..."

"Then we eliminate both threats," Helena finished.

"All those searches are running," Holt said.

Beside him, Marsh's typing slowed. "Voice match is processing. I'm running it through all the Intelligence Community databases I can access. Usually takes a few hours."

Hours they didn't have. Fuck. Holt racked his brain for

what else he could search and entered more parameters while his siblings grilled Victoria and Connor for more details. When his phone rang a couple minutes later, he expected Chris again, or maybe Avery or Mel, no doubt she had heard about this by now, but Warden Novak's name flashed on the screen instead.

Warden Novak or Amelia?

He shushed the others and answered the phone through his computer, the call piping through the speakers. "This is Holt."

"Babe, it's me," his ex-wife said. "You sitting down?"

That brick he'd earlier avoided landed in his gut, jagged and rough, and if he hadn't been sitting already, it would have dragged him down for sure. "You're on speaker," he replied. "What've you got?"

"I got Tessa to talk." Of course she had. Amelia had been their organization's best inquisitor, her ability to manipulate pressure points to the point of torture unsurpassed. "She didn't have a name, but I got enough out of her to run a trace and connect the dots. Her payments ran back to a single IP address. It was pinged about an hour before the latest post you flagged."

"You somewhere you can send it through?"

"No, but I memorized it." The smirk in her voice improbably made him smile.

She rattled it off, and the numbers rang a bell to him. He'd seen them before. He entered the IP address in a Finder window, searching their other data for a match.

Three dings.

"Fuck," Holt cursed. "That IP address appears in the

flow of funds to Samantha Pritchard's account and two others. It pinged an offshore bank, but I ran into a wall trying to get the Account Holder's name."

"Give it to me," Marsh said. "I can try to pull some strings with State."

"And the other two?" Hawes asked.

"One's another wall."

"Give that to me too," Marsh said.

The other... Holt couldn't believe his eyes. "A deposit to Detective Isiah Fletcher."

"What's the bank?" Amelia asked, the darkness in her voice like another brick added to Holt's gut.

"Royal Bank of the Caribbean."

"Fuck." A chair protested in the background as if Amelia had landed in it heavily. "Your grandmother has an account there. She had me run funds through there when she didn't want the three of you to find them."

"And you didn't disclose this to the feds?" Hawes demanded from over Holt's shoulder. If she had, Holt would have caught it three fucking days ago.

"The last I saw of it, the balance was zero. I thought she'd closed it."

"She must have had more money squirreled away," Helena said. "Moved it over."

"This is Rose," Holt said out loud, putting words to all those jagged bricks, to the anger that was raging through his veins, to the betrayals that kept coming like the AR fire and RPGs in the desert all those years ago.

"Yeah, babe," Amelia said. "I think so."

"She tried to trick the cartel into doing her dirty work,"

Hawes said, following his train of thought. "When that didn't work, she tried to leverage Fletcher. And when that didn't work, she went to the dark web for mercs."

"Because *we*," Helena said, "took away her army."

Brax's words from long ago thundered in his ears. "*Hulk out.*"

"Back away from the desk," he said to Marsh and Jax, unable to keep the tremor out of his voice. They moved at once. "Amelia, thank you. We'll be in touch."

With his friends safely out of range and the call with Amelia ended, Holt stood, inhaled deep, then unleashed his bottled-up growl, along with a swipe of his right arm the length of the desk, sending keyboards and peripherals flying. The freestanding monitor on one end was next, followed by the router on the other. He started for the nearest CPU but was blocked by Hawes on one side and Helena on the other, caging him in.

"We're not going to destroy everything again," Hawes said calmly, barely loud enough for Holt to hear over his raging pulse and heavy breaths, all the anger, all the pain he'd bottled up for the past nine months pouring out of him. "We don't have time. We need to find Brax."

"She did this," Holt seethed. "She took my wife, tried to take my daughter's future, *our* future, and now she's trying to take Brax. I'm done. This is over. The end."

"The loose end," Helena mumbled. "That's what she's after. Eliminate him or use him to tie all the loose ends back under her control."

Holt, practically snarling, whipped around, the

thought of Brax—of any of them—being a *loose end* maddening.

Helena laid him out on the floor faster than he could blink, a hand around his neck and a knee to his sternum. Marsh whistled his appreciation, but Helena's icy blues remained locked on Holt. "Stop it, Little H."

Hawes knelt beside them, a gentler hand on his shoulder. "It didn't go her way, which means we have an opening. We can use that."

Holt yanked back the heaving Hulk, relaxing a measure, and Helena responded in kind, backing off her hold. "How?" he rasped out. "For what?"

"If she wants to tie up the loose ends, then that's what we'll do," Helena said. "Our way."

"Checkmate." Hawes's deadly grin befitted the Prince of Killers. "Once and for all."

CHAPTER TWENTY-TWO

Avery and Maya were waiting for Holt in the lobby of SFPD headquarters. "He still here?" Holt asked as soon as he cleared the metal detectors.

Avery nodded. "Hasn't left all night."

"Where's his office?" he demanded, no time to waste. Hawes and Helena had gone ahead to MCS with Jax and Marsh, the latter two knowing the work needed to get a positive ID on the bank accounts and on Brax's kidnappers. A location too, and once obtained, an extraction plan. Holt had a different loose end to tie up.

"Other end of the hall from the chief's office," Maya answered. "I don't think—"

Holt didn't hear what else she said over the pounding of his boots as he climbed the steps two at a time. By the time he crested the stairs, however, Avery had caught up to him, and she blocked his path at the entrance to the short hall where Fletcher's office was located. He tried to juke left around her, but he was no match for the top operative's agility.

She glared him back a step, her dark eyes under-standing but firm. "Take two breaths, boss," she said. "You cannot go in there and assault a detective."

Not what he'd intended to do, but his clenched fists and clenched jaw indicated otherwise, his instincts not fully aligned with his brain. He took the two breaths she suggested and used them to wrangle his wayward instincts under control, Amelia's words from earlier in the week also flitting through his mind.

"*Bottle that anger,*" she'd said. "*Hold it for when you really need it.*"

For Rose.

Fletcher was a means to that end, not the end itself.

"Good," Avery said, recognizing his readjustment. "Now, listen. According to Maya, Fletcher is a good cop and genuinely likes Brax. He *wanted* to come work for him, and he *did not* want to pursue the investigation against him, but that's his job. He had to." Consistent with what Brax had said about the detective. "Do not jump to every worst conclusion."

Holt nodded, then strode beside her down the hallway, making a quick pit stop in Brax's office to grab a caramel candy out of the crystal dish, needing that connection, needing the sense of calm Brax always provided. The smell and taste of the candy weren't as good as having Brax there in person, but the sense memories helped center him a little.

Avery rapped twice on Fletcher's door.

"Come in," the detective called, then, at seeing who his visitors were, nearly fell out of his chair as he hurried to stand. "Is there word on the chief?"

"Nothing yet," Avery said as she shut the door behind them.

Fletcher's eyes cut to the door, to Avery, then to Holt. In the relative silence of this part of the station at this time of night, Holt swore he could hear the increased speed of the detective's breaths, the increased tick of his pulse. Fletcher wasn't a fool. He knew who they were, and he knew he was the prey in this situation. Nevertheless, he squared his shoulders and crossed his arms. He wasn't a big guy, several inches shy of six feet and closer to Hawes's build than Holt's, but the broad shoulders and toned forearms exposed by rolled up shirtsleeves spoke of time at the gym or more likely, in a pool. Would explain the faint whiff of chlorine in the air.

Curiosities Holt forgot all about with Fletcher's next words. "I'm glad you're here. I was still trying to figure out how to come to you without raising red flags."

Holt nearly swallowed the candy whole. "Excuse me?"

Fletcher gestured to the two guest chairs in front of his desk, then claimed his own again once Holt and Avery were seated. "One, you need to understand I respect the chief. He recruited me for the position here, and I jumped at the chance to work for him."

"And two?" Holt prompted.

"Two, almost immediately after I arrived here, I started getting anonymous tips about his involvement with your family."

"You opened an investigation?" Avery said.

"I had to, per protocol."

"Fuck protocol," Holt growled. "He recruited you."

Fletcher held up a hand. "I don't disagree with you. There was no evidence Chief Kane's personal life affected his professional one. I filed the case paperwork, poked around a little like I was supposed to, but I slow rolled it as much as I could until this Camino thing accelerated matters. At which point the chief read me in."

Holt leaned forward, elbows braced on his knees. "Read *you* in?"

"On you and your grandmother."

Holt bit the candy in half, molars be damned.

"Explain," Avery clipped, her voice relaying the same what-the-fuck tone as Holt's words would have if he'd been able to find them.

"How about I give you what you need instead?" Rotating in his chair, Fletcher retrieved the nesting doll off the credenza behind his desk and began unpacking them, each a different sugar skull design. From the smallest, he retrieved a key that unlocked his center desk drawer. He pulled out a flash drive and slid it across the desk to Holt. "The chief told me to keep a record of all the tips, including the metadata. Said you might need it."

Holt turned the small piece of plastic over in his hand. "He thought she was behind it."

"He didn't discount the possibility." Because Brax had clearer eyes than he and his siblings had when it came to Rose. "But he didn't want to raise it, unless he was sure, and for a while there, it was looking less and less likely."

"He kept you updated?" Avery asked.

Fletcher nodded. "He wanted to make sure everyone at the department stayed safe too, and that we were on standby in case anything went sideways."

That explained his reluctance to involve SFPD earlier tonight. Goddamn self-sacrificial streak strikes again.

"And the deposit?" Avery said.

Holt glanced up in time to see Fletcher longingly gaze at the tiny nesting doll in his hand. "She found my weak spot. Tried to exploit it and used the money as blackmail." He breathed deep, then began nesting the dolls back together. "Kane warned me she might try. That's on the flash drive too. I didn't give her what she wanted, and I didn't touch the money, but I take it she made her move anyway."

"We think so." Holt closed his hand around the flash drive and stood, Avery also rising beside him. "But this will help. Thank you, for it and for believing him."

"He's the most honorable man I know," Fletcher said. "No reason not to believe him. Just bring him back safe and let us know what you need. The department is behind you."

Avery was out the door first, Holt halfway over the threshold behind her when the last of the candy dissolved and he thought about what Brax would want for Fletcher, how he'd want to help but couldn't. Holt could, though. He rotated back around, unsurprised to find Fletcher fiddling with the nesting dolls again. "Rose will be taken care of," he said, "but if there's anything we can do to help, we owe you a favor."

"Thank you." Fletcher set the doll back down and wiped the misery from his eyes. "But it's taken care of."

MCS headquarters hadn't been this busy on a weekend night in a good long while. The first and second floors had cleared out at midnight, Saturday's second shift their last of the weekend, but the third floor buzzed with activity. Holt's team of hackers was processing evidence as fast as Jax or Chris could get it to them with Marsh hammering away at restricted access barriers. Avery, Victoria, and the rest of the available operatives waited in the conference room, ready to move as soon as they had a location and orders. And while Hawes and Helena made calls and arrangements, Holt cranked through the data on Fletcher's flash drive and all the other data at his fingertips, organizing, and if necessary, manipulating it to paint a picture that would put a stop to their grandmother—and possibly shutter their entire illegal operation. All the evidence the feds would need to tie at least a dozen operations to them—to Rose as the ultimate arbiter of their contract-targets' fates.

He transferred the last stack of files to his tablet, then rotated in his chair. "It's done," he said to his siblings. "Are you sure about this?" He was sure, no question, but he was also the one least likely to go to jail. Hawes's and Helena's efforts to keep him clean all these years had been even more evident as he'd parsed through everything.

"Would you do the same for Chris?" Hawes said. "For Celia?"

"Of course." Jail included.

"Exactly," Helena said. "And Brax has been a part of this family longer than either of them."

Humbled by his siblings' devotion, Holt hung his head, only lifting it again when Helena knelt beside him.

"I went to him," she said. "Right after he joined the department. The old chief had given him a stack of files on us. He looked wrecked that night, like everything made sense and didn't. I asked him if he loved you, and he answered *yes*, just as fast as you said *of course* a second ago. He promised to always protect you, regardless of who we were and what we did."

Wide-eyed, Holt glanced from his sister to his twin... who didn't look surprised at all by Helena's revelation. "You knew?"

Hawes nodded. "I knew he had kept you alive in the desert and that he was going to do the same here. That's all that mattered then. That's all that matters now."

"We keep him alive too," Helena said. "At any cost."

She rose, and a throat cleared behind them. "Showtime," Avery said from the doorway. "Mel's yacht just docked in one of the southside slips."

Holt considered her, their most loyal operative over the past year, the operative who'd saved his ass twice this week, the one who spoke for the operatives as a group. "Are you on board with this plan?" he asked, sure Helena had filled in her second. "Are the other operatives?"

"We're on board, boss. Contingencies are in place."

She cracked a half smile. "Not blind either. Fletcher was right. Brax is an honorable man, and we've seen what he's done, and we've seen the two of you together. You both deserve to be happy."

"Thank you."

He barely got the words out before Jax barreled into the increasingly crowded room. "We've got a location on the chief." They handed him a tablet.

"Probability?" Hawes asked.

"High," they replied. "Marsh got a voice match, and we got a match on the car. Both are tied to a suspected white supremacists' compound in the East Bay. Paramilitary sort. One of their members pinged the dark web ad."

"*This*," Hawes sneered, "is why we broke from Rose. She'd do business with anyone."

Helena's fingers twitched, the motion the same as if she were flipping knives in her grip, getting ready to throw. "Trying to fund their fucking cause and probably trying to frame someone for killing a police chief in the process."

"We're not gonna let that happen," Hawes said. "How do you want to play this?" he asked Holt. "This is your call."

This time of night, their operatives could be there in thirty, move in right away, and assuming the location was correct, rescue Brax and do some damage to a bunch of assholes in the process. But his siblings were right. Rose would keep coming for them, keep coming after Brax, Chris, Celia, and all their loved ones. After anyone connected to them who she could leverage, like Isiah Fletcher. She had to be stopped, once and for all, which was what Brax would want too, why he'd told Fletcher to copy all those files, why he'd let himself be taken tonight. So that no one else would be hurt. Holt couldn't let all this be for nothing. Brax had trusted him to find him, which he and his team had done. Now he had to trust Brax to hold on a little longer while he and his siblings finished this for good.

"Work with Jax to adjust the operation details based on this location," he told Avery. "Let us talk with the feds. See if we can work a deal. Then let's be prepared to move as soon as we've got all our ducks in a row."

"Got it, boss."

"And clear the conference room," Helena added. "We're gonna need it, and I want the operatives out of sight."

Avery and Jax left, and Holt wheeled back around, confirming once more that he had everything they needed on his tablet.

"If they go for this," Hawes said behind him, "then we go to Rose right away. I already called the warden at CCWF. They'll be ready for us."

"No," Holt said. He grabbed his tablet, stood, and turned to face his siblings. "I have to do this alone. It's long overdue, and CCWF is two and a half hours away. I need you two with the teams on Brax in case anything goes sideways."

"Fine, but Chris will go with you," Hawes said. Holt opened his mouth to object, but Hawes raised a hand, silencing him. "Like you said, two and a half hours away, in the middle of the night, and he's got experience staring down the devil. We're not sending you out there without backup either."

"Okay." Holt could live with that if that's what they needed to do their jobs, which were as important as the one he had to do. "I need Brax to walk out of there alive. I just fucking need him."

Helena clasped his one shoulder, Hawes the other. "We'll bring him home, Little H," she said. "Promise."

Holt drew them both into a hug. There were no two people he trusted more to bring the man he loved back to him alive.

───────

Holt had occupied the same room as US Attorney Dominic Price on multiple occasions. The federal prosecutor had handled Amelia's and Rose's cases, and he was family-friend-tight with Mel and Aidan, who were seated across the table with him. Nic also co-owned one of the best breweries in the Bay Area. Tonight, though, it hurt to be in his presence. To notice the same career military bearing and precision of the man Holt was missing. Different branches, but the Frog's cool blue eyes and his focus as he read over the materials Holt had compiled were at-attention sharp, as sure as his stance would be if he were standing.

"If this goes as planned," Helena said from Holt's right, "you add more charges to Rose's rap sheet and bust a bunch of racist, homophobic assholes for assaulting, kidnapping, and ransoming a LEO, and whatever other charges you want to pile on."

"And if it doesn't go as planned," Hawes said from Holt's other side, "you bust the same bunch of deplorables... and us."

"Either way," Chris added, "you make a hell of a bust."

Nic spun a black and blue titanium band around his left ring finger. "Your grandmother is already in jail for what will likely be the rest of her life."

"*Likely*," Helena said. "But if we want to be sure she stays there for all of it, this would do the trick, correct?"

"Correct," the prosecutor said, not giving away more than he had to.

"And if these additional charges stick, certain of her privileges would also likely be revoked, correct?"

"*Likely*."

Holt had the distinct impression Nic and Helena had played this game before and that they both enjoyed it, more than a little.

Aidan, somehow perfectly pressed and suited at two in the morning, leaned forward in his chair. "Look, I'm not opposed to clearing"—he gestured at the tablet—"a dozen-plus cases from the FBI's and SFPD's boards and adding more charges against Oscar fucking Torres."

Marsh had come through with confirmation Rose was the account holder at Royal Bank of the Caribbean and with the account holder's name on the other deposit Rose had made. It traced back to an incarcerated hacker Aidan and Jamie had put away several years back. Marsh had further confirmed Torres had charmed one of the guards into granting him access to a computer, the IP address of which pinged the one at FCI Dublin that St. James and Sam had been routing things through. Smartly, Rose had kept several layers between her and her dirty deeds, but she still wasn't smart enough to understand her grandkids and their allies would find her, would make the connection. Or what they would put on the line to protect their loved ones—especially Brax, who had never turned his back on them. On Holt.

"But you will be implicated if this goes the way of Scenario B," Aidan said. "I'm not even sure we can keep you completely out of Scenario A."

Hawes matched Aidan in style, albeit a bit more wrinkled at this point in the night, his suit jacket long since ditched and his sleeves rolled up. His Prince of Killers persona more than made up for it, his demeanor cool and calm compared to the Irishman's flickering fire. "But Holt is clean?" he asked.

"Yes," Nic replied. "From the look of this."

"And if we turn state's evidence?"

"No one will ever work with you again," Mel said. "Except me."

Hawes's icy exterior cracked, just a little, one corner of his mouth ticking up, but his burgeoning smile died with Helena's next question. "Jail time?"

"Minimal," Nic was quick to answer. "Maybe none, given your cooperation over the past year."

"The past four years," Mel said. "I can provide that evidence if needed."

"Thank you," Hawes said to her, then to the other two,

"If this is what we have to do to get Brax back and be done with Rose, then fine, we accept that risk as long as we get to keep MCS in trust for the next generation's legacy."

"I can live with that." Aidan stood and offered his hand. Hawes shook it, and Helena and Nic exchanged the same.

A shiver raced through Holt and he clasped his hands under the table. He was at bat now, and it was up to him to make sure Scenario A played out and not Scenario B. His family, Brax, his whole heart depended on it.

CHAPTER TWENTY-THREE

The police escort from San Francisco to the Central California Women's Facility trimmed the two-and-a-half-hour drive down to two. Chris's lead foot had also helped, but even at top speed, the trip was utter hell.

Chris had thankfully cut his fidgeting some slack, always asking for an update each time Holt picked up his tablet—either to check on Lily, sleeping soundly under the watchful eyes of Celia and her teens, or to check the status of their operatives moving into position. They'd surrounded the compound with the FBI and SFPD teams forming a secondary perimeter. No one had eyes on Brax yet, but the compound was bustling with activity in the middle of the night, and on the dusty road leading to its entrance, they'd found tire tracks that matched those of the getaway Jeep.

Chris had thanked Holt for each update but otherwise left him alone in miserable peace. Not that Holt would have rather engaged in idle chitchat. His mind was already too full, rehearsing what he wanted to say to Rose, mentally reviewing Helena and Avery's flawless raid tactical, imagining his life with Brax in the future, and replaying the one they'd already shared together in the past.

Stepping off the plane in Afghanistan, terrified to the point of shaking, until the tall, spindly captain lifted his shades, smiled, and assured Holt's unit—assured him—that he'd be taking care of them.

Experiencing worse terror the first time the raid sirens had blared, getting lost in his head and under a bed, until Brax had shared a piece of his own tragedy and gently coaxed Holt back from the memories of his.

Playing cards every week, surprising Brax with that first Hanukkah dinner, holding on with everything he had as they fell through the crumbling building's floor, afraid he was crushing Brax but not willing to risk letting go, doing everything he could to return the favor Brax had done him by getting on that mission and getting them to cover, under a fucking bed of all things.

Dancing close in a crowded club, Brax so uninhibited and sexy, so real, that Holt couldn't resist the desire churning through him, acting on it later that night.

And again over a decade later, recognizing the trust and desire for what it was, built over countless conversations, messages, and moments in each other's company.

Love.

Love he couldn't let slip through his fingers again.

He kept that thought—that goal—in mind as he waited in the visitation room, continuing to periodically check his tablet. After a few minutes, Chris, propped against the wall behind him, shifted, and Holt lifted his gaze. The door swung open and behind the uniformed guards shuffled in his shackled grandmother. CCWF was a maximum-security prison. It wasn't FCI Dublin where a nod would get Rose's cuffs removed; not that Holt would give that nod. While he and Chris could easily take Rose, she didn't deserve the consideration. And she wasn't giving them any consideration either, her glare cold and imperious, even as the guards secured her cuffs to the floor and table bolts.

She waited until they left before speaking. "Only one of you." Her icy blues flicked to Chris. "And you brought him."

Just this side of a sneer, which Chris returned in kind. "Good to see you too, Rose."

Holt forced himself to remain relaxed, to not hurtle to the end of his chair and demand she end this game. Instead, he focused on the changes—and not—in his grandmother. No makeup, her gray hair cut short, some weight loss, and dressed in the same jumpsuit as the other maximum-security prisoners. But the way Rose still carried herself, she might as well have been wearing Chanel and styled for a meeting with the governor. She thought she had the upper hand, always, despite the fact they'd foiled her previous attempted coup.

Holt's anger, earlier eclipsed by fear and worry, strained at the reins he was holding tight, bubbling to the surface and rippling beneath his skin. No way she could miss the blush hitting his cheeks. He did nothing to hide it or the leading edge of fury in his voice. "This isn't a social visit," he said. "Or a familial one."

"How's my great-granddaughter?"

Holt woke his tablet and opened the login page for Royal Bank of the Caribbean. He flipped the tablet around and set it on the metal table in front of Rose. "I'll tell you when you wire the funds to the criminals holding Brax."

"I have no idea what you're talking about," she replied without a flinch.

"Of course not." He reclaimed the tablet, minimized the bank's page, and opened the index of files he'd shown to Nic and Aidan. He laid the tablet back in front of Rose. "Like you have no idea about the crimes detailed in these files."

No physical flinch but the whites of her eyes became more visible.

"The FBI and the US Attorney's Office have been made aware of this evidence," Holt continued. "If Brax isn't released by the time Chris and I walk out of here, a copy of these files will be released to them."

Rose clasped her hands in front of her. "Those are not my operations."

"The evidence says otherwise."

"And if I say otherwise?"

"We're the ones who've built a rapport with law enforcement, starting with the man you had kidnapped."

Chris pushed off the wall and pulled out the chair next to Holt, the metal legs scraping over concrete. "What were you planning to do with Brax?" he asked as he lowered himself into it. He crossed one leg over the other, hands folded in his lap, the motions so eerily similar to Hawes's that Holt would swear it was his brother sitting next to him. He was willing to bet Chris intended Rose to notice the same, to be knocked unsteady by a proxy of the man who'd beat her once already. "Leverage him to take back control? Or were you foolish enough to think he'd turn on Holt, like you thought I would on Hawes?"

"You did."

"Not in the end, and I didn't spend a decade and a half in love with Hawes like Brax has been in love with Holt."

And there it was. The same grenade Chris had lobbed into an eerily similar situation nine months ago, only more plainly spoken now. Holt was no longer surprised by it. Acknowledged and accepted, celebrated and cherished, he would have thrown that truth bomb himself if he could. As it were, he had another for his grandmother. He finally let himself shift forward on his seat, let Rose see the conviction and fury simmering in his eyes. "There is no way I would have turned on him. I have loved that man for almost half my life, I plan to love him for the rest of it, and I will not let you or anyone else get in the way of that."

"You turn this over," Rose said, "I won't be the only one behind bars."

"Hawes and Helena are aware," Chris said. "They're prepared to make that sacrifice."

She shook her head, once, hard, the way she used to do when she chided her grandchildren for misbehaving. "Me and your grandfather, your parents, this isn't what we wanted—"

Holt lurched to the end of his chair. Far past done, it

was all he could do not to growl out his response. "One, you do not get to speak for the dead. Two, you wanted a legacy in *your* image. We want a fucking future in *ours*." He rolled up his right sleeve and slapped the outside of his arm, the tattoo a representation of everything he was trying not to become. "One that doesn't tear at our souls and drag us into darkness. One that I'm proud to leave my daughter. The same future Hawes fought for last summer."

Her eyes hardened, her knuckles whitened, and like Holt's, her pale skin reddened, no makeup to hide her temper. But she didn't speak.

"Or maybe this is vengeance?" Chris said, resting his forearms on the table. "More than just severing the loose ends *you* left dangling? It chafes, doesn't it? Knowing we're here because *you* made a bad deal, because Hawes and your grandchildren outsmarted you."

When she still didn't reply, her wrinkled lips pressed mutinously together, Holt stood and braced his hands on the table. He wouldn't loom over her, but he couldn't stay seated either. "Is he right?"

Silence.

"Everything you and Papa Cal built, everything Mom and Dad died for, everything we're trying to leave for Lily and the rest of her generation to come, you're willing to throw all that away for vengeance? To ruin a good man? To get back at us?"

A sneer splintered her façade. "You're the one threatening to do the same."

"For love. For our family. We're willing to give it all up to protect one of our own."

"He's not—"

Holt would have flipped the table if it weren't bolted down. He settled for bringing his hands down in an ear-splitting slap against the metal, a satisfying release of all the anger and pain he'd bottled up the past nine months. "He is. I wouldn't be here today if it weren't for Brax. He saved me multiple times over, and he offered to give himself up to save your great-granddaughter when pictures of them were posted, so don't tell me he's not a part of this family. And this family, *my* family, is ready and willing to do whatever it takes to save him." He jabbed a finger her direction. "Including from you. You want to continue to hold out? For vengeance, leverage, or whatever mistaken power trip you're on? You go ahead and make that mistake." He swung his finger toward the tablet. "I hit Send and all those files go to the feds. Everything they need to add a dozen more charges against you. Or you can pay the scum who answered your ad what they want and let us live our fucking lives the way we see fit."

Finally—*finally*—she flinched, but not out of fear. There was none of that in her cold, blue stare. Only surprise. As if she were really seeing him, really taking him seriously for the first time in his life, and not just seeing him as the designated punching bag who would continue to take her hits and suffer the brunt of her manipulations. "You found your spine," she said in a self-congratulatory tone. "If there's anything I've done right—"

He let the growl rip. "You had nothing to do with this. *This*, the me here today, is because of Brax, my daughter, my family, and our friends." He grabbed the tablet, brought the bank page back up, and shoved it within her reach. "Transfer the fucking money."

They stared each other down another long few seconds before Rose tilted forward, keying in the codes to make the transfer, as cool and casual as she could be, as if she were wiring funds for an everyday occasion.

The urge to flip the table again was strong, but Holt snatched up the tablet and straightened instead. He made a screenshot of the transfer confirmation, attached it to a different email he had drafted, and hit Send.

"What was that?" Rose asked.

Rather than answer, Holt opened the camera roll and scrolled to a picture from Friday night. Lily on Brax's shoulders, both of them covered in latke-goop. He flipped the tablet around for Rose to see. "Lily is better than she's ever been. She's going to grow up with two dads, a mom, and a family who loves her, and one day she'll know they were willing to sacrifice everything for her."

Rose cleared her throat and lifted her shockingly chastened gaze, the wind finally taken out of her imaginary-Chanel sails. "When will I see her?"

"That depends."

"On what?"

Holt handed the tablet to Chris and rolled down his sleeve. "On the terms you negotiate with the federal prosecutor. That sound you heard a second ago? That was me sending proof to the feds of your conspiracy to commit numerous crimes, including the kidnapping of Police Chief Braxton Kane. US Attorney Price will be here later today to discuss the additional charges against you."

Chris banged on the door to signal their exit, and it was almost loud enough to drown out Rose's gulp.

Almost.

"I'd suggest you call your lawyer." He didn't bother waiting for her reply.

Her gulp was victory enough. Chris's parting "Check-mate" was the Hawes-flavored icing on the fucking cake.

The sunrise lit his second sprint in as many days up the stairs at SFPD headquarters.

The man he loved striding across the bullpen, flanked by his brother and sister, Jax and Marsh, made his chest expand and his fingers tingle, love rippling all directions and framing the most welcome sight he could imagine.

The same man, the chief of police, meeting him, a digital assassin, in the middle of the bullpen and kissing him like he didn't give a fuck what his colleagues thought, smiling against his lips as Maya, Fletcher, and dozens of other officers cheered behind them, paved their path forward.

CHAPTER TWENTY-FOUR

It was noon by the time they all traipsed back into the Pac Heights house, but the aromas of breakfast wafting from the dining room were strong enough to knock Holt's stomach back a few hours.

Brax's too, judging by the grumble his belly made.

Following their noses, they found a spread laid out on the dining table—French toast dusted with powdered sugar, crispy bacon, bottles of maple syrup, and two pots of blessed, steaming coffee. And the swear jar sitting in the middle of it all, the strawberry plushie jammed inside it, just like they'd told Elisabeth to do.

Celia appeared out of the kitchen, wiping her hands on a dishtowel and eyeing the jar. "Do I want to know about that?"

Holt shook his head, stifling a laugh.

"Figured not. And figured you might need some food." Already in mother-hen mode, she took one look at the bruised and bandaged Brax as he appeared beside Holt and shifted into overdrive. "Damn, Chief." Tossing the towel over her shoulder, she hustled to their side, fingers lightly grasping Brax's chin so she could inspect his face. "You okay? Need anything? First aid kit's in the kitchen."

He gently clasped her wrist and lowered her hand, dropping a kiss on the backs of her knuckles. "Thanks, Cee, but I'm good."

"We swung by the hospital on the way here," Helena said before stealing a kiss from her girlfriend. "Nothing's broken. They x-rayed, bandaged, and sent him home with the good sh—stuff."

Footsteps thundered down the stairs, and Marco was the first to round the corner. "Can we eat now?"

Behind him, at a much more careful pace, appeared Celia's daughter, Mia, with Lily in her arms and the cats in her wake. As soon as Lily spied them, she made her intentions clear. "Ba-Ba!"

Holt didn't begrudge her in the slightest, facilitating the handoff to prevent his daughter from trying to make the impossible leap from Mia's arms to Brax's.

"Hey, princess," Brax murmured as he gathered her close. Eyes fluttering closed, he buried his face in her curls and inhaled deep before letting out a long, slow, contented breath.

Waves of peace rolled off him and lapped at Holt's heart, drawing him closer. He circled Brax's back with one arm, Lily with the other, holding his family tight, and looking on with more happiness than he thought possible as the rest of his family descended on the food.

Lily, while excited to see them, was not to be left out of

her favorite activity for long. "Yes!" she exclaimed.

Holt pulled out a chair for Brax and Lily and was about to claim the one next to them, when his phone vibrated. He pulled it out of his pocket, surprised to see a call from the warden at CCWF. He schooled his face, hopefully before Brax or his siblings noticed. "Call I need to take," he said. "I'll be right back."

Brax glanced over his shoulder. "Everything okay?"

"Yeah, fine," he said as Hawes stretched across the table to hand his niece a piece of bacon. She stuffed it in her mouth and hummed her approval. "Save me some bacon."

"No promises."

He dropped a kiss on both their heads, then ducked out of the dining room, across the foyer, and into the living room to answer the call. "This is Holt."

It wasn't the warden on the other end of the line. "Hey, babe," Amelia greeted.

He lowered the phone, checked the caller ID, then brought the phone back to his ear. "What are you doing at CCWF?"

"Is Brax okay?" she asked. "Are you and Lily?"

"We're good. Brax is a little banged up, but he'll be fine. We're all just happy to have him home."

"Good, I'm glad."

"Thank you for your help." Holt rested against the side of Lily's pack and play. "We couldn't have done it without you."

"It was the least I could do for my family."

"Thank you," he said again, fighting a sudden knot in his throat. Fighting the wisp of dread that ghosted up his spine. "Why are you there, Amelia?"

She was silent a moment longer before answering. "Making sure you get the happily ever after you deserve."

Stinging eyes joined the knot in his throat. "Amelia, don't—"

"I'm just keeping an eye on her. She won't bother any of you again."

He exhaled the breath he didn't realize he'd been holding. "Okay, thank you."

"Visitation here is once a month," she said. "I expect you and Lily and Brax to come see me in May."

He blinked fast a few times, swallowed hard, and when that didn't work, inhaled deep. "We'll be there."

The line clicked off and he exhaled another long breath, surprised at the call and how much it had affected him. How much he hadn't realized he'd needed Amelia's blessing and the peace of mind she was willing to give them all.

"Holt, you get lost in there?" Helena called. "The bacon is almost gone!"

"Coming!" He wiped his eyes and nose on his sleeve, gave his head a sharp shake, then stood and returned to the dining room.

He quelled Brax's concerned look with a kiss and an "All good," then dug into the plate Brax had made him. Everything was delicious, and their plates were clean in less than twenty minutes, though the house was no less full of pleasant sounds. Marco had cornered Jax and Marsh to talk computers, the cats were tussling in the corner over Marsh's cowboy hat, adding their claw marks to the ring of Lily-sized teeth marks around the brim, and Celia, Mia, and Avery were in the kitchen trading pastry recipes. A family at home for the weekend together.

Across the table, Hawes cleared his throat, drawing his and Brax's attention. "Notice you didn't take your badge back?"

Holt swung his gaze to Brax. "You what?" He'd missed that in all the commotion at the station—the reunion, the backslaps, the statements, and the sorting of evidence and follow-up appointments.

Brax drew a caramel out of his pocket, unwrapped it, and popped it into his mouth. "To be determined." He handed the shiny wrapper to Lily to play with. "My priorities are shifting." He clicked the hard candy against his teeth, once, twice, then cheeked it. "I want to be with my family."

Chris stretched an arm over the back of Hawes's chair. "As an ex-lawman, I got no complaints about working this side of the equation. Whole lot less rules."

Brax chuckled, and Holt's head spun. Had he had too much coffee, or had the world flipped on him again? "Brax, what's going—?"

Brax's fingers over his lips silenced his words. "We'll talk about it later," Brax said. "Right now, I just need a shower and you."

"And that's the cue for babysitters," Helena said,

pushing up from where she sat on the other side of Hawes. She rounded the table and plucked Lily off Brax's lap. She moved to turn, but Brax stopped her, a hand on her arm.

"Thank you, and not just for babysitting duty." He glanced across the table at Hawes and Chris, then back to Helena. "What you all did for me..."

"Small price for giving us back our brother," Helena said with a smile that lacked any of her usual coyness. One hundred percent genuine.

"And for the past six years," Hawes added.

Helena turned her smile on Holt. "A price we thankfully didn't have to pay, thanks to you." She dipped her chin and kissed his head. "Nice job, Little H."

"Thanks, Hena."

Of course she ruined—no, made perfect—the moment by knuckling his head, then encouraging Lily to do the same to Brax. They were all still laughing when Hawes waved them toward the stairs. "Go on up, we'll see you in the morn—afternoon."

"Try evening," Chris pretended to whisper. "Maybe."

Heat rushed to Holt's face and stayed there as snickers followed him and Brax up the stairs to the third floor. He was sure his face, his nose, his neck—all of him—was beet red by the time he shut the bedroom door behind them. "Thanks for coming back here," he said, eyes downcast, looking anywhere but at Brax, the sudden embarrassment silly yet inescapable. "Especially after that."

Brax's toes appeared in his line of sight, then his hands landed on his hips, backing Holt up until he bumped against the wall. Brax lifted his chin, forcing his gaze. "We needed to be with family."

"You understand their yours now? That we're yours?"

Bruises and bandages be damned, Brax's smile could have lit the whole house. "I do."

Holt gently cupped his cheeks, wanting to feel that smile, to capture a piece of it beneath his fingertips and in his memory forever. "Thank you for loving us."

"Thank you for giving me a family." Brax brought their lips together in a kiss filled with the same gratitude as his words, meeting its match in everything Holt was grateful for in return.

"Chris was right," Holt whispered against his lips. "If something happened to you, I'd fall apart or burn the world down."

Brax snaked a hand around his waist, between the wall and his ass, and hauled him close. "You're still here."

"And I almost burned the world down for you."

And closer, a knee shoved between Holt's legs, Brax's dick digging into his thigh. "Fuck, Holt, what you do to me."

Holt threw back his head and laughed in joy at the familiar words, at Brax's easy freedom to say them and at his own privilege to drown in them the rest of his fucking life. In this love, in the kisses Brax rained down his neck, and in the cock rutting close to his own, both growing harder by the second.

Holt righted his head, lips trailing along the shell of Brax's ear. "Thought you wanted a shower?"

"Fuck the shower," Brax growled into the crease of his neck. "Just need you to fuck me."

And fully hard. "Holy fuck."

Brax spun out of his arms so fast that Holt almost toppled forward, off-balance and bereft. Almost whined aloud. Until Brax shucked his shirt off over his head, the muscles of his back rippling. And as if that beautiful sight wasn't enough, he dropped his jeans and boxers, his tight round ass flexing as he added an extra sway to his hips on the way to the bed.

Holt tried not to pounce, not wanting to injure him any further, but it was a near thing. But Brax didn't seem to be in the bad kind of pain as they kissed, grappled, and stripped Holt too, both of them getting naked and tangled in the sheets together. Greedy touches and greedier kisses, only coming up for air when their greedy bodies demanded more. "Fuck, Cap, tell me where you want me 'cause I'm not going to last much longer."

"Don't think I've got multiple rounds in me this morning either." He drew him up by the wrist, both of them on their knees, chests and groins bumping. "Want to feel all of you in me. Nothing between us."

"Not helping," Holt gritted out.

The asshole in bed with him smiled, wicked and gorgeous, and Holt had to kiss him again to bank the rising tide of desire. It worked, but only for a moment. Until Brax pulled away and put on an even more wicked display—him on his knees, hands gripping the headboard, his ass thrust out in invitation. Holt had to grab the base of his dick to keep from coming right there.

Brax grinned over his shoulder. Fucker knew he was pushing Holt to the edge. "I trust there's at least lube around here."

Holt had never moved so fast in his life, snatching the bottle from the bedside drawer and coating his dick and fingers with a generous amount. But that was where fast ended. As hard as he was, as much as he wanted to bury himself in Brax, he wanted to make this good for him too, as good as Brax had made it for him the other night. And fuck if he didn't enjoy the push and pull of Brax's ass around his fingers, the moans and shivers he coaxed out of him with each nudge against his prostate, the torture he was inflicting on both of them.

"Now, Private."

The barked order was as good as a spank, precome leaking from Holt's dick. He caught it in his palm and stroked it down his length, adding to the slick of the lube. Ready, he lined up at Brax's hole and pushed in slowly. The heat was overwhelming, compounded by the heat of Brax's body as he bowed his back, forcing Holt to round over and around him. His knuckles whitened around the rail, his body tensed beneath Holt's, and for a second Holt considered pulling out, until the resistance around his cock eased, same as it had around his fingers, and he slid the rest of the way in. He wrapped his arms around Brax's front, hands splayed over his chest, fingertips weaving through the sprinkling of chest hair. Warm all over. Under his hands, under his body, around his cock. "Fuck, Cap, this—you—feel amazing."

Brax pushed off the rail, levering them both up to

kneeling, and fuck if that didn't feel even better, Brax spread over his knees, sinking down on his cock, both of them driving the motion.

Together.

Same as their hands moved, Brax's entwined with his, guiding them opposite directions, one over his heart, the other around his dick, jacking him together as they continued to rock. Faster and faster, Holt thrusting up, Brax slamming down until Brax, head tossed back on Holt's shoulder, tensed in his arms and spilled over their hands. The blast of sticky heat and the vise around his cock sent Holt over the edge right behind him, spilling into Brax and groaning against his neck.

Bodies and hearts satisfied, they fell together onto their sides, Brax still in his arms. Holt peppered the flowers and vines on his shoulders with kisses. "I don't ever want to go without this feeling again. Don't ever want to go without you again. I can't lose you, Cap."

"My answer hasn't changed, Private. You won't. I'll protect you."

Brax tried to burrow back into him, then grumbled when Holt rolled him over instead, wanting them face to face. For the promise he had to make, the question he had to ask. "And I you," Holt said. "Make it official?"

Laughter erupted, the body against his shaking. Brax threw a leg over his hip, bringing them even closer. "Did you just propose to me?" His smile was so big, so bright, reaching all the way to his eyes where it had been missing for too long.

Holt would happily spend the rest of his life making

sure that smile—his man—never got lost again. "Marry me, Braxton Kane." He stole a quick, hard kiss from the smile and the man he loved. "I want to spend the rest of my life with my best friend. If he does too."

Somehow, impossibly, wonderfully, Brax's smile grew even bigger. "He does."

III

BRAX

CHAPTER TWENTY-FIVE

Later That Year

Brax stood in front of the door at the end of the second-floor hallway, trying and failing to shake the sense of déjà vu. It had been well over a year since he'd last been there, helping to haul Hawes's moving boxes at the time. The only stronger sense in this moment was curiosity. What in the hell was he—was she—doing there?

Ignoring the thumbprint reader, he raised his fist to knock. It never landed, the door swinging open to reveal a gala-ready Melissa Cruz. Curls piled atop her head, she was dressed in an elegant green ballgown, emeralds around her neck to match, and sparkly heels that peeked out from the dress's thigh-high slit.

"Shit, Mel," Brax said. "We can do this another time. I didn't know—"

"Please, it's a TE gig I'd rather be late for." She ushered him in and closed the door behind them. "Besides, the real party's next week. Your crew still coming?"

New Year's Eve at Nic's brewery, Gravity. Talleys, Madigans, and the strays like him and Mel they'd picked up along the way. Ask Brax two years ago if that's where and who he thought he'd be spending the holidays with and he would have said impossible. But over the past year, the impossible had become possible, beyond his wildest dreams, including those he'd kept locked away for over a decade. "We'll be there."

"Excellent." Stepping past him, she sashayed on her high heels down the long entry hall of Hawes's old condo.

"I was wondering what happened to this place."

"Turns out it's right around the corner from our flat."

"Just turned out that way?"

She shrugged a single bare shoulder, exposed by the gown's asymmetrical collar. "Boat is good for mobility, but a stationary base of operations is good too, especially given the rampant seasickness in our ranks."

Brax's laugh died on a gasp as he cleared the end of the hallway. The large open area that used to be Hawes's living space had been completely transformed. Where the reclaimed-wood dining table had sat now lived a sleek conference table with black leather office chairs around it. In the adjacent seating area, near the seismic struts and big glass patio doors, were now matching workstations. The bolted in ladder to the panic room and wall-mounted TV still existed in the living room, but along the opposite wall, where a built-in desk and shelving unit used to be, was a state-of-the-art command setup—monitors, keyboards, speakers, peripherals—that rivaled and looked an awful lot like Holt's setups. Not the full-scale MCS or Pac Heights ones—this space wasn't that large—but comparable to the one at the house in Pacifica where they'd decided, with zero debate, to move in together. Finally, at the far end of the space, the kitchen looked mostly the same—save for an extra coffeemaker—but above it, the former lofted bedroom had been glassed in and converted into a private office.

Brax's stunned gaze traveled back to the wall of computers. "Do I want to know who helped build this?"

"Our friendly neighborhood hacker collective."

"Including my husband?"

She quirked a brow, and Brax failed to hide his smile.

"First night of Hannukah," he said. "On the beach in Pacifica. Just the family." After Hawes and Chris's big wedding in January, and Helena and Celia's Paris elopement, he and Holt had wanted something small, private, and close to home. A festival of love and lights where sand met the ocean. A celebration for them and their family.

"About fucking time. I'm happy for you, Brax." She squeezed his shoulder before crossing the room to lean a hip against the ladder. "I guess I know why you're here then."

"You had it right all those months ago. My priorities have definitely shifted." That night she'd come to him, he'd been so tired he could hardly think straight. *Quicksand*, he'd described it, the feeling of sinking with no way out, unable to juggle his increasingly large stack of conflicting priorities. The quicksand had only gotten denser, more aggressive, nearly swallowing him whole earlier in the year, but he'd survived by following his heart, by grabbing hold of the man he loved, and letting Holt and his family help pull him free. They'd been willing to sacrifice everything for him. Holt was giving him everything he could. More than enough. It was Brax's turn to do the same. "I can't have the life I want, the family I want, and be the chief of police. You were right. The decision is here, and I'd appreciate your help navigating through it."

"You're ready to walk away? The work you've done with SFPD—"

"I'm leaving the department in good hands." It had taken him longer to extract himself than anticipated, but everything was in place now. "Maya will continue the work we started, with Fletcher's help, and I'll be there to help too, in a civilian capacity, as needed." But that was the most he could give them. Holt and their family deserved the rest.

"All right, then," Mel said. "Follow me."

Brax followed her up the stairs into the overwatch office... with two desks. The far one was bare but for a laptop, chair, and lamp. The closer one, which Mel rested back against, was in use but minimally cluttered—lamp, chair, laptop, legal pad and pen, a framed ace of hearts playing card, a business card holder, and a stack of files. "I need a partner."

Brax snapped his gaze back to her face. "Tracking bounties?"

"Tracking bounties with a very specific crew." She grabbed the stack of files off the desk and held them out to him. "I hear you're particularly good with recruitment, with finding the best in people."

Déjà vu whacked him over the head again. Chief

Williams had offered him a stack of files six years ago, his first day on the job, and his life had been forever turned on its head. Everything he thought he knew about his best friend had been recast in a new, unexpected, terrifying darkness. Over the years he'd learned Holt was still Holt, and there were more layers—more light than dark—to the Madigans than those files depicted, but he couldn't help feeling like he was standing on the edge of a similar life-upending moment. Unlike Williams, though, he trusted and respected Mel. She was an ally and, more importantly, a friend. If she were about to up-end his life, it had to be for a good cause.

Accepting the offered files, he flipped through them, his jaw hitting the floor with each name he recognized. Some only in passing, others in a much closer context. "These are—"

"I love a good redemption story, don't you?"

He returned her earlier quirked brow. "Speaking from personal experience?"

"Abso-fucking-lutely." She reached for the business card holder, slid out a single piece of thick cardstock, and held it out to him.

Another offering. Another life-changing moment.

REDEMPTION, INC. the card read in silver-pressed foil, peaking out of the swirls of gray.

Like his husband's beloved fog.

And printed below the company name were his and her names. As cofounders.

He flicked the card against his knuckles, fighting a smile. "Confident much?"

"I've been called worse."

He laughed out loud as another once impossible future unspooled in front of him. Suddenly possible. All because a certain ginger-haired private had stepped off an army transport and into his life fourteen years ago. Holt had made the impossible possible for him—a life full of love and family—and had opened the door to another unexpected opportunity. A chance to make the impossible possible for others too.

"I'm in."

Thank you for reading!

For all the latest updates on new projects, sneak peeks, and more, sign up for Layla's Newsletter and join the Layla's Lushes Reader Group on Facebook.

Reviews are an invaluable tool when it comes to spreading the word about great reads. Please consider leaving an honest review for *Silent Knight* on Amazon, BookBub, or your favorite review site.

AUTHOR'S NOTE

Holt and Brax are U.S. Army veterans and a portion of this book involves their time in the military, at a fictional base in Afghanistan. I've tried to be accurate where possible, and the numerous blogs, message boards, and websites were most helpful for researching the environment Holt and Brax found themselves in during this period of their lives and after. That said, certain liberties, such as with Brax's orientation role and career path, have been taken for story purposes. All liberties taken and mistakes made are my own.

ACKNOWLEDGMENTS

I'd be embarrassed to tell you how many times I myself have read this book. Each time I went in to write or make an edit, I fell back into it with these two. I love them, a lot, and I hope you did too. Thank you for your patience. I know I've teased their story to death. I hope it lived up to the nuggets of angst I've dropped along the way. As we draw Fog City to a close, I really can't thank you all enough for your excitement, support, and love of these characters. I've loved writing this series—it feels the most me of any series I've written—and I can't wait to leap into the spinoffs (yes, plural).

Special thanks to my readers in the Lushes Facebook Group who have hung with me and cheered this couple to their happily ever after, to Kim who helps keep author-me running, to my sprint groups and author friends from keeping me on track, and to my agent Laura Bradford for the subrights support.

Thank you to the team that made this final book of the

Fog City series amazing: Wander Aguiar and models Grant and Robert W. for the stunning cover photography, Cate Ashwood for the stunning cover design, Kim, Rachel, Allison and Erin for the beta reads, Kristi Yanta for the book and series guidance, Susie Selva for her editorial expertise, and Lori Parks for the careful proofreading.

Finally, thanks to the PR professionals who help make my releases run: Nina, Kelley, Kim, Kayti and the entire Valentine PR Team and Leslie and the GRR Team!

ABOUT THE AUTHOR

Layla Reyne is the author of *Variable Onset* and the *Fog City, Agents Irish and Whiskey*, and *Trouble Brewing* series. A Carolina Tar Heel who now calls the San Francisco Bay Area home, Layla enjoys weaving her bi-coastal experiences into her stories, along with adrenaline-fueled suspense and heart pounding romance.

You can find Layla at laylareyne.com, in her reader group on Facebook—Layla's Lushes, and at the following sites:

facebook.com/laylareyne

twitter.com/laylareyne

instagram.com/laylareyne

amazon.com/author/laylareyne

bookbub.com/authors/layla-reyne

Ingram Content Group UK Ltd.
Milton Keynes UK
UKHW021119180423
420361UK00014B/1009